COMPULSION

GILLIAN WELLS

Copyright © 2025 Gillian Wells

Ebook – 978-1-7638265-0-2
Paperback – 978-1-7638265-1-9
Hardcover – 978-1-7688265-2-6

All rights reserved, including the right to reproduce this book or portions thereof in any form whatsoever. Apart from any fair dealing for the purpose of research, private study, criticism or review, no part of this publication may be reproduced, stored in or introduced into a retrieval system, or transmitted in any form or by any means (electronic, mechanical, photocopying, recording or otherwise), without the prior written permission of the copyright owner.

FOR BEAR WITH ALL MY LOVE

FOR THE TEAM AT AUTHOR SERVICES AND
ALL MY SUPPORTERS WHO HAVE HELPED MY
WRITING JOURNEY THANK YOU

PROLOGUE

THE BIG BLACK dog stopped in the middle of the track and looked directly into the headlights. His eyes blazed with fire from within. *Black Shuck*, the woman thought, then she shook her head. *Don't be silly. He was a mythical dog in darkest Suffolk, not out here in the outback.* She shivered—good thing she was driving slowly. The animal stared at the car—or her?—for a few more moments then disappeared into the bush. Scared before, she was now even more jittery as she eased forward slowly, the track getting rougher and rougher. What would she find when she got there? Would it be good or bad? Various scenarios spun round and round in her head.

CHAPTER 1

TWO YEARS EARLIER, Ginny Harrison was feeling rather stressed, as every time she sat down to create in her workroom, the phone rang, or her husband needed her help.

The fourth time it rang, she snatched it up. "Who is it? I'm busy."

Silence for a moment, then a male voice asked, "Is this Mrs Harrison, the hat lady?"

She didn't recognise the voice and decided it must be a new customer, though it wasn't normal for a man to ring.

"Yes, yes, it is. I'm sorry. I have a lot on just now. How can I help you?"

"My name is Charles Unwin, and I would like you to make a hat for my wife—specifically for the Melbourne Cup. It's the first time we're going, and we want to make a good impression."

"I see. What have you in mind? Has she got her outfit yet?"

"No, we thought we'd start with the hat and then find an outfit to match."

"It's harder to do that. Look, make an online appointment—tomorrow arvo at three if that suits."

"We just moved into the district. We will come to you."

"You know how to find me?"

"Certainly." Charles Unwin hung up without saying another word, leaving Ginny staring at the phone.

"Rude prick," she muttered. She returned to her work.

She was a milliner, much to the surprise of many people since she lived on the outskirts of a small outback town. But hats were lightweight and easy enough to pack. It was rare, however, for her customers to come to her. Mostly, they were from the cities, but in the modern world with Facetime and Zoom she managed well matching hats to outfits and people. She loved what she did and knew she was very good at it. Word of her abilities had spread, and she had as many clients as she could cope with but always had difficulty turning people away.

She was just getting started again when she heard her husband calling her. She sighed. She'd thought he was organised for the morning. She and Jeff had been married for twentyfive years. They'd had a cattle property—a few sheep too. They'd had a good life, hard but fulfilling. Then Jeff had hit a rock when on the quad bike late one afternoon. The bike had landed on top of him, paralysing him from the waist down. Ginny knew he hadn't hit a rock on purpose, but she was frustrated, as she had said time and again to be back before dark. It had been twilight, and the rocks had been hidden in the long, dead grass. Once they knew the extent of his injuries and that he would never walk again, they had made the decision to move to town. Ginny had an Arab horse she adored, so they'd managed to find a place with enough room for a horse, some hens, and a good-sized vegetable patch.

Ginny had done a millinery course at college back in the UK. She then came to Australia backpacking and met Jeff. He'd been tall, good-looking, and full of fun, and they had clicked straight away and married within a very short time. Her parents had come out for the wedding, and she had been back to the UK a few times, though not since Jeff's accident. She had four brothers and one sister who all had children, so her parents were taken up with enough grandchildren that they didn't worry about Ginny's child-free life. For herself, the urge to have kids wasn't very strong, so she hadn't minded when Jeff said he didn't want children. He came from a large family and reckoned it was bad enough when the Harrison tribe got together without more "brats" around.

Up until Jeff's accident, Ginny had helped on the property and hadn't thought about millinery; now it was a lifeline. Making hats brought in much needed income, and it also helped her. Jeff didn't cope with his disability. He railed against it but wouldn't do anything to help himself. He refused help from physiotherapists, doctors, and counsellors. Instead, he wallowed in his misery. He became a stranger overnight—a once vibrant man who'd been full of life was reduced to an empty shell, needy and miserable.

Although it was a small town, the internet had made her business possible, and it was unusual for anyone to come see her, though of course a few locals did. Sitting at her workbench, she shook her head. Charles and his wife sounded like city types. She didn't think they would last long out here. Jeff rang his bell again and, heaving a sigh, Ginny went to see what he wanted.

"You forgot to fill my water bottle," Jeff said peevishly. "I finished my coffee, and I'm thirsty."

The house, and all within and outside it, was specially designed for him. It had taken most of the money they had got when they had sold and moved. Jeff had the equipment to do many things himself, but he chose not to.

Ginny said nothing. There was no use arguing—she just filled his bottle. "I'll be in at lunchtime. Is there anything else?"

Jeff bit his lip, hesitating. He lowered his eyes, and tears of self-pity threatened to fall, but he shook his head, and Ginny returned to her workroom.

CHAPTER 2

THE NEXT AFTERNOON, it was very hot and humid. Ginny had the air con going in her room, but it still felt sticky and airless. It was quite a large room they'd had built onto the original house. One end was her workspace and the other a mini showroom where she displayed the many different styles of hats and material colours that she had available. She had large hats, small hats, perchers, fascinators, and other miscellanea. Most of her hats were made of sinamay, but she had materials for straw and felt hats. A variety of trimmings were available: feathers, silk flowers, ribbons, and many other bits and pieces.

The time of the Unwins' appointment came and went. Having finished the piece she was working on, Ginny fiddled about waiting, but as it seemed to get hotter, she decided to give up for the day. Jeff was resting as he normally did when it got very hot. He had his own bed, and Ginny had helped him out of his wheelchair and onto the bed earlier. He was now fast asleep. It was strange; some days he could sleep really well and on others not at all. It was the same at night.

She went through to the kitchen and poured herself a cold drink. She stepped outside onto the verandah for a moment. *Sure to be a storm before too long*. Almost on cue, she heard an enormous clap of thunder.

Millie, her horse, had a good shelter she could go in, so Ginny wasn't too worried about her, but their dog, Puck, hated thunder and, big bumbling animal that he was, she'd have a difficult time calming him down if the storm was very loud.

She was about to go back inside when she saw a big 4WD car drive in. It must be the Unwins—nearly two hours late.

Feeling very annoyed, she went back through the house to her room, glancing in the mirror as she did so. On the rare occasions she had clients come, she always tried to look quite smart. No one would take her seriously if she was unkempt. She had dark hair that she had twisted into a loose bun, and wisps were escaping. She had quite a pretty face, though her nose was too big—at least she thought so. Her figure was her best bit. She was curvy and quite tall. Squaring her shoulders, she opened the door as the Unwins alighted from their car.

The woman was nearer, so it was her Ginny first saw. She was a very big woman—tall and muscular. She had big breasts and rather chubby legs, which were straight with no shape, and she wore very short shorts. They did nothing for her, and Ginny thought she would be better covering her legs up. She had a handsome face and blonde hair. Her husband was also tall and thin. He had dark hair and a pencil moustache. He was quite good-looking.

From the back seat, a scruffy boy got out. It was difficult to tell how old he was, but Ginny thought he must be about eighteen or nineteen. He was handsome with dark, curly hair, large eyes, and a full mouth. But he was wearing a torn shirt and looked as if he needed a good wash.

The woman marched up to the door looking very purposeful. Ginny opened the door just as she got to it.

"I'm Margarita Unwin and have come to see you about a hat for the Melbourne Cup," she announced in a booming voice.

"Of course you are," Ginny said. "You are rather late. I was about to get on and do my other jobs. Is it possible to come back? Do you live nearby?"

Margarita Unwin tossed her head. "Not my fault we are late. It's Alex. He made us late. We're here now, and I don't want to come again, thank you."

It was on the tip of Ginny's tongue to say she would have to if she wanted a hat made, but she decided to let it pass. She'd just get rid of them as quickly as possible. She stood aside, and all three came into the house.

"Perhaps you'd like to sit." Ginny indicated a small sofa in the showroom. She spoke to the husband and son.

Margarita was already marching around, looking at the samples Ginny had displayed.

"What do you have in mind?" Ginny asked her.

"Something that will stand out. I don't want a run-of-the-mill thing."

"Colour?"

"Orange or shocking pink."

There was something about this woman that was really getting under Ginny's skin, and she knew she would find her patience shattered by the end of the day.

A long consultation started. Choosing the style of the hat was the worst because Margarita kept changing her mind. Charles tried to speak two times, and both times, Margarita shushed him.

Alex finally burst out, "For God's sake, Mum. Make up your mind, or we'll be here all day!"

"Do not speak to me like that!" Margarita bellowed.

Silence reigned. Nobody moved or spoke, then Charles said mildly, "It's OK, my dear. Alex was only trying to help."

Margarita glared at her husband then turned her back and continued her quest to find the right style. Ginny then realised that Margarita was more likely to go for something that she had tried to steer her away from. Eventually, a large hat with a big brim was chosen. It suited her, as she was a big woman, and a small hat or percher—which she had originally been looking at—wouldn't have been right.

Next came choosing a colour. But there was a terrible noise. Thunder had been rumbling during the entire consultation, but no one had taken any notice of it—all being concerned with hat picking. The Unwins didn't flinch at this particular crash. However, Ginny knew what it was. She had heard it before.

"Jeff! Sorry, I'll be back in a minute," she told the Unwins.

She rushed through the house to their bedroom. Jeff had tried to get into his wheelchair and had somehow fallen on the floor. He lay, helpless, between the chair and the bed. Ginny always told him to wait until she was there, but once or twice he hadn't, and he'd fallen before. This time it was worse, as he was in a very difficult position. He'd likely banged his head on the wall behind the bed, and his legs were half under the bed. He was sprawled on the floor, looking dazed and very uncomfortable.

"My God, Jeff. Why didn't you ring if you wanted to get up?"

"I did. You didn't answer." His speech sounded slurred, but then again, he often didn't bother to speak properly.

Having moved the wheelchair out of the way, Ginny attempted to lift him into a sitting position, but it was no good. He was heavy and not helping her.

She put the wheelchair in a different place and said, "If I help you sit up, can you hang onto the chair?"

"I'll try."

Just then, they heard a noise and saw Charles Unwin standing in the doorway, an embarrassed flush colouring his cheeks.

"Um, can I help?" he asked. When Ginny nodded, he came forward, crouched behind Jeff, and heaved him up and into the wheelchair quite easily. No mean feat, as Jeff was a big man and, in his current state, something of a dead weight. Charles had acted so quickly that Ginny hadn't had the chance to process this unexpected turn of events.

"Thank you. How did you know that I—that we . . ." Ginny trailed off.

"Margarita was fussing because you had gone, so I was trying to prevent any unpleasantness. My wife can be . . . difficult. I'm sorry I—"

Ginny held up her hand. "Don't be. I am so thankful you came to help. You are grateful too, aren't you, Jeff?"

Jeff nodded. He was feeling ashamed as he always did at times like these. He knew, deep down, he made life for Ginny harder than it needed to be, but somehow, he couldn't help it.

"Go see to your customers, Ginny. I will be OK now," he muttered.

"You're sure? Your head. Did you hit your head?"

"Nah, it's fine. Go."

Jeff had hit his head, but it didn't hurt.

Reluctantly, Ginny turned to go and was almost surprised to find Charles still standing there.

Ginny couldn't decide if Margarita knew what had gone on, but she was more conciliatory when they returned and didn't ask any questions. Alex hadn't moved from the sofa and was playing with his phone, though he looked up and startled Ginny by giving her an enormous wink. Finally, they sorted out what to order: an orange hat with a large brim and shocking pink feathers as a trim around the crown. It would certainly be very different from any other. Margarita told Ginny she would have an outfit made to match and had already found fabric she wanted.

Ginny hastily worked out the cost of the hat, which came to quite a large slice of money, but the Unwins seemed unfazed by the price, much to Ginny's relief.

While all this was going on, the rain had started and turned into a deluge. Charles looked out the door and asked, "Do you mind if we wait a few minutes? I'd like the storm to subside a little before we leave."

"That's fine. Would you like a drink while you wait?"

All three declined, but Ginny felt compelled to wait with them by the door. "Did you move into town recently?" She decided to make small talk.

"We bought the Taylor place a few weeks ago," Charles said.

Ginny's eyes widened. They must be loaded since they'd bought the biggest cattle station around the area, and she had heard it had gone for several million dollars.

"Oh, I see. I rather thought you were more, um, maybe not country people. Sorry, that came out wrong."

Alex burst out laughing before his parents had a chance to answer. "Well said. Mum hates the country, and Dad doesn't know one end of a cow from another, and as for horses . . . well!"

"Alex! Hold your tongue!" Margarita was livid, although Charles didn't seem that worried by Alex's statement.

"Oh, um, it'll take you a little time to settle in, but if you want to know anything, do come and ask. Jeff and I had our own place a while ago, not as big but the principle is the same. Gosh, that's a lifestyle change. I admire you for taking such a big step." Ginny was gushing, but she wanted to calm the waters and felt sorry for Alex.

Slightly mollified, Margarita muttered, "Thank you." She still looked angry, and when Ginny glanced at Alex, he winked again. The urge to laugh suddenly overtook her, but she managed to turn it into a gasping cough.

Charles peered outside and announced that he thought the rain was easing.

Just then, Puck, who had been hiding under Jeff's bed, came charging into the room and cannoned into Margarita, knocking her backwards onto the small sofa, which creaked ominously when she landed.

"Oh my God, I'm so sorry. He hates thunder. I'm sorry." Ginny was mortified, and to her horror, both Alex and Charles roared with laughter. She badly wanted to join in but didn't think she should.

Looking very ruffled, Margarita got to her feet, and with as much dignity as she could manage, she made for the door. Her menfolk followed her out. Charles stopped as he got to the door and said in a low voice, "Thank you for everything. I like your dog!" Then he winked at Ginny.

As she watched them drive off through the rain, Ginny shook her head. What a strange family they were. She had thought Margarita ruled the roost, but she wasn't so sure now. Maybe Margarita was all bluster, and Charles just knew the right way to handle her.

CHAPTER 3

WHEN GINNY CHECKED on Jeff, all humour left her. Jeff was pale and sweating. "My head hurts," he said in a weak voice. Ginny immediately went to him and looked at the back of his head where she guessed he had hit it. "You said you didn't hit your head, but there is a lump here. You did hit it."

Jeff nodded then wished he hadn't, as his head swam even more. He couldn't see straight as it was.

Ginny didn't like the look of Jeff at all. "I'm going to ring the doctor," she said.

Having rung the local doctor, Ginny managed to get Jeff back onto the bed. He seemed more hopeless than usual and gave her no help at all. She got him a drink of water—luckily, she had a proper drinking vessel since he couldn't or wouldn't sit up. She wasn't sure if he even understood what she was saying.

It seemed ages before Dr Harvey came. Ginny fussed round Jeff all that time and told him about the Unwins, though he took no notice of her words. She told him she had thought Margarita was the boss but now wasn't so sure. She tried to make him laugh about Puck's antics, but it didn't work. He seemed almost comatose.

Dr Harvey examined Jeff and asked him some questions. He didn't really respond. The doctor pulled Ginny to one side. "I'm sorry, my dear, but he needs to go to the hospital. I think he may have had a small stroke, but his chest isn't good either."

"When it's so hot and humid he does struggle. I try to keep the house as cool as I can, but it's been very hot today, and that storm we had earlier doesn't seem to have cooled things off."

It was a long wait for the ambulance. Dr Harvey waited too. He didn't say anything, but Ginny picked up on his anxiety.

When the ambulance arrived, everything happened quickly, and before Ginny knew it, she was alone again. She had said she would follow them to the hospital because she wanted to ask Jo, her friend and neighbour, to look out for Puck and keep him overnight if she stayed at the hospital. Millie would be all right, but the chooks would need shutting up too.

She packed an overnight bag for herself. The day was drawing to a close, and she wasn't sure what would happen next. As it turned out, she was halfway to the local hospital when a nurse called her to say Jeff was being transferred to Brisbane by air ambulance.

She now had a four-hour drive in front of her. She pulled over and drummed her fingers on the steering wheel. Maybe she should go back home and reorganise everything, as it was obvious Jeff's condition was serious. She would need more than the few things she had brought with her. Reluctantly, she turned round and retraced her route. Luckily, she had only driven about fifteen kilometres.

Jo was collecting Puck when she pulled up to the house. "Hi, Ginny. I already shut the chooks up. Why are you back?"

"They sent Jeff to Brisbane, so I came to take a few more bits with me. Can you keep Puck for a few days and watch Millie for me, and of course the chooks too? Take all the eggs."

"Kids will be pleased—they love scrambled eggs at the moment." Jo was quite a bit younger than Ginny and had two children: a boisterous five-year-old called Marcus, and a thoughtful three-year-old called Mary.

"Well, help yourself to the veggie garden too. There are beans galore, and the asparagus and tomatoes are coming on."

"Thank you, honey. You OK?"

"I will be once I know what's up with Jeff."

Ginny was just getting back into the car when her mobile rang. It was an unknown number, and she nearly didn't answer it. As the Bluetooth hadn't had a chance to take over, Ginny answered it while she drove towards the road.

"Mrs Harrison, my name is Sarah Duval, and I am a senior registrar at Princess Alexandra Hospital . . ." By this time, Ginny had pulled over. There was something in the woman's voice she didn't much like.

"What's wrong?" she demanded.

"I'm so sorry, Mrs Harrison, but your husband passed away before he got here. They just informed us. He couldn't be saved."

Ginny stared into space. Nothing seemed real at that moment. Then the registrar spoke again. "Mrs Harrison? Mrs Harrison, are you there?"

"Yes." Even to her own ears, her voice sounded a long way away.

"Unfortunately, there are formalities to go through. I'm sorry to ask, but do you know what undertaker you will be using?"

Ginny shook her head then managed to say she had no idea.

"Can you let me know as soon as possible?" The doctor spoke briskly.

"Y-yes, of course, thank you." Ginny hung up. She wasn't sure if the woman had finished speaking or not, and she didn't care.

She sat still for some time, then she drove slowly to Jo's house. She felt as if she were in some strange land and nothing was real.

Jo came out to the car, as she had seen Ginny drive in. "What did you forget?" When she glimpsed Ginny's face, she paled. "Oh God, Ginny. What happened?"

Ginny got out of the car. She was trembling. "Jeff. He . . ." She started to sob, deep racking sobs with no real tears.

Jo put her arms around her and guided her to the house. Puck saw and understood his mistress was upset and pushed his nose against her hand. Jo sat her down. Her children came rushing up but then stopped, and Jack, Jo's husband, shepherded them away. "Come on you two. It's bedtime." He glanced at Jo, who nodded.

After a time, Ginny managed to get herself under control enough to speak. "A doctor just rang. Jeff passed away before he got to the hospital. The woman asked me what funeral director I'll use! I don't know. I can't think. I can't believe all this. Why, why did he die? Why didn't he wait until I was with him? This isn't real, is it, Jo? I'll wake up in a minute, won't I?"

Jo was completely out of her depth. She was young, and death hadn't ever touched her before, but she knew her friend needed her support and comfort, so she said, "I expect they will investigate why he died so suddenly, and I will help you sort out any arrangements that you need. What about his family?"

"I'd better ring them." Ginny took a big breath and tried to pull herself together.

"Look, Ginny, I think you should stay with us tonight. You shouldn't be on your own."

Ginny laughed bitterly. "I will be now, won't I? Thank you, but I will go home now. There is so much to sort out, or will be tomorrow. Thanks for everything. I'll speak to you tomorrow."

Ginny got to her feet and gave Jo a quick hug, then, with Puck at her side, she got in her car and drove the short distance back home.

CHAPTER 4

THREE WEEKS AFTER Jeff's death, Ginny woke in the middle of the night. The hat!

Margarita Unwin had arranged to pick it up the next day! Ginny had forgotten all about it and had done nothing towards making it. She flew out of bed and looked at the clock. Two thirty in the morning. It was the first night she had slept this long, and now she had to get up!

Puck thought it was great when she appeared, and he immediately wanted to go out. He'd been an outside working dog in his youth, but only a few days before Jeff's accident, Puck had badly broken a back leg. Overnight, he became an indoor dog since the break was high up, and he needed lots of attention. He was of an indeterminate breed. He was big and rustybrown with a coat like a poodle, but his physique more closely resembled a kelpie. Jeff had found him wandering at the side of the road, and no one ever claimed him. He was getting on in years, and since Jeff had passed away, he was even more devoted to Ginny.

Ginny was too befuddled with sleep to make a good start on the hat. It took about forty hours to block a hat and that was more time than she had left, plus she had to trim the hat and match the colouring. She would just have to work extra hard and hope for the best. Luckily, she already had the materials she wanted, else she would really be stuck. But she had to colour the feathers to a shocking pink and hoped the sinamay she had in stock, which was orange, could be dyed the correct shade.

As she worked, she thought back over the last few weeks. She tended to block out the bad bits, like Jeff's autopsy and the fiasco of finding an undertaker who would bring the body home. Every decision had been stressful. Jeff's mother had come to stay for a few days, and most of his family had come to the funeral service. Ginny got on all right with Janice, Jeff's mother, but they had never been thrown together in such a fashion and both found it hard. They didn't really know each other that well, and Janice had never understood their decision to not have children. She viewed it as unnatural, though at least she hadn't brought it up often. She had gone home the day before, much to Ginny's relief. She desperately wanted to be alone to process what had happened and how her life was now changed forever.

As Ginny worked on the hat, her mind went into overdrive, and tears poured down her cheeks, almost as if a tap had been turned on inside her head. She stopped, stood up, and stretched. The last thing she wanted was for the beginnings of the hat to get wet and be destroyed. Taking some deep breaths, she sat again. She had loved Jeff with all her being even though she had often lost sight of that after his accident. He had become a stranger, but sometimes the old Jeff would appear briefly. He had made her exasperated many times, but deep down, she still loved him to bits—even the cranky, sad man he had turned into. How was she going to manage without him?

Her thoughts swirled as she worked. Daylight came, and sunlight streamed into the room, so she stood and switched off the lights. She heard a small, sharp bark. She had forgotten about Puck and left him outside, much to his annoyance. Letting him in, she made herself another hot drink and sat once more to work.

The day passed, and Ginny made herself drinks, but she didn't really eat. She was too wound up and worried. She hated working under pressure. Day turned into night again, and she still had a way to go.

She woke with a start. She had nodded off. Looking at the clock, she saw it was two in the morning. She was still sitting at her workbench with Puck curled up at her feet. He sat up and put his head on her lap and looked at her with his big brown eyes. "Oh God, Puck," she said. "I never fed you yesterday. Come to that, I didn't really eat either."

She got stiffly to her feet and fed the dog then made herself a sandwich. Then it was back to work.

At eight o'clock, the phone rang. It was Charles Unwin. "Hello, Ginny. Um, we've decided not to go to Melbourne this year. We will, of course, come and pick up the hat at some point, as my wife will want it for other occasions, but it's no longer wanted this week. By the way, I'm sorry to hear of your husband's passing." He gave a small cough.

Many answers passed through Ginny's mind. She was in turn angry, relieved (as she hadn't finished the hat), and let down. Ultimately, exhaustion won out.

She was silent for so long that Charles asked, "Ginny, are you there? I said—"

"I heard you. Thank you for letting me know." She hung up before he had a chance to say more. *Serves him right. He hung up on me that first time.*

She went to her bedroom, stripped off, and got into the shower, then she lay on the bed thinking she was so dog-tired she would sleep. However, sleep eluded her. Her mind was in overdrive, and she was extremely annoyed with the Unwins.

When did they decide not to go? They said they would pick the hat up today, so they must have decided before. They are a very odd family, that's for sure. I wish I could talk to Jeff about it—it might have made him smile if I could joke with him.

These last thoughts made her cry. At last, she fell into an exhausted sleep.

Puck growled and barked, jerking Ginny awake. She sat up, disorientated for a few moments. Someone was at the workroom door, and she was naked! She flew up and grabbed a robe. Looking at the clock as she pulled it around her, she saw it was twelve thirty. She'd had about four hours of sleep, maybe less.

Feeling dishevelled, she combed her hair with her fingers as she went through to the workroom. Opening the door, she was startled to see both Charles and Alex standing there looking uncomfortable.

"This is a bad time, I can tell," said Charles. "You sounded so angry, so I thought we had better come and apologise in person. Well, Alex and I did. We brought you some flowers."

Ginny then realised Alex was holding a large bunch of flowers that must have come from Roma. There was nowhere in their little town to buy flowers such as those. It was the biggest bunch Ginny had ever seen.

She stood aside. "Come in and sit down. I'll just go and get dressed." She fled before they answered her.

She hurriedly dressed in a clean shirt and shorts and brushed her hair, though she left it loose. No time to put any make-up on. She looked at herself in the mirror. She was pale and had dark rings under her eyes—they were still puffy from her crying session. *What the hell does it matter?* She returned to her guests.

"I'm sorry. The truth is, I have been trying to finish your wife's hat because I haven't done much with it. The hat got put on the back burner after Jeff passed away." Ginny had decided to be honest.

"I am very sorry. It must be tough, to struggle with work as well as your husband dying," Charles said in a very gentle voice. His kindness immediately brought tears to Ginny's eyes.

She covered it up by asking, "Shall I take them since they are for me?" She held her hand out for the flowers.

Alex didn't let go of them. Instead, he said, "Show me where your vases are, and I will arrange them for you, if you like, that is." He, too, spoke in a gentle voice much like his father.

Ginny was now very flustered. The kitchen, which was normally neat and clean, was like a bombsite. She had let more than just the hat slide over the last few weeks.

"No, no, it's all right." She spoke to his back as Alex marched off with the flowers. Leaving Charles sitting in the workroom, she hastily followed Alex. Not stopping to see his reaction to her messy kitchen, she dived into the laundry and found a large vase that had never been used. It had been a wedding present.

Alex deftly set about trimming the flowers and arranging them artistically in the large vase, chatting away as he did so.

"Mum has absolutely no sense of style. She needs Dad and I to choose things for her. God knows what she would look like without our help. Same with the house, decor, and furniture. I discovered I like design, and flowers come into that. I'm getting quite good at arranging them, I reckon."

"Yes, you are." Alex really was making a good job of his self-appointed task. She watched him for a few minutes then suddenly said, "Oh, your father." She had forgotten all about Charles and rushed off.

He sat on the sofa in the workroom, flicking through an old magazine that Ginny had been meaning to throw out for ages. He seemed very relaxed.

"Alex doing a good job?" he asked.

"Yes, yes, he is."

"You are surprised—I can tell. Alex is very artistic. I think his paintings are wonderful. He has an eye for colour and style, and he has pretty much restyled the inside of our house. Margarita hates all that. She says it's not manly, which of course is ridiculous. It has caused quite a lot of friction. He was at university studying to be a vet of all things, but he dropped out. I'm not sure what he is going to do, but I think a course at TAFE may be the answer. He loves animals but wants to pursue other options."

Just then, Alex appeared in the doorway with his arrangement. It was magnificent, and it made Ginny gasp.

"Where would you like this?" Alex asked, struggling a bit to keep control of the large vase.

"In here. I spend most of my time here. Thank you. Thank you both so much! I don't know what to say. I've never had flowers like them. Can I get you a drink?"

Both men opted for a cold drink, and Ginny went to the fridge, thinking she had some light beer left over from the wake. She didn't, but there was a bottle of white wine, and she decided one drink each wouldn't hurt. Getting glasses, she had another strike of inspiration and got out some crackers and cheese. Once she'd arranged everything to her liking, she called for her guests to join her on the verandah.

"Heavens, Ginny! There was no need to go to this trouble," Charles said.

"It's well past lunch, and I haven't eaten much today, so I thought we could share this. I appreciate your flowers and your visit."

Alex grinned. "Looks good to me."

They each nursed a drink, and the cheese and crackers went down well. Ginny found the father-son duo very easy to talk to. She couldn't help noticing that Alex was extremely goodlooking and was much tidier than the first time she had seen him. His father was a handsome man too.

After a bit of small talk, Ginny said, "If you don't mind my asking, where is Margarita today?"

"She went to Sydney to see friends and family. She misses them. Not cut out for the rural lifestyle at all," Charles said. "You know the saying, 'when the cat's away'?"

Ginny was slightly shocked that Charles would talk of his wife in this way, especially to someone he hardly knew. She would find out over time that Charles kept nothing to himself and always said exactly what he was thinking or feeling. It could be very disconcerting. Alex was much the same, she would discover.

"Oh," she said. "It must've been difficult for her to move out here."

"She liked the idea of it as much as anyone, but the reality is not what she hoped for," Charles admitted. "It has always been my dream. My grandfather owned a big cattle station in the Territory. I don't remember him at all. Through bad investments and bad luck, he lost it all to the banks. He committed suicide when my father was very small. My grandmother moved around and finally settled in Sydney. She found a wealthy husband, and we Unwins have never looked back until now. It's in my blood. I was a property developer in Sydney, sold up, and here we are."

"Oh," Ginny said again, not sure what to say next. They were out of her league—that was plain enough. Jeff had life insurance, but it wasn't very big, and they hadn't had that much left over from the sale of the farm after they had customised the house for Jeff's needs. She would have to be careful with her finances until she was sure where she stood.

The afternoon quietly slipped by. Alex had a wicked sense of humour and was also something of a mimic. Several times, Ginny found herself laughing out loud—something she hadn't done in a very long time.

At last, Charles stood. "We must go." He grinned. "Now we've killed the bottle and eaten all your cheese!"

Ginny panicked a bit. "Are you OK to drive?"

"I didn't drink as much as Dad. I'll drive," Alex said. Charles threw him the keys and, having thanked Ginny again, they left but promised they would be back soon to pick up the rather redundant hat.

Ginny watched them go. Alex blasted the car's horn as they drove off, and Ginny smiled. Then she rather sadly cleared up the remains of the crackers and took everything into the kitchen. *Charles is lucky to have a son like Alex.* Then it struck her; if she and Jeff had decided to have children, maybe she wouldn't feel so alone and lost?

CHAPTER 5

FOR THE NEXT few weeks, Ginny was busy going through documents related to Jeff's passing. She also felt like she was permanently handing out his death certificate, which was very depressing. Everyone expressed their sympathy, and she appreciated this, but it didn't take the ache away. The evenings were the worst, and sometimes she would just sit and let the tears flow. Jo popped round when she could, but with two young children and a busy life, she rarely had time to visit. Jo finally told Ginny to see the doctor because she had lost weight. She looked haunted and gaunt. She wasn't sleeping either. She was back in the bad place she had been in when Jeff first had his accident.

Finally, Ginny agreed. She would visit the doctor after Christmas, which was just a few days away now. Against her better judgment, she went to Jeff's family for Christmas, but although they tried hard to welcome her, she felt like an outsider. She was glad to return home. Puck had gone with her, and he seemed glad too.

Dr Harvey asked her lots of questions, took her blood pressure, then sat back and looked at her. "Ginny," he said gently. "I can't find anything physically wrong with you. I think you need to speak to someone regarding coping with grief. I can give you some sleeping pills, but that's about all I can do. What do you say?"

"No on both counts, but thank you, doctor. Well, I might want to accept sleeping pills to take sometimes, but I don't want to speak to anyone. I will work through this in my own way. I don't mean to sound ungrateful."

After returning home, Ginny decided to ride Millie. She hadn't ridden in months. Millie was getting fat and was very unfit. Ginny was horrified by how fat she had become and resolved there and then to start riding daily again.

So she started a new regimen. She would get up and ride Millie first thing before it got too hot, then she'd do her other chores, have breakfast, and busy herself in her workroom. Afternoons were either for work or anything that took her fancy.

For a time, this seemed to really help. She also realised she was freer than she had been for a long time. That thought made her feel very guilty, though, so she squashed it down.

One morning, she was just about to go outside to ride Millie when her phone went, and much to her surprise, it was her mother.

"What's wrong?" Ginny asked. They spoke once a week on the phone and always at the same time unless either of them had a prior engagement. This was unusual.

"Nothing, sweetheart. Dad and I were talking, and we think it'll be lovely if you come over. It's going to be our sixtieth wedding anniversary in a couple of months, and we'd like you to be there."

Ginny was aware of this but had put it on the back burner. She could afford it, she supposed, but would need someone to look after the animals. Someone to live in would be best. "I'll see what I can organise, Mum, I promise. It's the animals that tie me down now."

As she came off the phone, she felt really defeated. Puck was one thing, but what about Millie? She was an elderly horse and needed a bit of TLC. Who did she know who had the time and inclination? She would have to ask around in town. A week later, she still hadn't found the ideal solution and was beginning to think that was it. Coming out of the hardware store where she had gone for a few odds and ends, who should she see but Charles getting out of his big 4WD.

"Ginny! Long time no see. How are you? I feel guilty about not popping over after we shared the wine and cheese. Life has been hectic. We need to pick up the hat too."

Ginny was pleased to see him. He was a nice man. Pity about his wife, else maybe they could all be friends. She couldn't imagine being friends with Margarita.

"Have you time for a coffee?" Charles asked after they exchanged pleasantries.

Ginny still hadn't got used to the idea that she had nothing to rush home for, and she hesitated. Giving herself a shake, she replied, "Yes, great, thank you. I'll see you over there. If you tell me what you would like, I'll order."

Five minutes later, they were sitting opposite each other in the small cafe. Charles was telling Ginny all about his business and how he was enjoying life "out in the sticks." Finally, he ran out of steam. "Sorry, Ginny. I have done nothing but tell you all about my life. How are you, really?"

This threw her slightly. She wasn't one for airing her troubles, so she said instead, "I am trying to find someone to look after my place, so I can go and see my folks back in the UK, which isn't easy. I could get Jo, my neighbour, to look after Puck, though that's not a good long-term plan. I really need someone to live in."

"Aren't there agencies for that sort of thing?"

"There are, yes, but I worry about Millie and the hat business. I can get ahead with orders, but there will always be orders to take and maybe some to post. I'm just not sure what to do."

Charles looked very thoughtful, then he said, "I might have a solution to your problem."

"Oh, what is it?"

"Alex. Ever since we ate your cheese and drank your wine, he has been on at me to ask you a question." Charles stopped and looked uncertain.

"Goodness, what question? You look worried. It can't be that bad."

For the life of her, Ginny couldn't think what it was that was worrying Charles so much.

"Well, you might think so. He wants you to train him in millinery!"

Ginny stared at Charles for several minutes until he finally said, "Sorry. I guess it's a bad idea, but it has really fascinated him ever since we came that first time."

Ginny pulled herself together. "It's fine. I am just so surprised, that's all.

I need to think. I, well, I could help, I suppose. It will certainly help me if he is willing to come and stay at my place, then I can go and see my folks."

"Good. I'll tell him."

"Hang on. There are all sorts of things to sort out first, even if he is willing to come and stay while I am away."

Charles brushed all that aside. Ginny would learn that Charles and Alex were two people who knew exactly what they wanted and would move heaven and earth to get it.

Charles seemed quite excited, and it wasn't long before he took his leave.

Ginny hadn't even finished her coffee when he left. She watched him get in his car while she sat near the window. *My goodness. What have I done, getting mixed up with the Unwins in this way?*

The next morning, she had just got back from her ride on Millie when a strange new 4WD came flying into the driveway in a swirl of dust. *What the hell. Who's this silly bugger driving like a madman?* Out jumped Alex, grinning from ear to ear. He ran to Ginny, and before she had a chance to speak, he threw his arms around her and gave her an enormous hug.

"Thank you, thank you. This is wonderful. Tell me what to do. Can I help unsaddle Millie?"

Ginny, still recovering from the hug that she had begrudgingly enjoyed, said, "First of all, slow down. Then introduce yourself to Millie. She doesn't always take to strangers, especially men."

Millie, however, had already decided she liked this young man and pushed her nose against his stomach, searching for a treat. Ginny looked on in surprise. "Well, that's a first. Never seen her take to someone that quickly before." Then she remembered Charles mentioning Alex having an affinity with animals. It certainly seemed true.

Having sorted Millie out and given her breakfast, Ginny showed Alex round her property. She told him what needed to be done and where the chook food was. Ultimately, she listed everything that needed doing to maintain the place. Then she asked, "Have you had breakfast? You must have left home early."

"Just a cup of coffee, but don't worry, I'm fine." Alex suddenly seemed unsure of himself, and Ginny guessed it was because he wasn't sure if she was going to let him do any millinery.

"Right. First things first, breakfast and then your first lesson. You won't be paid to start with, as you are going to be in charge here and look after the place, yes?"

"Oh yes, Ginny. I am so pleased. It's difficult at home, as Mum gives Dad and I hell. It will be so good to get out of the way for a bit. Have you booked your flights yet?"

"Not yet. I only spoke with your father yesterday, and I wasn't sure what was going to happen. It's all been very fast."

Alex grinned. "Us Unwins always do everything at top speed."

Ginny was embarrassed that she could only offer toast or cereal for breakfast, but Alex didn't seem put out, and over the next few days, Ginny found he didn't worry about anything much and was very easy to please.

She spent the morning showing him the various materials and accessories she used for making hats: ribbons, feathers, artificial flowers, silk, felt, sinamay, straw, bindings, and the sewing machine. She tried to explain how everything worked and went together. Alex took everything in. "Do you want to write it all down?" she asked. "There is so much to remember."

"Nah, I'll remember."

Ginny was doubtful but didn't push it. They had lunch, then Ginny said, "Lately, I've tried not to work in here in the afternoons, but we can do a bit more if you like. If you have never used a sewing machine, you might like to have a go on some scrap material."

She found Alex's weak spot. He got in muddle after muddle. He tried to go too fast to start with, and the two pieces that he was supposed to be stitching together ended up a real mess. Ginny got the giggles at one point, and Alex joined in. It took them a while to get serious again. Ginny looked at the clock. "You've an hour's journey ahead of you to get home. I think you should get a move on."

Alex looked as if he wanted to argue but went on his way. Ginny watched him go and was suddenly overcome with a wave of loneliness. She had enjoyed her day. He was good company, and it had been fun.

CHAPTER 6

THE NEXT DAY, he didn't turn up, and Ginny found a terse message on the answering machine from Margarita saying that Alex wouldn't be coming. *Oh dear, sounds as if she isn't happy. Maybe she is putting a stop to it all before he learns anything. I hope she will let him come and house-sit at least.*

Ginny had spent the previous evening booking flights to and from the UK. She had phoned her mother, who was very excited about Ginny's visit. She was now worried but decided to sit on it and not panic. She had three weeks before she went. She had been lucky to find a flight so close to her ideal departure date, but since she was only one passenger, it was easier.

Ginny found it hard to concentrate that day. Her mind kept returning to Alex. He had been such great company, and his wicked sense of humour had been good for her and had lifted her out of her grief. That day seemed very dull in comparison. Though she was tired, she found it difficult to sleep that night and hoped she wasn't getting back into the bad sleep cycle she'd had earlier.

After a night spent tossing and turning, she was just getting herself some breakfast when Alex came speeding into her driveway. She went to the door to meet him and found she was inordinately pleased to see him. "Alex! Hi. You made it today!"

He grinned at her as he came round the car. "Sure have, and I stopped at the bakery for pastries on the way here." He waved a brown paper bag in the air.

Sitting at the kitchen table, Alex said, "I have a big favour to ask. I don't know how you'll feel about it." He stopped speaking and looked unsure of himself.

"Won't know until you ask."

"As you know, I don't get on with Mum—well, no one does, really. So the thing is . . . I was wondering if I could stay here from now on. I know I will when you are away, but can I start now?"

Ginny was taken aback. She wasn't sure what to say, but after looking at the plea in Alex's big brown eyes, she threw caution to the wind. *Why not. He will be staying soon, anyway.*

"So long as your father is happy with the arrangement, then it is OK with me. But you'll have to help get your room ready."

Alex let out a whoop, and Ginny thought he was going to hug her again, but he didn't. She felt strangely disappointed then berated herself. She really was being silly.

She had only one spare bedroom, and it was in an almost self-contained part of the house—a bit like a motel room with a jug and cups and an en suite bathroom. She and Jeff had designed it that way in case they ever needed a nurse to live in. Ginny was now thankful they had. It had its own entrance off the verandah, so anyone sleeping there could come and go as they wished without disturbing anyone in the main house.

Ginny led Alex through and tutted at herself because the room and bathroom, though not filthy, were dusty and smelt stale. She threw open the windows and, having got bedding from the cupboard, told Alex to make the bed up. Currently, it had just a cover over a bare mattress. She set about tidying the bathroom and cleaning it. It was quite spacious with a bath, shower, and basin, plus a toilet hidden around the corner. Several small spiders got a nasty shock, and she was slightly ashamed.

"I'm sorry. This is a bit untidy and dusty. No one slept in here much—only Jeff's parents when they came . . . they came—" Tears flooded her eyes, and she stopped speaking. Alex stepped towards her and lightly put his arm across her shoulders and gave her a gentle squeeze.

"It's OK. I understand. Please don't get upset," he said gently. With a big effort, Ginny pulled herself together, and they proceeded with the task at hand.

When they finished, another thought struck Ginny. She would have to feed Alex, and provisions were low since she hadn't been bothering to eat much. A trip to the supermarket was next on the list. Alex insisted on going with her, which was a good idea. He told her what he liked and didn't like as they walked round with the trolley. He wasn't exactly fussy but liked the more expensive items that Ginny mostly avoided. She was rather horrified by her bill at the end.

As they came out of the shop, Jo turned into the car park, saw Ginny, waved, then came over. Ginny introduced them and told Jo that Alex was going to be staying and looking after her place while she was away.

Jo, after talking to them both for a few minutes, pulled Ginny's arm. "Can I have a word with you?" Ginny allowed herself to be led a short distance away.

"What is it?"

"Do you think it's wise to have a young bloke like that living in? After all, you hardly know him, and the gossips are going to have a field day."

Ginny stared at her friend, and as Jo opened her mouth to speak again, Ginny, who had been wrestling with her thoughts and anger, said, "It's no one else's business, for a start. I am old enough to be his mother for God's sake, and I like and trust both him and his father. Got it?"

Jo flinched and immediately backed down. "I'm sorry. I meant no harm. I was just playing the devil's advocate."

"Maybe, but it suits me to have some help. I'm teaching him millinery, and it's a good hour either way for him to go home on rough roads. It seemed the sensible solution."

"I'm sure it will be fine. I just worry about you Gin, that's all."

This annoyed Ginny all over again, as she hated being called *Gin*. Her real name was Genevieve, but as a child, she'd called herself *Ginny*, and it had stuck.

As they drove home, Alex picked up on Ginny's annoyance. "Did your friend upset you just now?" he asked. That was something else Ginny would learn: Alex was always upfront about asking questions and voicing his opinions. He was always careful not to be hurtful.

Ginny found herself telling Alex what Jo had said. He looked thoughtful. "I don't want to put you in an embarrassing situation. I won't come to stay until you go away."

"Rubbish. The age gap between us is huge. What are you? Twenty? I am forty-six, nearly forty-seven. Who in their right mind would think there was anything other than a working relationship between us?"

"I hope we are friends too," he said. Ginny, who was driving, glanced across at him.

"Yes, friends, of course." Somehow, she felt sad saying it.

CHAPTER 7

AFTER THEY HAD eaten supper, which Alex helped her prepare, he asked if it was all right to get his music out of the car.

"Yes, but what do you mean?"

Alex looked embarrassed. "I'm trying to teach myself how to play the banjo, but I'm not getting on very well."

Ginny laughed. "Don't ask me for help. I don't play an instrument, and Mum always told me I was tone-deaf. But of course you can bring it in. That room is yours for the time being, so go for it."

Alex said goodnight, went out to his car, and returned to his room through the outside door off the verandah. A bit later, Ginny heard rather odd strumming coming from his room. She smiled to herself. It was good to have someone else in the house. Puck laid his head on her lap. "You like Alex too, don't you boy. You be good while I'm away."

Weeks flew by, and it was time for Ginny to leave. Ginny had taught Alex as much as she could in the short time he had been living with her. Because she was teaching him millinery and how to care for her animals, she'd worried it would be information overload, but he took it all in his stride. They'd fallen into a companionable existence. Alex gave her space and spent most of his own time in his room. Each night, she could hear him trying to master his banjo, and it made her smile. They worked together but spent their leisure time apart, though they ate together. Alex had initially offered to help prepare dinners, but Ginny had rejected the idea since she liked to cook and have the kitchen to herself.

She was driving herself to the airport. Alex and Jo had both offered to take her, but Ginny wanted to be independent and wanted her car there when she returned four weeks later.

Ginny had a wobble in her step when she left, as she felt strange leaving everything in Alex's care. Had she gone mad? She hadn't known him or his family very long, and he was so young! Would he cope with everything, or would she come home to a disaster? She worried the whole of her long journey, but when the plane touched down in the UK, all her concerns flew away. Greeting her parents, who were waiting at the airport to meet her, was very emotional.

It was quite a long drive to their home in Suffolk, but Ginny chatted the whole way, and the time passed very quickly.

"The family all wanted to come and say hello, but I persuaded them to visit one at a time. I thought meeting them all at once would be rather much for you," Amy, Ginny's mother, said.

"Good thinking, Mum. I am already feeling odd. Jet lag is a strange beast. I know it makes one feel that nothing is real." Ginny then gave an enormous yawn.

Amy and Roy, Ginny's parents, had moved into a smaller house three years before, so Ginny hadn't been to their house, though she had seen pictures. It was a pretty cottage. The walls were plastered and painted Suffolk pink, and it had a pantile roof. Tulips in full bloom, as it was now well into spring, lined the driveway like miniature soldiers in a guard of honour. "Oh wow. Dad, Mum, what a pretty house! John and Laura are happy in the old house, are they? I've never asked."

"They seem to be, though their children are getting very grown up now, so they might want to downsize in a few years," Amy said.

Ginny loved the house and said she'd like a tour, but no sooner had she got inside than tiredness overtook her, and after having had a quick drink in the kitchen, her mother showed her the room upstairs. Ginny had the quickest shower she'd ever had before falling into a deep sleep.

When she woke, it was dark, and she glanced at the clock; it was seven thirty at night. She had slept since three in the afternoon. She groaned. She probably wouldn't be able to sleep later.

However, she surprised herself. After eating a lovely dinner and catching up with more family gossip, she retired to bed again, feeling sleepy. She had told them more about Jeff's accident and illness now than they had known before. Talking things over on the phone or even occasionally facetiming was never the same as face-to-face conversations, and now she could really tell her parents everything. She'd cried too, but they were healing tears.

They were eating breakfast the next morning when the door flew open. "Boo! Boo!" Ginny's sister, Jane, rushed in and enveloped Ginny in her arms. She was younger than Ginny, and she had always called Ginny *Boo*. No one knew why or where it came from, but it stuck, though Jane was the only one who used it nowadays.

Both women had damp eyes as Jane said, "You look well. Your hair is lighter. Have you lost weight?" Ginny scrambled to answer Jane's questions, and her sister kept on talking.

"Kids are at school, but they will catch up with you later. We're all coming for dinner. Did Mum tell you?"

"I think she mentioned it, but I seem to be in a brain fog just now," Ginny said.

Jane hugged Ginny again. "So sorry to hear about Jeff's passing—not that I ever managed to meet him, really, but I know he made you very happy until his accident."

Tears overflowed in Ginny's eyes. She couldn't help it. "At least we had a good life together until then. It changed him, and thinking back now, I imagine he was pleased to go. He hated what he had become. It made him so unhappy to be stuck in that wheelchair. I know some people cope better than others. Jeff had always been so full of life. It was a cruel thing—that accident. It robbed him of his dignity and his pleasures, like going out to see to the cattle, fencing, and mustering. Everything he loved vanished in a heartbeat. He just found it so hard to accept how his life had changed."

Ginny found herself immersed in family as never before. Only Jane was younger than her. Her four brothers ranged in age from John, who was fifty-six, down to Doug, who was forty-eight. Amy also joked that it took her and Roy a while to learn how to make babies, but once they got the hang of it, they made the most of it. Ginny was forty-six, and Jane was only sixteen months younger than her, so the two of them had always been close as children.

Two evenings later, John and his wife, Laura, and Jane and her husband, Clive, came for dinner. Ginny still had to catch up with her other brothers, and her mother had told her she was doing it in stages, so by the time it came to the celebrations, Ginny would have seen all the close family beforehand. In some ways, it was very strange. Her brother was almost a stranger, and Ginny had never actually met his wife, though they had been married for twenty years. Ginny had gone to Australia before that. Paul had married before she went, and she had also met Luke's wife. Doug had looked like a confirmed bachelor and had only been married a few years. He'd left it late and had married a woman who already had three children.

It was a pleasant evening, though Ginny felt strangely out of it. Her parents saw John, Laura, and the children regularly. Actually, they saw all their children and grandchildren regularly—everyone except her. Without meaning to leave Ginny out, they talked about things she knew nothing about: teachers at school and residents who had moved in or out of the village. Ginny realised how removed she was from their lives. They all loved her, as she did them, but their lives were so different, and in some respects, they were strangers. It made her sad, though she also understood it had been her decision in the first place. The fact that she had no children also set her apart.

Over the next few days, she gradually met her other brothers and their partners. She liked Paul's wife, Marie, and she'd met her before just like Luke's wife, though they hadn't been married. Finally, Doug and his tribe of stepchildren arrived. Amy had warned Ginny they could be testing. As it turned out, they were. Gloria, Gordon, and Gavin. Gloria was thirteen, and the other two were eleven and nine respectively. One minute, they were rude, and the next, they were wheedling that they wanted something. Ginny thought they were spoilt brats, but of course she kept it to herself. The more she saw of them the less she liked them, and it made her glad she hadn't had any herself.

In some respect, she felt rather like a celebrity, as family and others she met wanted to know all about her lifestyle and Australia, but on another level, they were all immersed in their own lives.

She and her mother had a lovely two days out once she settled in. They went to Cambridge and shopped till they dropped. Ginny had forgotten how she loved John Lewis and Marks & Spencer. They had a late lunch, then they wandered round King's College Chapel and walked down to the river. There weren't any punts out, as it was a rather windy, cloudy day, but Ginny enjoyed it. She hadn't been in Cambridge since her mid-teens, and everything had changed. She hardly knew where she was. It didn't matter, though, and her enjoyment wasn't in any way spoilt.

The next day was bright and sunny, and her mother suggested they go to Bury St Edmunds and look around Abbey Gardens. Ginny, who'd loved to go there as a child, jumped at the chance. It had changed but not much, and she relived some of the things she had liked most as a child, especially the aviary. The birds were so exotic to many, but to her, most were normal. The gardens were just starting to be a blaze of colour for the summer, though one or two beds had only just been planted up so were behind the others. Ginny found there was more information about the abbey than she remembered, and she reinforced her memories. They had a lovely lunch at Angel Hill and had a peek inside the Angel Hotel where Charles Dickens had stayed; he then featured it in *The Pickwick Papers*.

It was now only a few days before her parents' party, and she and her mother had bought new dresses in Cambridge. Ginny found she was getting excited. She couldn't remember when she last went to a party.

The party would be held at a local hotel, taxis had been organised so people could enjoy a drink or two, and there were rooms available for any who had come far and wanted to stay the night. It would be a sit-down dinner with dancing afterwards. Her parents had splashed out. Ginny had spent more than she had intended on her dress, but it wasn't every day she had the chance to go to a party. It was a long, pale-blue dress with silver threads running through it. With her dark, slightly curly hair hanging loose, she would look stunning.

On the evening of the party, Ginny found herself sitting between her father and brother John, and she enjoyed their gentle teasing about how lovely she looked. John asked her where the gauche teenager who had been such a pain in his bum went. There was much laughter between them, and as Ginny got into her stride, she soon teased him back. She had forgotten the art of being a younger sister, but it was coming back, and the meal and speeches all passed by in a happy blur.

Then the band arrived to get ready for the dancing. Ginny didn't know when she had last danced and was grateful that after dancing with her mother, her father whirled her around the dance floor. At least she didn't make too many mistakes and tread on his toes too much.

Various relatives and acquaintances from the past asked her to dance. She was grateful that, though they all offered condolences, no one dwelt on her bereavement. After dancing with Douglas, she got herself a glass of cold water. While she sipped, a tall, grey-haired man whom she had vaguely noticed earlier came up to her and asked, "May I have the next dance, please?" Ginny smiled. This was all very old-fashioned, as was his request.

"Do you mind if I sit this one out? I am feeling quite hot and longing to have a sit down. I'm not used to all this."

He smiled at her. He wasn't at all good-looking. His large nose overpowered his slightly receding chin, but he had nice grey eyes; when he smiled, he looked quite good.

"In that case, do you mind if I join you?"

"I'd appreciate the company. I thought I'd sit on the terrace. These long summer evenings are something we don't get where I live."

He followed her outside, and they found two cane chairs to sit on. "This is a lovely hotel. Mum and Dad are lucky it isn't too far away. I'm Ginny, by the way."

The man bowed his head slightly. "I'm Graham, Graham Rolf. I'm a friend of your father's. Sadly, I have only met your mother once or twice."

"Is your wife here?" Ginny looked round, feeling suddenly uncomfortable.

Graham snorted. "No, thank God. I'm divorced with two kids. One is in America, and one lives with my ex."

"Oh, how old are they, then?"

"My son in America is thirty, and my daughter is twenty-five. She just had a relationship end; hence, she went home to Mummy."

He sounded rather bitter, so Ginny said nothing. He peered down at the drink he had brought out with him, and she studied him for a few minutes. There was something sad about him that made her feel sorry for him. As if he felt her gaze, he raised his head and looked into her eyes.

"I am sorry you lost your husband. You must miss him so much."

This immediately brought tears to Ginny's eyes. Her throat closed, so she only nodded in response.

"Tell me about your home and what you do. You make hats, I hear. Is that right?"

Grateful for the change of topic, Ginny launched into describing her home and her business. From then on, they both relaxed and shared stories and incidents and laughter. Graham asked her to dance again, and she found he was an excellent dancer. They spent the rest of the evening together.

When everyone was leaving and going their separate ways, Graham asked her if he could ring her tomorrow. "You are staying with your parents, so I have their number." Ginny nodded, though she was suddenly unsure. From their conversations, she had worked out that he was about sixty—quite a lot older than her. Younger than her parents but older than she liked the thought of.

Back in her parents' kitchen, Amy made hot chocolate for herself and Ginny. Her father announced he would stick with a nightcap of whisky.

"I got the impression that Graham likes you, Ginny," Roy said.

"Um, yes. Well . . . he asked if he could ring me."

Her parents exchanged looks. "He's a nice man. You could do worse," Amy said.

"Maybe, but he's a lot older than me."

"He's sixty-six. I know because he had a do at the golf club when he turned sixty-five last year," Roy said.

Ginny pulled a face.

"Remember, it's just a number. It has nothing to do with how people are. Some people are old at forty or fifty. Age is just a number that has nothing to do with reality. He is fit and healthy, as far as I know, and well off too. He is also full of life and great fun," Amy said.

"Well, he may change his mind. What else can you tell me about him?"

"He's divorced. He owns that factory out on Hadleigh Road—they make components for tractor hydraulic systems. Never met his wife. I think it wasn't a very happy marriage for a long time before they separated. He lives out towards Bury in a big house. He must rattle around in it like a pea in a drum," Roy said.

Ginny spluttered in her mug, laughing at the picture her father painted.

While lying in bed that night, she thought about her conversation with Graham and realised she had found him attractive but couldn't imagine him as a lover.

CHAPTER 8

GINNY'S MOBILE BUZZED. Although she'd muted it before going to bed, it disturbed her enough to wake her. She blearily looked at the clock and saw it was seven thirty—late for her. She picked up her phone, but it had already stopped ringing. *Oh God. It was from home. What's wrong?* She fumbled for a minute or two then rang back, trying not to think about how much it was costing.

"Ginny! How are you? Just thought I would update you and tell you all is well." Alex's cheery voice came over the phone loud and clear.

Ginny felt cross, then relieved. "You gave me a fright. I thought I said to only ring if there was a problem."

"Well, yes, but we are all missing you: Millie, Puck, and me. I thought you might be worried about the business and all."

Alex sounded very downcast and deflated. Ginny was sorry she had spoken rather sharply.

"It's OK, Alex, and it's good to hear from you, really. It's just that I was worried for a minute. Tell me how you are. Are you coping with those orders you had to send out? Did you get them posted in good time?"

For the next minute or two, they talked about hats then finished the conversation. Alex assured her Millie and Puck were fine too. As Ginny put the phone down, a wave of unexpected homesickness swept over her. She missed her animals and her business. She even missed Alex. She shook her head. What was she thinking? He worked for her and was her student. Feeling cross with herself, she scrambled out of bed and went to have a shower.

When she got downstairs, her mother was sitting at the kitchen table. "Hello, dear." She yawned, and Ginny glimpsed her tonsils. "Good party last night. Didn't expect to see you yet, though. Dad is still sound asleep."

"I would've slept longer, but Alex rang from home and woke me up."

"This being the man looking after your place? You said he's very young. How old is he?"

"Twenty."

"Goodness, taking care of your home is a big responsibility. Is he up to it? Aren't you worried?"

Ginny shook her head, clasping her hands around the mug of coffee her mother had placed in front of her. "No. He is very good with animals and a talented artist. I have confidence that all is well."

"That's good, then." Her mother seemed to have lost interest. She asked Ginny what she wanted for breakfast.

The morning passed quietly since everyone was still recovering from the night before, then at lunch, the phone went again. It had rung several times throughout the morning as friends and family touched base to show their appreciation for the party. Amy picked up the phone and beckoned Ginny over. "It's for you," she said.

As Ginny took the phone from her mother, she guessed who it was. "Hello."

"Ginny, how are you today? I hope you're not suffering from sore toes after all the dancing we did."

"I'm good, Graham. Thanks for the concern. How are you?"

"I am well, thank you. I was wondering if you would have lunch with me tomorrow. I could pick you up at about twelve thirty?"

Ginny hesitated for a moment but remembered what her mother had said the night before. "Thank you, I'd like that."

They made small talk for a few more minutes then hung up. "You look thoughtful. Everything all right?" her mother asked her when she returned to the kitchen where her mother had set out a cold lunch.

"Graham just asked me to lunch tomorrow, and I said yes. I'm not sure it's wise, but I remembered what you said last night. I don't want to lead him on, though. I'm going home in just over a fortnight, after all. There is no future for us."

"He knows that, so it's up to him. Have fun while you have the chance. I'm sure Jeff wouldn't want you to sit and be miserable. You're still young, and you've had a hard few years. Enjoy what comes your way."

Ginny gave her mother a hug. "Thanks, Mum. You're right. I need to take any chances for fun when they come along."

The rest of the day passed quietly, though some of the family popped in later in the day to mull over the party and compare notes. Paul teased Ginny about making out with Graham, more to get a reaction than anything, but Ginny didn't rise to the bait. She just smiled and said he seemed like a nice man.

The next morning, she couldn't decide what to wear and got herself quite hot and bothered about it. Amy teased her gently and told her she was acting like a teenager. This made Ginny stop and take stock. *Why am I getting so het up about it? It's just lunch. If he doesn't like me in broad daylight and wearing normal clothes, then it's his loss.*

It was a cool day, so she opted for a pair of light cotton trousers and a green top, which was quite low cut but not too revealing. It was her personal favourite, and she felt happy in it.

Graham was on time, and he pecked her on the cheek when she came out of the house, just as he had when she had said goodnight after the party. He opened the car door for her and generally fussed over her to ensure she was comfortable. She enjoyed the luxury of being a passenger in his Mercedes.

He drove towards the coast then stopped at a small village pub. "They do the most wonderful Sunday roasts here. Small and out of the way it may be, but it's special," he said. They got out of the car.

He wasn't wrong. The food was superb, and Graham was a great companion. They hadn't really talked of personal things at the party. Instead, they had danced more than anything. Now, Ginny found they had common ground because Graham was also an avid gardener. He didn't know much yet since he'd only begun dabbling now that he was semi-retired. Ginny loved her garden, though she didn't have much time, and grew more vegetables than anything else.

He also regaled her with stories of his life and work and made her laugh.

Then, towards the end of the meal, he said, "Tell me about your husband. Jeff was his name, right?"

Ginny, having had more wine than Graham since he was driving, suddenly felt more serious than she'd felt a few minutes before.

"What do you want to know?"

"He was in a wheelchair, I understand. Why? How did that happen? Was he always like that?"

Sudden tears gathered in Ginny eyes, and she turned her head, so Graham didn't see.

"No, he had a bad accident. He was on a quad bike, and it rolled, trapping him underneath. He broke his back. It happened four or so years ago. I'm sorry, Graham, but I don't want to talk about it. That accident changed our lives forever." With that, Ginny got to her feet and made for the bathroom.

Graham watched her go with a frown on his face. He'd put his foot in it big time. When she came back, however, she appeared to be back to normal, or at least how she was before he'd started to talk about her husband. He'd been curious since he didn't know any details. In fact, no one outside her family did.

"Sorry about that. It's still raw. After all, it hasn't been a year since he passed away."

"I know, and I'm the one who's sorry. That was crass of me. Now, would you like coffee or tea before we go?"

The rest of the afternoon passed pleasantly. When they got back to her parents' house, Ginny asked him in.

"Thank you, but no," he said. "Maybe next time. Have dinner with me Tuesday?"

"Thank you, but Jane and her husband are coming over. They are going on holiday at the end of the week, and Mum wants us to have a nice meal together before they leave."

"Ha, OK. We will have to have dinner another night, then." He had come around to her side of the car, and he kissed her gently on the lips. Ginny kissed him back equally gently. It was a nice kiss.

"See you soon," he said as he got into the car. Ginny nodded and watched him drive away. *He's a really nice guy.*

On Wednesday, Ginny found herself going out for dinner with Graham. This time, they went into Cambridge, which was a rather long drive, but Graham seemed unfazed by this. The restaurant was small and romantic, with booths rather than tables. Ginny was rather horrified by the prices in the menu then told herself he'd brought her here, so it was up to him. She was going to give the entrée a pass, but Graham insisted, and Ginny found the portions appropriate, which was a relief as she felt she was getting larger by the day. They both chose a duck dish for their mains, and Ginny reckoned it was the best she had ever tasted.

The conversation flowed easily; neither found themselves at a loss for words. Ginny felt totally relaxed and enjoyed herself more than she had in a long time. Graham had one glass of wine which, as he had ordered a bottle, meant Ginny drank more than her share. It also meant she was quite giggly by the time they finished their meal. Later, she wondered if this had been a ploy on Graham's part.

When they got back to her parents' house, Ginny asked him in again.

"Thank you, but it's late. I have to pass. However, I do want to ask you something." Graham took a big breath, his knuckles white around the steering wheel.

He cleared his throat. "You'll be going home next week. I'd like it if you'd come to the coast with me for a couple of days. I was thinking Aldeburgh. I realise I am rushing you, but you'll be gone soon, and I like your company. I—" Graham ran out of words.

Ginny was startled by this request because she hadn't seen it coming. She shook herself mentally and said, "Thank you for a lovely evening and your invite." She paused, remembering what her mother had said. *Why should I decline? It might be fun, and if it isn't, I won't see him again for a very long time, if ever. What do I have to lose?*

"I'll join you," she said.

Graham jumped out of the car, came around to help her out, and gave her an enormous hug. "Great. I'll pick you up about nine on Friday morning. Is that OK?"

Ginny nodded, and Graham planted a kiss on her lips, then he positively danced round to the driver's side and sped off, not waiting to see if Ginny got inside the house. Ginny was highly amused. *He's acting like a teenager.*

CHAPTER 9

GINNY BOUNCED BETWEEN being excited at the prospect of the weekend and being consumed with self-doubt. Would she be sharing a room? A bed? She didn't know what to think and chickened out of asking her mother for her opinion. When she had told Amy and Roy about going to the coast with Graham for the weekend, they had simply told her to enjoy herself. It was a good time of the year to go on a trip since the school holidays had yet to start.

By the time Friday morning came round, she was a bundle of nerves and almost felt sick. However, Graham, apart from obviously looking forward to the time away, didn't seem any different. Somehow, his consistency allayed Ginny's nerves.

Their first stop was Snape Maltings—the old maltings had fallen into disrepair but had been refurbished a few years ago. Now, the old maltings had become a small artisans' village. There were shops selling all sorts of homewares, furniture, and clothes. The shops sold everything one could think of. There were art galleries, a large restaurant, a theatre, and many delightful nooks and crannies. Not all of the buildings had been refurbished yet. The mellow bricks, soft sunshine, and meandering river all had a soothing effect on Ginny. They had a light lunch after wandering around, then they dived back into the shops. Ginny admired clothes, jewellery, paintings, and lots of odds and ends.

"There are so many things I could take home if I could afford it and if it would fit in my suitcase," she exclaimed.

Graham laughed as she admired a bookcase. "You'd certainly have a problem bringing that home," he said.

Once Ginny had exhausted her wallet and her feet, they drove to the hotel. Ginny didn't know what to expect but was relieved to find Graham had booked two rooms next to each other. Neither made any comment on this since they were still strangers and were both feeling their way in the relationship. Also, they were conscious that their time was limited.

"I'll let you get settled and see you in the bar in, say, an hour. Is that OK with you?" he asked.

"It suits me well. See you then."

Ginny unpacked the few things she had brought and tried to decide what she would wear for dinner, as she knew they were going to a well-known restaurant. She had brought two outfits for the evening, so it didn't take her long to choose a deep-red top with a boat neck. She had bought navy trousers to go with it. She knew she looked good in it.

She lay on the bed and dozed off.

She woke with a start to the sound of her mobile ringing. Blearily, she looked at it. Her landline number in Australia. *Oh God, what happened?* Her hand shook as she answered it.

"Alex, what's wrong?" she asked.

"Hi! Nothing's wrong, nothing at all. I just wanted to hear your voice. You said you'd keep in touch, but I haven't had any messages from you for a few days, and I was worried. Are you OK?"

Ginny let out a breath she hadn't realised she was holding. "Yes, I'm fine. Sorry I forgot about texting or emailing. I've just been busy, you know. I'll be on my way home this time next week, in any case. Are you sure everything's all right?"

They chatted for a few minutes, then they hung up. Ginny felt guilty because she hadn't kept in touch on purpose. Her feelings towards Alex confused and alarmed her. She had thought distance would clarify them; instead, she was even more unsure. *This is so stupid. He's young enough to be my son, but—don't go there. Don't think about him. If I do, the hurt will be too great. I don't need more hurt, but . . . God, what should I do? Concentrate on Graham. Think about now, and let the future take care of itself.*

Ginny jumped off the bed and into the shower, trying hard to rid herself of her thoughts about Alex and forcing herself to think about Graham instead. She knew he was a nice guy: kind, decent, and perhaps loving. If she let Graham make love to her, would she stop thinking about Alex? She acknowledged to herself, for the first time, that Alex had been in her thoughts throughout the trip.

With her mind still in turmoil, Ginny met Graham at the bar. They ordered gin and tonics and chatted about the day and what they had seen. Ginny forced herself to concentrate on the conversation. Then Graham pulled a small package out of his pocket and placed it on the bar top in front of her. "For you, Ginny," he said

Mystified, she unwrapped the small box. It contained the pretty little pendant she had admired in the antique jewellery store at Snape Maltings. "Oh, Graham, it's beautiful, but I can't accept this. And how did you buy it when I was with you the whole day?"

"I got it when you went to the toilet, and why can't you accept it? It's a gift for a beautiful woman, which you are. Here, let me." Graham rose, took the pendant, and fastened it around Ginny's neck. It was a teardrop-shaped ruby set with tiny diamonds, and Ginny remembered the expensive tag that had been on it.

"Graham, it's too much. I hardly know you, nor you me. I—" Graham held up his hand to stop her protests.

"Please accept it, and make me a happy man. I know you are returning to Australia in less than a week, but I intend to visit you soon if you'll allow it."

Ginny was now completely out of her depth. What could she say?

Did he really intend on coming all that way to see her? It seemed too far-fetched for words. She decided to go with the flow. What else could she do?

They walked along the seafront to the restaurant. "Pity it's a shingle beach. Walking on the sand would have been fun," Ginny remarked.

"You'd have to take your shoes off to walk on the sand. I think this is better." They were walking along a concrete path behind the beach. Ginny wasn't sure she agreed with this but let it pass.

Graham had done his homework as far as the food was concerned, and it was plain the staff were expecting him. Ginny wondered if he had been there before—maybe with other women. It didn't make her feel envious but slightly unsettled.

However, they had a superb meal, and they both had quite a bit to drink, so Ginny once again found herself feeling a little giddy as they walked back to the hotel.

When they got upstairs, Ginny hesitated outside her room, and as she fiddled in her bag for her key, she debated whether she should ask Graham in or not. She needn't have worried. He took the key from her when she found it and unlocked the door, then he asked if he could come in.

"Yes, of course. Would you like a cup of tea?" Part of Ginny's mind rebuked her for how ridiculous she sounded, but she suddenly felt more sober.

Graham didn't answer. Instead, he put his arms around her and kissed her, his tongue probing her lips apart gently. Ginny gave in to the kiss, responding with a strange kind of detached feeling, as if she were standing outside her body and watching herself.

"Ginny, you are so desirable," Graham muttered, drawing his head back. His hands creeped under her top and then he released her bra. Taking Ginny completely off guard, he pulled her top off before disposing of her trousers and panties. She knew he was thoroughly aroused because when he'd kissed her, she'd felt his erection through their clothes, but she hadn't expected this level of urgency.

With his lips back on hers, he steered her to the bed. Without more ado, he climbed on top of her and thrust his erection between her legs. Tearing her mouth away from his so she could speak, she said, "Graham, slow down, for God's sake."

He looked down at her and winced. "God, I'm sorry, it's just—it's been so long since I— since I made love to a woman. I . . ."

Feeling sorry for him, Ginny reached up and put her arms around his neck. "It's been a long time for me too."

They moved slowly for a minute or two, but it wasn't long before Graham thrust into Ginny again. Ginny was only now getting aroused. She had come to realise she didn't fancy him. He was a nice guy, but she didn't desire him at all. However, she was trying hard to match his desire. Within moments of entering her, he climaxed, leaving Ginny feeling disappointed and frustrated. She drifted off to sleep soon after, the alcohol helping her escape into oblivion. When she woke a little later, Graham was snoring gently bedside her. She carefully got off the bed and went into the bathroom. She decided to have a shower because she was sticky and uncomfortable. When she returned to the bedroom a few minutes later, Graham was awake.

"Sorry, I was a bit too eager. I'll do better next time, I promise." He held out his arms to her. He looked so sad and forlorn. She went to him and allowed him to kiss and caress her. This time, she was more aroused and wanted him more. But when the time came, he climaxed too soon, and she was left feeling deflated, though she didn't tell him. For the second time, he fell straight to sleep.

She lay beside him, thinking. Maybe he was always like this. Or maybe, like he'd said, he was out of control because it had been a long time since he had made love to a woman.

When she woke in the morning, Graham was gone. She guessed he had returned to his own room sometime in the night, and a bit later, when he knocked on her door, this was confirmed.

At breakfast, they were a bit awkward together, but as time went on, they both relaxed and got back to the companionable state of their times before. Graham was good company, and he made Ginny laugh, though he could be serious too.

Graham had booked a table at the hotel that evening. They lingered a long time after dinner, then they moved to the bar, both unsure of where the evening would lead them when they went upstairs.

When they made love for the third time, she was very aware that Graham was trying hard to slow down, and although it was better, Ginny was way behind him and left feeling disappointed. When Graham asked her if it was all right for her, she said yes. She had faked it a bit, but she was sorry for him. One thing that had surprised her was that she hadn't been turned off by the fact he wasn't in the first flush of youth. He was no Adonis and never had been, but she had hardly noticed that. He was such a nice man, so she was happy to kiss and cuddle him, but a good lover he was not. The wrinkles on his face and his knobby knees didn't concern her at all. It was merely his lovemaking that was lacking.

Perhaps he's always had a problem. But why should I care? I'll be gone soon, and I'm not likely to see him again unless I come back for another visit. That's not on the cards, in any case. I've a business to run, animals to nurture, and all sorts of commitments. Then there's Alex! Ginny hurriedly shut that thought down. What on earth had got into her, lusting after a boy?

They returned from their weekend trip, and when they got to Ginny's parents' house, Graham accepted her invitation inside. He stayed for a meal and was reluctant to leave. Ginny watched him and her father discuss politics and realised with a shock that Graham was nearer her father in age than her.

Later, she walked him to the door. "Thank you for a lovely weekend and the beautiful pendant. It was too much."

He smiled at her. "When can I see you again? I've really enjoyed myself. It's been marvellous."

"Mum has got me catching up with everyone this week, and I leave on Saturday. Maybe we can have lunch on Friday?"

Graham opened his mouth to protest but shut it again. This woman had really got under his skin, and he felt like a teenager again after a long time feeling lost, lonely, sad, and somewhat redundant. However, he had known from the outset that she would be leaving soon and had her family around her to see. Swallowing his disappointment, he agreed to meet on Friday. He gave her a lingering kiss and took his leave.

"How was your weekend? Was it OK?" Amy couldn't resist asking when Ginny returned to the sitting room. Her father had gone to bed, but Amy was agog to hear how Ginny had got on.

"Mum, we already told you what we did and saw."

"Yes, but did he behave or make a pass!"

"Mum!" Ginny was slightly shocked. Finally, she said, "He made a pass, but it didn't mean anything—at least not to me. He's a nice guy, but that is as far as it goes. Now I'm off to bed. Night." She kissed her mother and escaped as quickly as she could.

Amy sighed. She had hoped Graham would sweep Ginny off her feet, and she would return to the UK permanently. Knowing Ginny had no family in Australia made her worry.

CHAPTER 10

ANOTHER ROUND OF family visits. It was more emotional this time because no one knew when she would be back. Ginny, caught up in the moment, almost forgot about Graham. In the midst of all this, Alex phoned again to tell Ginny all was well, and he was looking forward to her return. Again, Ginny got cross with herself, as visions of Alex kept intruding into her thoughts. What was the matter with her?

Friday came around all too quickly. Graham wanted Ginny to spend the whole day with him, but she wanted to spend time with her family and said she'd see him in the evening. Reluctantly, he agreed.

He was early picking her up. He hadn't said where they were going, and Ginny hadn't worried, thinking it was up to him. As it turned out, he took her to his home.

It was a large, Georgian house with a short gravel drive sweeping up to the front door. Manicured lawns and rose beds decorated the right side of the house, and on the left, there was a brick wall separating it from the neighbour's property. Ushering Ginny in, Graham led her through the house and into a large white-and-chrome kitchen. It wasn't homey, and it lacked character. It was like something out of a glossy magazine. Graham fussed over the final dinner preparations since he hadn't managed to finish setting the table before he picked Ginny up. It was a cold meal, which didn't matter as it was a very warm evening. Looking out the window towards the back garden, Ginny spied a spa.

"Goodness, what a beautiful garden, and you have a spa! Do you use it much?"

"A bit. I thought we could have a dip together later."

"I haven't brought anything to wear in it, sorry."

"Birthday suit is fine by me, and no one else can see, so don't worry about that."

Ginny wasn't too sure. Graham had seen her body, but somehow this would be different. She gave a little shiver. Graham was a good cook and had made a salmon mouse and a very decadent chocolate dessert. He also was very generous with the wine. Ginny noticed he wasn't holding back and guessed he intended for her to stay the night. He wouldn't be driving. She felt she was being railroaded and wasn't comfortable.

Then came the moment when Graham said they should get in the spa. Ginny felt backed into a corner and started to refuse, but Graham was so crestfallen that she gave in.

It was strange, she thought later. Graham's body looked more youthful than it had in Aldeburgh. Maybe it was the dim light. The sun had nearly set, as it was high summer and didn't get that dark before ten at night.

Ginny had skipped across to the tub as quickly as she could, so she could hide under the water. They had only sat in it a few minutes before Graham kissed her and caressed her breasts. Perhaps the water factored into her arousal, but Ginny was more turned on this time than she had been before, and when Graham lifted her out of the tub and took her on a lounger, she enjoyed his advances more. Unfortunately, he was still way ahead of her.

"I got the bed ready, dear. I intend to make love to you again shortly," he whispered.

"I'm sorry, but I am going home—back to my parents' house. I can't stay the night. I need to be there."

"But I can't drive you. I drank too much."

Ginny was fairly sure he'd done it on purpose, so he could persuade her to stay.

"I'll ring Dad. He will come and pick me up. I'll do it now if you don't mind. It will take him twenty minutes or so to get here."

Graham looked as if he would argue or make a fuss, but in the end, he didn't. They got dressed, then they sat waiting.

"Ginny, I don't want you to disappear from my life. We'll keep in touch, won't we? We can use Facetime or whatever."

"Yes, of course, but we will have to keep tabs on the time difference. I have been rung in the middle of the night a few times, and it's not funny."

After hugging and kissing her fervently, Graham finally let her go when her father turned up. Ginny was highly embarrassed, but her father looked straight ahead and spared her some blushes.

"I'm guessing Graham didn't want you to leave?" he asked as they drove away.

"It would appear not. He's a nice guy, but he's twenty years older than me!"

"Does that matter? Like your mother would say, age is just a number. It's how you behave that matters. Teenagers can be like old men sometimes and vice versa. I don't know Graham terribly well, but he's always seemed much younger than me—at least I always thought so. Not that I've thought about age much, I have to say. Mum and I are the same age, as you know, so it's never come up before."

"No, I suppose not."

Several hours later, Ginny thought about what her father had said as she sat in her seat in the plane heading back to Australia and Alex.

He had offered to meet her at the airport, but she had refused. Her flight would get in late at night, so she had booked a hotel for the night. She surprised herself by sleeping well. She had left her car in the car park, so the next morning, she got behind the wheel and started the drive home. It would take five hours, but she figured she wouldn't hurry. She had hardly left the car park when her phone rang through the Bluetooth.

"Ginny, hello. Are you OK? I tracked your flight, so I know you landed. When are you setting off?"

Ginny couldn't help smiling at Alex's enthusiasm.

"I just set off, so add five hours or so, and I will be there."

"I will be so pleased to see you—so will Puck and Millie. Drive carefully, won't you?"

"Of course. See you then." Ginny hung up before Alex had a chance to say anything else.

Her feelings seemed heightened—not diminished as she had hoped.

She didn't analyse them. She hadn't before, and now wasn't the time, but she was filled with a mixture of suppressed excitement and foreboding. The road seemed to stretch ahead endlessly. Would she ever get home, and did she want to? She would have to confront her feelings.

What feelings, though? I am making something out of nothing. We're friends, that is all. I am old enough to be his mother, for God's sake. As for him, well, I'm just someone who is part teacher, part employer, and part friend. That is all—it has to be. It can't possibly be anything else. There is no way in the world he could possibly want to make love to me. No way! Why am I thinking about that, in any case? Oh God, it's because I want him. Graham woke a sexual need in me, and I want Alex. I want him desperately. That's it, then. I will give him his marching orders when I get home . . . for both our sakes.

On and on, for kilometre after kilometre, her thoughts spiralled. She stopped for a comfort break, still wrestling with her emotions. She suddenly had a thought. What if she didn't go back? She could phone Alex and say she was delayed and tell him to go home to his parents. Would it work? She doubted it but thought it was worth a try. However, her phone was dead. She had forgotten to charge it overnight. She chucked it onto the passenger seat in disgust as she got back into her car. Even the damn phone wasn't helping.

By the time she turned into her driveway, she was exhausted by her thoughts, the journey, and jet lag.

She climbed out of the car. No one seemed to be around, not even Puck. It was quiet and peaceful, and nothing seemed different. In one way, she felt as if she hadn't been home for months, and in another, she felt like she hadn't moved an inch.

Hauling her baggage out of the car, she went in through the workroom door. Looking around, she noticed all was neat and tidy, and there was a flower arrangement on the small coffee table in the waiting area.

Moving through the house, she found everything was sparkling. There was no sign of Alex, but she saw his car parked down by the chook run, so she knew he couldn't be far away. Taking her case into her room, she saw a small vase of fresh flowers on her nightstand and a big welcome home banner over the head of her bed. This made her feel uncomfortable, as this was her room, and in some ways, she felt Alex had no business entering her space. She shook her head. It was a lovely gesture, and she shouldn't be crabby about it. Just as she came out of her room, a big brown bundle launched itself at her.

"Puck! Down," Alex said loudly as he gathered Ginny in his arms and gave her a big hug. She was caught off balance, as she hadn't seen either of them coming, and was almost cross to be caught out. She pushed them both away.

Alex looked at her curiously, then he said, "You look amazing. The holiday really did you good, I can tell."

Ginny blushed slightly. "Thank you. How was everything? It all looks good, I have to say. Thank you for looking after everything so well."

"Do you want an update on the hats now? Shall we do that first?"

"No, I'm too tired. It can wait until tomorrow. A coffee or tea is what I need right now."

They moved into the kitchen and were soon telling each other about their experiences over the last four weeks. Ginny didn't mention Graham, though. Later, while she lay in bed, she wondered why she hadn't, but it was none of Alex's business.

For the next few days, they both settled back into the routine they'd had before. Ginny told Alex he should go home for a rest and, a little to her surprise, he agreed. He then let slip that his mother was being very difficult and had been over several times trying to get him to return home.

Ginny's curiosity was aroused. She hadn't liked what she had seen of Margarita, and her relationship with both her husband and son seemed strange.

"Why doesn't your mum like you working for me? Do you know?"

"Mum is very controlling. She gets that from her father—my grandfather. He's . . ." Alex paused and seemed to be choosing his words carefully. "He's a property developer and nightclub owner and has lots of business interests in Sydney. Dad, as you know, had business in Sydney—that's how Mum and Dad met. I rather think that when Mum decided Dad was the man for her, he didn't stand a chance. Dad is following his dream out here, but Mum spends most of her time in Sydney. When she is here, she expects me to be at home. She doesn't like it if I'm not. Dad has to be in Sydney more again now because Mum made such a fuss."

"Gosh, she must spend a lot of time travelling, then—going to and fro."

"It doesn't take that long in a helicopter," Alex replied.

"No, I suppose it wouldn't." Ginny felt silly and realised again how different their lives were.

"I'll take off tomorrow, if that's OK?"

"Course it is. Go for it."

"Thanks. Mum only ranted and raved at me when she came over. She didn't do anything else bad."

Ginny blanched. The possibility hadn't occurred to her. "It never crossed my mind that she would."

Alex gave a sudden grin. "That's OK, then," he said.

While curled up in bed that evening, Ginny thought about their conversation. She wondered exactly what Margarita's father was like. Alex hadn't said much more, only that his father's parents were both deceased, and he'd never really got to know them. Ginny had the distinct impression that he was a little scared of his other grandfather. She wondered how honest he was.

She lay in bed, unable to sleep for so long that she ended up oversleeping, and Alex had already eaten breakfast and fed the animals before she got into the kitchen. His dark eyes appraised her. "You look like you didn't sleep well."

Ginny shook her head. "Thought I was over jet lag but seems not." She yawned, then she noticed his bag sitting by the door. "You off, then?"

"Yep, if that's ok? I'll be back soon."

"That's fine."

Alex gave her a quick hug, patted Puck's head, then he left with a wave.

Ginny frowned. She felt let down. "I thought we'd at least have breakfast together and a chat. Puck, what do you think?"

Puck looked at her, smiling his doggy smile and wagging his tail. Ginny sighed. She suddenly felt very alone. She hadn't been on her own for weeks and weeks and had got used to company.

Ginny threw herself into her hats. It was what she had done when dealing with Jeff while he was alive and after his passing. Now it was different, and her mind kept wandering—wandering to deep dark eyes, a broad smile, and strong arms. She shook her head, went outside, and saddled Millie. She hadn't ridden since she had come back, and although Alex had exercised Millie occasionally, it hadn't been much. Millie had put on weight and was in a silly mood. Trotting down the gravel road away from home twenty minutes later, Millie shied at a piece of paper lying on the road. Ginny hadn't been paying attention, so she found herself hanging onto Millie's mane and dangling halfway off the saddle. Millie was feeling mischievous and full of beans, so she decided this was something she could make the most of and bucked, sending Ginny flying off the saddle. She landed in a heap on the road. Millie looked at her, then she ambled over to the grass at the roadside and started to nibble it.

Ginny sat up. She was winded but didn't think she had broken anything. She knew, however, she would have some enormous bruises to contend with later. She suddenly felt like crying, though why she wasn't sure; it was silly. She had fallen off countless times over the years, so why was this time any different? She should have been paying attention.

She scrambled to her feet and walked towards Millie who, seeing her coming, tossed her head and trotted off a few paces before grazing again. "Millie, come on, girl. Don't mess me about. Come on and let me catch you."

Ginny crept up towards Millie, holding out her hand. Millie looked at her contemptuously and, tossing her head, trotted off a bit further. She was having a great time. She'd let Ginny catch her when she was ready, not before.

Ginny could hear a car coming, and sure enough, a big silver ute appeared over the rise. It was plain, so it likely belonged to a farmer. Millie was nearer the ute than Ginny, and Ginny hoped the driver would see Millie was loose and stop. He didn't. He drove by her. Millie, not worried by vehicles, hardly raised her head. She was enjoying the grass too much.

"Stupid bloke," Ginny muttered as the car got to her. A big, burly man stuck his head out of the driver's window. "Not a good idea to let your horse graze like that. It might—"

"I'm not letting her do anything! I fell off. Can you help catch her?"

The man looked Ginny up and down, and a smirk creased the corners of his mouth.

"What's it worth?"

"What do you mean? I need to catch my horse. Please, can you help?"

He gave a big grin. Ginny noticed he had a tooth missing, though he didn't look that old. "I can, but it will cost you."

Ginny shivered. She finally realised what he wanted. "Forget it." She stomped off towards Millie who walked away again, but Ginny could tell she had nearly had enough of this game.

Ginny heard the driver get out of his car, but she didn't look round and continued walking towards Millie. "Please, Millie, don't do this to me," Ginny said quietly. The man's footsteps thudded behind her. A shiver of fear ran down her back.

Millie lifted her head and looked at Ginny. Millie didn't like strangers, and maybe that was why she thought Ginny was a good option. To Ginny's surprise, Millie came to her. Ginny grabbed the reins just as the man caught up to her.

Ginny turned and glared at him. "I can manage now, thank you," she said primly.

"Want a leg up?"

"No. I can manage."

He grinned at her, shrugged his shoulders, and ambled back to his vehicle. Ginny let out a breath. She decided he was fairly harmless—probably just thought he'd try his luck. Scrambling onto Millie's back once more, she decided to go back home rather than continue their ride. Millie behaved impeccably. She'd had her fun, so she'd be good.

It was all a blessing in disguise, however, as the incident made Ginny focus more on the important things in her life, such as her business, animals, and daily chores. She went to see Jo and had a catch up with her and generally settled down into her life once more. Alex rang briefly to say he wouldn't be back for a while. He was going to Sydney. Ginny assumed he was going to appease his mother.

Good. It will give me time to sort myself out and stop thinking about him. It's purely lust on my part, and I'm too old to be lustful, silly woman. From then on, every time Alex popped into her mind, she shut him out.

Graham took to ringing her every little while, and she enjoyed their chats. She acknowledged that he was a nice man, but she didn't love him and didn't think she ever would. The spark needed for love wasn't there.

Ginny tried to be more social than she had been before. She had been restricted by Jeff's reluctance to leave the house, and he hadn't taken kindly to strangers, so they had been rather reclusive. Now, Ginny joined the local

Country Women's Association and a craft group in the little town where she lived, so she made new friends. Winter was drawing to a close, and spring was just around the corner. Soon, she was taking orders for the Melbourne Cup, and it brought back memories of last year and her introduction to the Unwins. She ruthlessly closed the door on her memories.

Spring also brought Jeff to the forefront of her mind. Jeff had been gone nearly a year, and she still hadn't sorted out all his clothes and belongings. She didn't know why it was so hard to part with them, it just was. Silly, she knew, but she couldn't help it.

So she made a pledge with herself. She would pull her socks up, square her shoulders, and focus on important tasks. She spent a whole morning going through Jeff's things, and although she made two trips to the local Salvos, she still had quite a lot of items that she couldn't quite bring herself to part with.

She still had too much time on her own, however, and if she wasn't careful, Alex invaded those times. Thinking hard about the whole situation, she realised it wasn't just lust on her part. She had grown used to not having a sex life after Jeff's accident. Also, her experience with Graham had been off-putting. Maybe the romantic part of her life was over, though deep down, she knew that wasn't the case. With Alex, she was drawn to his deeply caring nature, his sense of humour, and the way his eyes sparkled with mischief.

His eyes . . . God, those wonderful eyes of his. It's almost as if he can see into my soul. Stop it, Ginny, stop it. She thought her feelings were definitely more than lust, but that didn't help her at all. In some ways, it made her situation worse.

Walking out of the hall where she had attended a meeting about forming a book club in town, she met the farmer who had refused to help catch Millie. She recognised him and sidestepped around him with her head down, hoping he didn't recognise her.

"Not on your horse today, then. Fallen off again, have you?" He sniggered.

Ginny stopped and looked him squarely in the face.

"What is it with you? Why are you so obnoxious?"

To her surprise, and probably his too, his demeanour changed. He opened his mouth, then he shut it again. He looked shamefaced and muttered an apology before walking away with his head down.

Jo came up to Ginny then. "Fancy a coffee? Was Jem being rude as ever? If he was, take no notice. He can't help himself."

Ginny agreed to the coffee, and once they had settled themselves at a table, she asked about the man.

"That guy, you say his name is Jem. I haven't seen him around town before. Who is he? Where does he live?"

"The other side of town from us. His wife committed suicide about three years ago. Everyone said it was his fault—that he mentally abused her. Actually, it's been longer than three years, now that I think of it. It was before you and Jeff moved to town and before I married. Anyway, the rumours got so bad that he became a recluse, and no one saw anything of him. While you were away, it came out that she'd been mentally unstable. Her mother, who lives in WA, came across to see Jem. They were all worried about him apparently. Alice, that's his stepmother, heard about the stories and put a notice in the local paper telling everyone that her daughter Mary suffered from mental illness. When Mary had a miscarriage, the loss pushed her over the edge. The paper posted an apology to Jem, and he is seen in town occasionally now, but he is very bitter. You can't blame him, really, but it makes everyone shy away from him."

Ginny told Jo about falling off Millie and what Jem had said and done.

"He's harmless enough. He's not that old, but he looks it. I expect it was just a little game he was playing."

"How old is he?"

"I'm not sure. Maybe late forties or early fifties?"

"Oh." Ginny felt sorry for him now.

They chatted about mundane things until Jo asked about Alex. "When is he coming back, or should I ask *is* he coming back?"

Ginny mentally squared her shoulders. "I honestly don't know. His mother rules the roost. Before, I thought Alex wasn't under her thumb and was his own man—his dad too—but from what I understand, Margarita has the upper hand at the moment. She was against him learning millinery—said something along the lines of it being a feminine profession. Charles stuck up for Alex, but I haven't seen him since Alex came to work for me.

It's been a long time since Alex left. I imagine he won't come back. Thankfully, my time teaching him has been paid for. I really don't know what is going on. He phoned me a few times, but the calls were very brief, and I learned nothing from them." Ginny's eyes suddenly flooded with tears, and she turned her head, hoping Jo hadn't seen.

When she got home, she reprimanded herself. *What was I thinking, allowing myself to be upset about Alex? He is nothing—just a passing figure in my life. Why worry about him?*

"Because you love him," a small voice in her head said.

No, that's not possible. He's too young.

All these thoughts swirled round in her head, just as they had every time she thought about him lately.

CHAPTER 11

TWO DAYS LATER, Charles Unwin turned up. Ginny was surprised to see him getting out of his 4WD and met him at the workroom door. "Hello, Charles. I don't imagine you are looking for a hat?"

"Hi, Ginny. No, I just thought I would pop by and see you, as I had to come to town."

"Come on in. Would you like a coffee, tea, or cold drink?"

"Coffee would be great, thanks. I also wanted to tell you about Alex. He is in Sydney, and I'm not sure when he will be back. Marcus, his grandfather, and Margarita are not keen on him being here and learning millinery. To be perfectly honest, I filed for divorce. I can't take any more nonsense from that woman. Her father will give her anything she wants. She wanted me once, but I'm not so malleable as she thought I would be. I just felt the need to explain since I suggested Alex come here in the first place."

Ginny smiled at him. Alex took after his father. "No worries. He looked after the place so well when I was away, and that was a huge help."

For the next half an hour, they talked companionably, and Charles asked about her trip. Then he looked at the time and got to his feet. "I must go. Thank you so much. Would you mind if I call in again next time I come to town?"

"Of course not! Thank you for updating me."

Ginny followed Charles to the door. He turned and gave her a hug and kissed her on the lips.

"Thanks, Ginny," he muttered.

Ginny watched him go, her feelings all over the place. He was so like Alex. *No, Alex is like him,* she corrected herself.

A couple of weeks later, Ginny took a hat out to a woman on a cattle station on the other side of town. She didn't normally do this, but Carol, the woman in question, had broken her leg in a riding accident and couldn't drive.

"Hi, how are you getting on?" Ginny asked when she arrived. "Do you really want this hat? If you're not going to Melbourne next week, I can keep it and give your money back." They had already had this conversation, but Carol was still adamant that she wanted the hat.

"Thanks, but it turns out we are going," Carol said. "Transport for me and my leg is all arranged. Wheelchairs, crutches, the lot. I even managed to get accommodation for the flights, taxis, and hotel. I am seriously looking forward to it. Have you been?"

"No, it's a step too far for me. I'm always so busy. Now, let's see how this looks."

Ginny left an hour or so later after spending a pleasant afternoon with Carol. She hadn't known her that well or for that long, but she was very comfortable with her and had enjoyed the afternoon immensely. The afternoon had sped by, and she was much later than she had intended. She decided to take a different road home, as the gravel road that was coming up was a shortcut. Once she set out on it, she realised she'd made a mistake. The road hadn't been graded for some time and was very rough, so she had to go quite slowly. Then she came to a better bit and put her foot down. Suddenly, her steering went, and she had a job to control the car. She'd had a blow-out in the front.

"Damn," she said aloud as she scrambled out of the vehicle. She was lucky she hadn't gone off the road when the tyre went. The car had been difficult to handle.

Heaving a sigh, she hurriedly started to prepare to change the wheel. Luckily, the boot was fairly clear, so it was easy enough to lift the floor to access the spare tyre, jack, spanner, and the other tools she'd need. It took her several minutes to get the jack in the right place, and she was conscious of the fact it was rapidly growing dark. The torch she had in the glovebox was useless. The battery was flat. She finally got the wheel off the ground, but for the love of her, she couldn't budge the nuts on the wheel. They were stuck fast.

She decided to ring Matt, who worked at the local garage. It was about twelve kilometres to town—too far to walk in the dark—and she'd rather not call the RACQ. However, there was no signal on her mobile. She walked one way—no good. She walked the other way—no good. She didn't fancy walking all the way home in the dark. *Why oh why did I take this road? If I'd kept to the bitumen, someone would have come along. I may not even have had a blow-out.*

She kicked the car in frustration. She felt like crying, but that wouldn't help. She tried and tried to release the nuts on the wheel and managed two, but there were eight in total. Her hands got sore, and finally, she gave up and crept into the driver's seat. She had a bottle of water but nothing to eat, and she was hungry. She didn't know how long she sat there trying to decide what was best to do when she saw headlights coming up the road behind her.

She jumped out of the car when the vehicle neared her. The driver stopped and got out. Ginny was about to ask for help, but the words died on her lips when she saw who it was. Jem. He'd been no help before. Would he help her this time?

"You again," he said. "No horse this time. Your modes of transport give you grief, it seems."

"Are you able to help or not because if not, just drive away, but have the grace to call someone for me when you get a signal on your phone."

"Hold your horses. Ha ha, I just made a joke! I'll help you. Women are pretty bad at changing tyres."

"I'm not normally, but the nuts are stuck."

Jem bent down and had a look. Muttering, he went to his ute and came back with a small canister of lubricant. He sprayed some on each nut, then he proceeded to unscrew them easily. "They got a bit dried up and stiff, that's all."

Ginny stood back and watched him. His movements were swift and sure, and before long, her car was once again ready to roll.

Heaving her blown tyre into the boot, he grinned at her, revealing the gap in his teeth. "I seem to be making a habit of finding you in trouble."

"Yes, you do. Thank you so much. Can I give you something?" Ginny was uncertain how to proceed. When he'd offered to help catch Millie, he'd wanted something worth his while. She hadn't liked the implication, and now she was worried all over again.

As if he had read her thoughts, he said, "Nah, no worries—just helping out. I think I upset you last time when your horse chucked you off. Sorry. I wasn't in the best place that day." He tapped his head, and Ginny took it to mean he'd been upset. "It was actually supposed to be a joke, but it didn't come out as one, did it. Sorry."

Ginny smiled at him and decided she quite liked him, though she didn't know him very well.

"You'd better be on your way," he said. "There's rain coming, and these old roads get greasy."

"I will. Thanks again." Ginny held out her hand, but he ignored it. Instead, he dipped his head and hurried back to his ute. Ginny got the feeling he was upset again. She drove home slowly, not wanting more mishaps and also thinking about Jem. She felt sorry for him and didn't like the idea of his help going unrewarded.

The next morning, she got busy and made a rich fruit cake. She had decided to bake Jem a cake as a thank you. She wasn't comfortable not acknowledging his help. If he hadn't come along, she might have been stuck on the road for hours, as no one else had passed that way while she'd been there.

She set out that afternoon. She knew where he lived, as his driveway led off the road where she'd had the puncture. She stopped on the way through town and dropped her tyre off. The guy questioned her a bit about where it had happened and if she had managed. He was just being friendly, but she kept the information to herself for reasons she wasn't sure of.

She set off up the drive. She felt nervous, partly because she wasn't sure what reception she would get.

The house was a typical Queenslander and looked spruce and well-maintained. There was a patch of lawn at the front, and Ginny could see a vegetable patch off to one side. Further on were some sheds. Jem's ute was parked to the side.

She had put the cake in a large plastic container and, holding it carefully, she climbed the verandah steps and knocked as loudly as she could.

For a few moments there was silence, then a huge dog appeared from around the corner of the wraparound verandah, barking loudly. It took Ginny by surprise, making her jump. She dropped the cake container with a clatter.

"Bruno, what the fuck is it?" an angry voice shouted from inside. Jem burst through the door, nearly knocking Ginny off her feet, as she had bent down to retrieve the cake. She straightened up, and for a heartbeat, she and Jem stared at each other.

They both tried to speak at once. Jem raised his hand, silencing her, and asked, "What's this, then? What are you doing here?" He didn't look angry—more confused than anything. Bruno sat by his master and smiled at Ginny with a big doggy grin.

"I, um, I made you a cake as a thank you for helping me yesterday."

Jem stared first at her then at the cake container, which was still upside down on the floor. To her surprise, he burst out laughing, then Ginny joined him. For a few moments, they were both helpless, then Ginny bent once more to pick up the box and cake. Quelling her laughter as much as she could, she said, "I think my offering might be the worse for wear now. It was a fruit cake, and as I said, it's a thank you."

Recovering himself, Jem said, "You'd better come through, and we'll see what the damage is."

He led the way down a short passageway into a large, airy kitchen with doors opening onto a spacious deck. Ginny couldn't help noticing everything was spotlessly clean. His home wasn't what she had expected, though what that was she had no idea.

She put the cake container on the bench top and lifted the lid. The cake had split in half but, on the whole, it had survived remarkably well.

Jem peeped at his gift over her shoulder. "That looks delicious, and it will get broken up anyway when I eat it. Would you like to have a coffee and a piece of cake with me?"

"Thank you, Jem. I'd like that." She perched on a stool and watched him as he put the jug on and set about making coffee. He faced away from her, so she allowed herself to stare. He was of medium height but very strongly built, and his hair, which was a dull blond, was receding slightly. He had quite a plain face, but when he smiled, he looked almost handsome—except for the missing tooth. Ginny wondered why he hadn't had a false one put in since it was right at the front.

He rummaged in the cupboard for mugs and plates. "I don't have visitors, so everything is at the back of the cupboard," he said by way of explanation.

"If you pass me a knife, I'll cut this cake," Ginny said.

"You think it wants cutting? I thought you were just breaking it up!"

Ginny snorted another little laugh. "Not the ideal way to share a cake!"

He passed her a knife, and once they each had coffee and cake, they naturally gravitated to the chairs on the verandah. Afterwards, Ginny would be surprised about how comfortable she felt with him compared to the first time she had met him. But he seemed relaxed and not at all like what she had thought.

"How long have you lived here?" she asked.

A shadow passed over his face. "It's been over twenty years now. We bought it when we got married."

"I heard about your wife. I'm sorry."

Many emotions passed across Jem's face: anger, bitterness, sadness, and resignation.

He turned his head towards her, and she was shocked by the pain in his eyes.

"I keep telling myself that I did nothing wrong, that I helped Mary as much as I could, but those buggers in town had me down as guilty without knowing anything at all. I won't forgive any of them for that. The only reason I helped you and spoke to you is because I know you weren't part of it all. Otherwise, I'd have left you to sort your own horse out. I wouldn't have even stopped."

Instinctively, Ginny touched his hand. "I'm glad you did, Jem. Thanks. You certainly saved me last night too. I didn't fancy a walk home in the dark. It's quite a long walk. I might have got lost!"

Jem grinned at her and tilted his head, appraising her. He said, "Nah, somehow, I don't think so. I think you are a strong woman. You know what you are doing."

They talked some more, and Ginny left with a whole new perspective on Jem Wakefield.

CHAPTER 12

NOVEMBER LEACHED INTO December, but Alex didn't return, and Ginny was beginning to think he wasn't coming back. Jo had invited her over for Christmas, but she had said no. She'd found the anniversary of Jeff's passing harder than she had expected, and it had left her feeling very depressed. Jeff's family had also invited her for Christmas, but again, she'd refused. Never very close to any of them, she now felt more alienated. Jeff's siblings were all married with children, and like her family, they didn't understand why she and Jeff had remained childless. Deep down, Ginny now regretted that.

She kept herself busy on Christmas Day and had conversations later in the day with family in the UK. Then Graham rang, and she picked up an underlying current in their conversation. He wanted to say something but didn't. She didn't press him; he would tell her if he wanted to. Maybe he'd found someone else. Ginny realised she didn't actually mind if he had.

She had seen Jem a few times in town, and they'd had brief conversations. She vaguely wondered what he was doing for Christmas but decided it was none of her business.

To her surprise, he turned up on Boxing Day with a roughly wrapped parcel. She heard a car and went to the door. She was very surprised when he appeared out of the driver's side. He looked embarrassed and uncomfortable, and after seeing her standing in the doorway, he grinned sheepishly.

"Hi, um, I hope you don't mind me rocking up like this. I brought you something. Um, I don't know if you like home-made wine, but . . . um."

Ginny couldn't help it. She burst out laughing. He looked quite comical, clutching the package of wine. His hat, which had nearly blown away when he'd got out of the car, rested at a rakish angle on his head. Puck had been asleep, but he now came bounding up and put his paws on Jem's shoulders and tried to lick his face. This sent Ginny off into even more gales of laughter. Afterwards, she wondered what had been so funny.

Recovering somewhat, Ginny beckoned Jem in. "I'd be delighted to sample your wine. Did you say you made it yourself?"

"Yes. I had so much fruit two years ago that I made wine with it. Didn't know what else to do, and I hate seeing food go to waste. This is made from oranges. It's more like a liquor, really, but see what you think."

It was very nice—not too sweet or bitter. "This is very good. How much did you make? How many bottles?"

Jem looked sheepish again. "Over twenty bottles. Well, actually closer to thirty."

"Oh my God, it will take you ages to drink that lot."

Jem nodded. "And I have another batch that wants bottling."

Ginny got some cheese and biscuits out, which stirred up her memory of Charles and Alex turning up with flowers. It made her feel sad for a moment. Would she ever see Alex again?

By the time they finished the bottle, Ginny was feeling quite drunk, though Jem didn't seem tipsy at all. Ginny worried about him driving home, so she plied him with strong coffee and insisted on making some sandwiches. He really seemed sober, and she hoped he was. They had chatted companionably about everything under the sun but nothing personal. Now, Ginny said, "I'm worried about you driving. You've had quite a bit of wine, and I feel quite drunk. I am sure if I got to my feet, I would fall over."

Jem grinned. "I haven't had as much as you. I was watching my step. Don't worry."

Ginny looked at him sharply. "Did you set out to get me drunk?"

"Nah, not really. You often look sad, so I thought it would do you good to have a few drinks."

To her surprise, Ginny's eyes flooded with tears. "Thank you," she said, sniffling, "but you're sad too."

"Yeah, well, I suppose. It's tough. Your husband didn't like who he became by the end, did he? No more than my wife liked the person she became. Perhaps they are happier now." He patted her arm.

Jem took his leave soon after, saying he'd bring her a few bottles of wine, as she'd had the idea to give any customers who came to the showroom a taste of his wine. She told him it wouldn't be many because most of her business was online. He seemed happy enough, saying it might help shift some of it.

Charles appeared two days later. He brought a package containing smoked salmon, many different cheeses, crackers, and a bottle of champagne.

"I came to repay you for your hospitality. I'm rather late, but never mind that. Better late than never."

As they had before, they sat out on the verandah and chatted about the weather and the price of cattle. Despite the mundane topics, Charles fidgeted in his seat and hesitated to meet her eyes. He had something to say. Suddenly feeling worried, Ginny sipped her drink. Her heart hammered in her chest.

"Thank you for taking Alex under your wing. I'm not sure what is going on in Sydney, and I am hoping he will return. His mother is very controlling. He seems to be under her thumb. I find you very attractive, to be honest, and once I am free, I would like to visit you. Maybe take you away somewhere? Nothing heavy, but maybe we could have some fun. I really like you and . . ." Charles trailed off and suddenly looked very uncertain. Ginny had never seen him look so unsure.

Ginny sat, dumbfounded. She didn't know what to say. In many ways, she hardly knew him but in others she did. He was an older version of Alex, and the more time she spent in his company, the more aware she was of their similarities.

Finally, she managed to say, "That's very kind of you to say. This is a surprise and something I need to think about. I—" Charles leaned over and put his lips to hers, easing her lips apart with his tongue. She let him kiss her deeply for a few moments, then she gently pulled away from him.

"Please, Charles, don't rush me."

"I am trying hard not to, which is why I haven't said or done anything before. With your consent, I will come again in the New Year. Next week?"

Feeling totally confused, Ginny nodded, and Charles took his leave soon afterwards but not before kissing her fervently.

CHAPTER 13

SHE DIDN'T SLEEP well. Thoughts of Jem, Charles, and Alex swirled round in her head. She liked Jem; he was a good man, though she suspected he could be difficult if pushed. Then her thoughts turned, as they always did now, to Alex. After she'd acknowledged to herself that she loved him, she'd found it harder and harder not to think about him. She wondered what he was doing and thinking, and what sort of Christmas he'd had. Her thoughts turned to Charles.

What the hell do I do now? Why is it that two people who are so alike don't affect me in the same way? Is it just lust with Alex? No, it's not. I don't understand it. Why is it that I love one and not the other? What is it with human beings that makes us love a particular person? Some women are so beautiful and yet others so plain, but men still love the plain ones too. What exactly is love? It's a very strong emotion, but it isn't rational. It must be something no one understands—something that is deep within us. We don't choose who we love. Love just happens, even if we don't want it to.

The next day she went for a good ride on Millie, then she settled down to get some hats made that were on order. She worked later than normal, and it was starting to get dark when she roused herself to go and shut the chooks up and feed Millie, who hadn't got that much grass and always had a short feed, in any case.

While she was down in the paddock, Puck gave a short, sharp bark and raced away towards the house. Ginny saw headlights in the driveway. *What now? I don't feel like visitors. Maybe it's Jem? I hope not. I am feeling antisocial.*

It seemed darker than ever as she retraced her steps towards the house. She first noticed Puck, who charged round like a lunatic, then strong arms lifted her off her feet, and a kiss was planted on her cheek. Alex!

"Where did you spring from?" She gasped when he set her back on her feet.

"Sydney. Was going to the station, but as I got nearer to here, I thought, Why bother." He shrugged. "I decided to come here first."

His voice seemed deeper, or did he only sound this way because she hadn't heard him speak for so long? When they got inside, she thought he seemed taller and more muscular too.

"How are you?" they asked in unison, then they both laughed.

Ginny let Alex speak. "I'm good, and you?"

For a fleeting moment, Ginny thought they sounded like two strangers speaking, and a small frisson of sadness passed through her.

"Good, um, how long are you here for?"

Alex spread his arms wide. "For as long as you want me." His gesture unnerved Ginny, and she quickly looked away. "Do you want a drink? Tea? Coffee?"

"Hang on." Alex rummaged in the bag he had brought in with him and stood up, waving a bottle of champagne under Ginny's nose. "I thought we could celebrate. You will still teach me, right?" He suddenly looked less sure of himself.

"Of course. I'll get some glasses. What about food—have you eaten?"

"Let's have some of this first. Ginny, I've missed you!"

Again, Ginny felt uncomfortable. She had to keep her feelings and desires in check. Alex must never know how she felt. The embarrassment would be huge, and they wouldn't be able to carry on. No, she had to hide her feelings, and they would get back on track.

Once they were sat at the table, Ginny managed to forget the war going on inside her, and they chatted away as they had before.

"I just realised we haven't sat and talked like this for months—since before you went to the UK. That is over six months," Alex suddenly said.

"Well, times goes quickly when you are living it up in Sydney."

Alex drew a breath. "Actually, it wasn't all good. I spent some time with my grandfather, Mum's father. He is one weird guy."

"Oh, you don't like him, then."

"Not really. Is it all right if I put my things in my old room?"

"Of course, and while you are doing that, I'll get us something to eat."

At first, Alex's return was strange, but it wasn't long before they got back into the routine they'd had before Ginny went to the UK. Alex wanted to know all about it, as he hadn't lingered to hear much when she'd first returned.

One morning, Ginny asked him why he had stayed away so long. She had refrained from asking before, but she was curious. It seemed so odd.

Alex looked embarrassed. "Well, as you know, I went to Sydney with Mum. Her father wasn't well, so I agreed to go. Anyway, while I was there, I met this girl. She was hot—I mean *hot*."

Ginny felt sick. Alex dating wasn't something she had really thought about. Jealousy flamed in her heart, but she managed to keep her voice neutral.

"Oh, what happened? Is it over?"

Alex looked surprised by the question. "Yeah, it was just sex, nothing more. Didn't really like her as a person. She was a bitch, really, but—" He left the sentence hanging.

"Was she upset when you left?"

"Hell no. We broke up a couple of months ago. I would have been back sooner, but Mum, well, Mum isn't keen on my career choice and made it difficult."

"What about your father? How does he play into all this?"

"Dad is living his dream as a big cattle man. I'm not sure he knows what he is doing, but he has some good people working for him. He came to Sydney a couple of times to see us but—" Alex shrugged. "He and Mum don't get on, and Grandfather doesn't like Dad. I was going to swing by and see him before I came here, but, well, I didn't. The urge to see you was too great."

Ginny's heart lurched at Alex's words. *Oh God, how I love you, Alex Unwin.* She took a deep breath and didn't look at him. She kept her eyes on the hat she was attaching a frothy lace decoration to.

"Your dad came out to see me a couple of times. He looked well."

Charles hadn't visited since Alex returned. He must know Alex was there and was playing it cool.

Alex was surprised and said, "I didn't think he came this way much, and he has more people working for him now than he did. I think Grandfather likes Dad to stay away on the station. Maybe he helps with wages, but I'm not sure."

"But your mother has officially let you come back, though... hasn't she?"

"Well, yes. She wanted me to go to TAFE in Sydney, but to my surprise, Grandfather thought coming here and having you teach me would be better. I think, deep down, he is worried about the drug scene. He thinks I am out of all that here."

Ginny looked at him sharply. "You're not into that, are you?"

"Nah. I tried some speed at a party a few weeks back, but it just made me feel nauseous. In any case, I don't want to stuff my life up like I know so many people have."

"Good. Now let me see how you are doing with that binding." Ginny turned her attention back to the job at hand.

The next few weeks flew by. Ginny found it harder and harder not to let her feelings show. She was completely besotted with Alex, and every little thing made her heart race. Many times, she would look up from what she was doing and see his large dark eyes on her, watching her, but not in a bad way, and when his eyes met hers, he always smiled his wonderful smile. Then Ginny would drop her head down, focus on what she was doing, and pretend she hadn't noticed anything.

Jem called in a few times with more wine. Ginny had given some away but not much, and it was becoming an embarrassment, though Jem didn't seem to notice. He seemed to like Alex, and they talked about horses, dogs, and cattle. A couple of times, they became so immersed in their conversation that Ginny almost felt left out. Graham also kept up his regular phone calls and hinted he might come and pay her a visit, though Ginny didn't take it seriously.

Halfway through February, everything changed. Valentine's Day. Alex gave her a card. It wasn't a day she or Jeff had ever worried about, so it rather went over Ginny's head. He had made it himself, and inside, it contained a simple statement: "To the most wonderful woman in the world. Please be my valentine."

Ginny's eyes bounced between the card and him.

"I didn't think it was worth mailing, as I was sure you'd know who it was from," Alex said.

Ginny gave him the briefest hug she could and fled to her room. Again, her heart had descended into turmoil. She sat on the bed, trying to get herself under control. *I can't do this. I have to tell him that I can't teach him any more. It's just too hard. I love him so much. I am a sad old woman.*

She squared her shoulders and headed to the kitchen, but who should be there but Jem, sitting and talking to Alex.

"Alex tells me it's Valentine's Day. He thought I came for that reason. Sorry, but no. Haven't celebrated it for years. I just dropped in with that magazine article I was telling Alex about the other day."

Pulling herself together, Ginny grinned. "Jeff and I didn't celebrate either. Coffee? Tea?"

By the time she finished making drinks, Ginny's resolve melted away, and she said nothing about Alex leaving.

A fortnight later, all her good intentions went out the window. They were both sewing. Alex used the machine while Ginny stitched a large flower onto a hat that was an expensive commission piece. Somehow, her needle slipped and dug deeply into her finger. Blood flowed. Hissing in pain, she dropped the hat, not wanting to get blood on it. Her first finger bled profusely. Before she realised what he was going to do, Alex took hold of her hand and put her finger in his mouth, sucking the blood. Heat and desire flooded Ginny's body. She felt like fainting.

"No." She snatched her hand away and rose so quickly that her chair overturned. She rushed to the small bathroom near the workroom.

She slammed the door behind her and, gasping for breath, leaned her head against the mirror. After a few moments, her heart rate slowed, and she washed the blood away. She found a Band-Aid, and although the cut was still bleeding a little, she put it on, then she opened the door. *This is it.*

Alex will have to leave. I can't control my body or my thoughts any longer. I'll tell him now.

Alex stood near the door, waiting for her, stark naked. His desire hung heavy between his thighs—on display for her. Without a word, he took three steps to Ginny and picked her up in his arms, his lips hungrily seeking hers. Ginny was powerless to stop now, and their tongues danced with abandon as they kissed.

Alex took her to her room and placed her gently on the bed. Without speaking, but keeping eye contact, he eased her top over her head and unclasped her bra, then he pulled her shorts and panties down. Ginny trembled and let him do what he wanted. Her need was so great, but at the same time, she felt weak and vulnerable. She didn't want him to see her naked. She was old, after all, or old compared to him. She felt ashamed of her body.

With a voice rough with desire and emotion, he said, "Oh Jesus, Ginny. You are so beautiful."

Ginny twitched, warmth radiating throughout her body. She was going to speak, but Alex knelt beside her and took her already enlarged nipple into his mouth. Instead of speaking, she wrapped her arms around him to pull him closer.

Urgency overwhelmed her. "Please, Alex . . . please, fuck me. Please." He nodded frantically, plunging into her. "I want you so much," she gasped. They both climaxed quickly. They had been waiting so long for this moment.

Alex rolled off her, panting slightly. It was a hot day, and Ginny had switched the air con off in her room earlier to save power. They were both bathed in sweat. Ginny leaned over and got the remote. Cool air soon wafted over their bodies. She looked at Alex and found his eyes on her. She didn't speak, partly because she didn't know what to say. She had broken all her self-imposed rules. *What the hell did I do? It's too late now, and that was all so wonderful.*

Delighted, she started to kiss him—light butterfly kisses on his eyelids and cheeks. She licked the salty sweat from his chest and stomach, then she moved down, finally kissing his manhood gently. She nibbled the head while stroking his length, then, at last, she took him into her mouth. Earlier, Alex had been moaning with pleasure, but now he made an almost guttural sound, and it wasn't long before he came down her throat.

Ginny lay back, content. Even if he disappeared from her life forever, she thought she could cope with anything after such amazing sex.

"Ginny, my Ginny, you are the most wonderful and amazing woman to walk this earth. I never imagined anything as wonderful as what we just shared. I love you so much. I'll always love you."

"Shh." Ginny didn't want him to say those things. He was so young. He had so much life in front of him. "Just live for now, Alex. Enjoy now, please."

They rested for a little while, both quiet, then Alex pulled her towards him again, but Ginny was ready for him. Pushing him back, she sat astride him, surprising him again.

They stayed in bed the rest of the day. Towards evening, they got up and saw to the animals then ate a light supper. They showered together, which took a long time, then they returned to bed.

Ginny woke in the morning to find Alex still deeply asleep, and as she lay there, savouring every minute of their lovemaking, a sudden thought hit her. They hadn't taken any precautions. She hadn't reached her change quite yet. Was it possible to get pregnant? She had been on the pill with Jeff, but once he'd had his accident, she had stopped because he wasn't capable any longer. Graham had used a condom, but in the heat of the moment with Alex, she had completely forgotten about protection. She had been too carried away by the fact that Alex actually wanted to make love to her. The thought still overwhelmed her.

She turned her head to look at him and saw he was awake. He started to kiss her, but she pushed against his chest. "I just realised you might have made me pregnant yesterday! We didn't use any protection."

Alex lay back and looked at her, a frown on his face. "I assumed you were on the pill."

"I was a long time ago, but Jeff . . . Jeff couldn't have sex any more, so I stopped."

Alex was quiet for a minute, then he said, "We'd have to be very unlucky for you to get pregnant so easily. I'll go to town later and get some condoms. In the meantime . . ." He nuzzled her breast. Ginny pulled back slightly. "Stable door. Horse is bolted," Alex mumbled.

Ginny gave in. He was right. It was too late for now, but after this morning, they'd have to be careful.

CHAPTER 14

TIME SLID BY, and neither of them spoke of the future. Ginny knew there wasn't one. Alex was too young, but she would always love him, so she lived in the present and didn't worry about the future. As for Alex, he was besotted. Such a beautiful woman loved him. She was beyond his wildest dreams in bed, and she was funny, kind, and generous. He didn't consider the future either, at least not to start with, but three weeks into their new relationship, he decided to take things further.

One night, after they had made love, he said, "I love you so much. Will you marry me?"

Ginny felt as if her heart had stopped. "Are you serious? You can't mean it."

"Ouch, you know how to hurt someone. Of course I mean it. What do you think?"

"I'm sorry. I didn't mean anything by it. It's just, well, there is a huge age gap between us. I'll be old, and you'll still be a young, sexy man."

Alex raised himself onto his elbow and looked down at her. It was a moonlit night, and he could see her face plainly in the silvery light.

"Ginny, I love you. I don't care that you'll have wrinkles one day. I don't care that your hair will get thin, and you won't be as mobile. It isn't just the sex, though that is marvellous. It's you—your humour, your personality, your generosity, your kindness. All those things and more."

Ginny's eyes flooded with tears. "I love you too, but marriage is a huge step. Let's just think about it for a little longer. I want to marry you—I just think we both need a bit more time. What on earth would your parents say?"

Alex flopped back on the bed. "I think Dad would come round. He likes you, so I don't think he would be a problem. Mum, well . . . I'm of age, so she can't legally stop me. Her father isn't a nice man. I think we need to do it quietly, then it will be too late for objections."

Soon after this conversation, Alex fell asleep, but Ginny couldn't. Her mind was in turmoil.

What do I do now? I can't hurt Alex, but I can't marry him! He is too young, and what on earth would Charles think? I should never have gone to bed with Alex in the first place, but I couldn't stop. I couldn't hold back. The urge was too strong. I was compelled to give in. No, that is an excuse. What to do, what to do . . .

Jem visited soon after and warned her that the gossips were having a field day in their little town. Jem thought it was great that Ginny had found love, but he warned her she might meet some nasty gossips when she next went shopping. After Jem left, Jo phoned her. Alex was outside feeding Millie. Jo got straight to the point. "People are saying you and that young bloke Alex are openly living together now. Is it true?"

"Yes, and before you ask, he is younger than you."

Jo sucked in a breath. "God, Ginny. What are you thinking?"

"When an older man has a relationship with a much younger woman, on the whole, people accept it. There might be a few snide remarks, but most people brush it off and consider him a lucky man. That's not the case with Alex and me, now is it? I am some sort of harlot or bad woman who's seducing a young man."

"Yes, but Alex can't—he can't . . . He can't really fancy you. I mean, he could have anyone."

"I'm going to hang up before I lose my temper. Quite apart from anything else, it's no one else's business. Bye."

Ginny hung up and found she was shaking. She didn't want to tell Alex. *I'll tell him in the morning. We will wait to get married. After all, it's only been just over a month. Oh God, a month. My period. I haven't had a period. Oh, please don't let me be pregnant. That would be the last straw. I'm too old for chil-*

dren. It was too late to call the doctor, and sleep would now be completely impossible. *I need one of those testing kits, but I dare not get one in town. Everyone will know.*

In the morning, as soon as possible, Ginny rang the local doctor. She knew Dr Harvey well because of Jeff. She managed to get an appointment for later that day. She decided to put one issue to rest for now. She would tell Alex she wouldn't marry him before she found out if she was pregnant. If the test came back positive, she could have an abortion without telling him. He'd be upset, but for his sake, she needed to be strong. She loved him too much to allow him to be caught in some sort of trap.

Alex was busy repairing the chooks' hut and run, which were getting rather the worse for wear.

When she got to him and he smiled his wonderful smile, her resolve nearly crumbled. "Alex, I've been thinking about your proposal. I won't marry you. It wouldn't be fair to you. In fact, I think we should take a step back."

"What the hell does that mean?" For the first time ever, Alex sounded angry. Ginny mentally wriggled, her resolve faltering again.

"Well, maybe we shouldn't sleep together for a time, or at least—"

Alex was hurt. "I'm not good enough for you. Too young and stupid I suppose. Fine. If that is what you want, I won't touch you. I'll be in my room." He chucked his tools down and stormed off to the house.

Ginny watched him go, upset with his reaction but unsurprised. She would put it right later when he had cooled down.

Ginny sat at her computer instead of picking up the hat she was working on. She always looked at hat emails straight away, but she had two email accounts: one exclusively for hats and the other for personal matters. She hadn't opened her personal email in over a week. There weren't many, but there was one from Graham. He had decided to come out to see her. He said it was a spur of the moment decision, and he would be there in five days. He hoped that was OK and asked her to pick him up from the airport.

Ginny stared at the computer screen, dumbfounded, then she hastily looked at the flight times he had given her. He was arriving today! In fact, his plane would be touching down about now. She was nearly six hours from the airport. There was no way she could drop everything and head off. In any case, why hadn't he rung her to discuss this? *Stupid bloody man will just have to wait. I'll pick him up tomorrow. Oh hell. What will he make of Alex and me? What do I do now?*

She knew Graham's mobile number from when she was in the UK. She waited for about an hour, then she tried it, but it went straight to voicemail. She decided to leave a message for him to ring her as soon as possible.

Ten minutes later, he rang her. "I just got into the arrivals hall, but I can't see you."

Anger gathered in her chest; however, she quelled the feeling as much as she could. "I'm sorry, but I didn't get your message soon enough. Can you find a hotel? I will be with you tomorrow."

Silence for a minute. "Graham, are you—"

"I'm here, yes, sorry. I was expecting you to pick me up. Um, I'll do that. I'm sure a taxi driver will direct me to a hotel nearby. I'll let you know where I am. Looking forward to seeing you and your place tomorrow."

You'll be lucky, Ginny thought. She wasn't game to do the drive in one hit. Then inspiration hit. If Alex came, they could split the driving, and it would be one way to introduce Graham to Alex that wasn't too confrontational.

The next thing she had to do was tell Alex about Graham arriving. She knocked tentatively on his door. He opened it a moment or two later, and before she could speak, he wrapped her in his arms and kissed her long and hard. Ginny was too confused and upset by all that was happening to resist.

"Is that the guy you told me about from the UK? The one who took you out dancing or whatever it was."

"Yes. I missed his email, and he is already here. Will you come with me tomorrow to pick him up?"

"Course, no problem. We can share the driving."

"There is no easy way to say this, but I don't know what he will make of our relationship."

Alex shrugged. "As I see it, it's no one else's business but ours. You love me, and I love you—end of story."

"But—"

"I love you. It will be fine. As for all that other stuff you were saying outside, well, it will have to wait. We will talk later, but now I'm going to finish the chooks' run."

"OK."

Ginny had an awful feeling that her life was spiralling out of control. The feeling was amplified that afternoon when the doctor confirmed she was pregnant.

"I'm too old," Ginny said despairingly. "I turned forty-eight this year. I can't have a baby now."

"Do you want a termination? What does the father want?"

"He doesn't know yet. I don't know what I want either. How long do I have to make up my mind?"

"Ideally, the sooner the better. The smaller the foetus, the easier and..." The doctor carried on talking, but the mention of the foetus brought it home to Ginny. This was real, a real baby, and she missed a lot of what the doctor said. Her mind was like a whirlpool.

She got to her feet, somewhat unsteadily. "I'll make an appointment soon," she muttered and fled.

She trembled in her car. *What do I do? What will Alex say? Oh God, what a mess.* She took several deep breaths. Sitting there wouldn't resolve anything. First of all, they had to pick Graham up the next day, then she would talk to Alex. Maybe she shouldn't tell him, but then again, it was his baby too.

When she got back, Alex was waiting for her. It was plain something was very wrong.

She hadn't said she was going to the clinic, and he asked, "Where have you been?" This threw Ginny, as it was out of character for Alex to speak like this, but before she replied, he said, "I got a phone call from Mum. Dad had an accident. I have to go." It was then that she saw his bag packed at his feet.

"Is he OK?"

Alex just shook his head. It seemed he didn't know.

"Now?" Ginny asked.

"Yes, darling, now. I'm sorry." Tears streamed down Alex's face. Ginny stepped up to him and put her arms around him.

"Shh, it will be all right. Shh. What happened? Is he in hospital?"

Alex just shook his head, muttering something she didn't hear. He pushed her gently away and made towards the door. As he stepped through, he turned his face towards her and chokingly said, "I will always love you. Remember that, always."

"But Alex, wait. Alex!" She ran to the door, but he was already in his car and doing a sharp U-turn. He was gone in a swirl of dust and gravel. Ginny caught sight of his face, and it was contorted in pain, tears still streaming down his cheeks.

Ginny thought vaguely about getting in her car and following but dismissed that idea as foolish. Alex was driving like a man possessed. She didn't want any other accidents to happen. What had happened to Charles? It must be very serious for Alex to be in such a state. She tried Alex's mobile, as he had Bluetooth, but his phone must have been switched off, or maybe he was in a black spot.

She accepted the fact that he had driven off worried out of his life but was confident he would be in touch soon. He was young and maybe a bit melodramatic. It couldn't be that bad, surely. She had more pressing things to worry about. She would set off to collect Graham early tomorrow and then she would have to tell Alex she was pregnant.

God, what a day. Everything happens at once. That is three things today. Maybe it will be OK now. I think I will wait and tell Alex face to face about the baby rather than over the phone—that wouldn't be right. His reaction will help me decide what to do.

With these positive thoughts in her head, she managed to go to sleep quite early. She missed Alex in her bed.

CHAPTER 15

THE NEXT MORNING, she wasn't as quick off the mark as she'd hoped. She had the animals to see to, and she was sick, extremely sick, so it was quite a bit later before she set off. She rang Graham from the car to tell him she was on her way.

"See you soon," he said.

"Not very soon—about five hours from now."

"Five hours! Are you detouring somewhere on the way?"

"I live quite a long way from the airport. I'll drive as fast as I safely can."

"Oh, I didn't realise. I'm sorry. It doesn't look that far on the map."

"It depends on the scale of the map. Anyway, I'll see you in a bit."

Ginny hung up. She was surprised how well she had slept considering everything that was going on. Her thoughts kept her company for most of the drive. She'd had only a drink before she left, as she had felt so nauseous, so she got a large packet of chips from the service station and nibbled on them, but the sick feeling returned. It was two in the afternoon when she finally reached the hotel. Graham was sitting outside waiting for her.

"Ginny!" He enveloped her in a bear hug and went to kiss her, but she turned her head, so he kissed her cheek rather than her lips.

"You look tired. You had such a long drive. I'm so sorry about messing up your day. I had intended to arrive on your doorstep as a surprise, then I got cold feet about doing that, so then I sent the email but still thought to surprise you. It wasn't until I looked at the map that I thought it was too far out to get a taxi!"

"I need a few hours to relax before we set off. Do you know where we can go so I can rest?"

"I actually booked the room for tonight as well. I did that this morning. I was lucky they let me. I suddenly thought I should have a backup plan, supposing something happened and you were very late. I didn't fancy trawling around looking for somewhere else."

The hotel didn't do lunch, but Graham took Ginny up to his room, then he went off and got some sandwiches from a bakery nearby. When he got back to the room, Ginny was asleep on top of the bed.

He looked down at her, thinking he would let her sleep for a little while. She looked tired. There were dark circles under her eyes. He was surprised. She somehow looked quite different from the person she had been in the UK.

Ginny woke with a start and looked round, disorientated for a moment. "Alex?"

Graham gave a small cough. Ginny then focused.

Graham gave another little cough, and Ginny sat up. "Oh, Graham. I'm sorry."

"Don't be. You look tired, and as you told me, we have a long drive in front of us."

They shared the sandwiches. Graham had also bought two coffees, which Ginny was grateful for.

Not long afterwards, they set off. Ginny kept up a commentary of her life, partly out of nerves and partly because it stopped her thinking about Alex too much. She hoped against hope he would be there when they got back. An hour into their journey, Graham fell asleep. Jet lag had kicked in. Ginny glanced across at him. He wasn't a pretty sight. He had his head back and his mouth open, and he was snoring so loudly it almost made her ears ring.

Ginny tried to block out the noise by thinking about her predicament. What on earth was she going to do? First things first, she had to tell Alex and see what he thought. They'd had nearly two months of intimacy and joy. Ginny didn't think she had ever been so happy. She had forgotten the difference in their ages. He was just Alex: her lover and her soul mate. She knew she would love him until her dying breath. She'd loved Jeff, but this was far deeper. She couldn't explain it. It didn't make sense, but that was how it was. She knew Alex thought a lot of her, but she was wise enough to know he was only just starting out in the adult world at twenty-one. She had decided to make the most of what time she had with him but knew he would leave her at some stage. This pregnancy was a complication she could have done without. *Maybe I should have a termination and not say anything? But that wouldn't be right either. What shall I do?*

With a big snort, Graham woke. "Sorry, I think I dozed off. Have I missed much?"

"You slept for a good hour, so you missed over a hundred kilometres of scenery."

"Oh, it's dark, or nearly dark. It gets dark very early here, doesn't it, and it is very quick. The sun is there, then it's gone."

"Even at the height of summer, it's dark here soon after seven. Other states have daylight saving, but we don't. I'll be on kangaroo watch now. They're a bit like deer in the UK. They seem to have a suicide mission sometimes and just leap out in front of you. Most cars are completely written off after hitting one."

"Even a big vehicle like this one?"

"Yep, it's been known. I'm going to pull in at the next servo for fuel. If you want the toilet, now's your chance."

Graham shifted in his seat. He did but hadn't been game to say for a reason he couldn't explain. Ginny was different. She had been on holiday before, and she was at home now and leading a busy life. He suddenly felt like a trespasser. He'd felt close to Ginny in the UK, very close, and had come out here to ask her to marry him. Now he realised that was a very naive idea, and he may have made a big mistake. He had been told he had the very early stages of Parkinson's disease, and he had thought if he married Ginny, a much younger woman, she would be the ideal wife to look after him when life became difficult. Plus, he loved her. Now he wasn't so sure.

As good as her word, Ginny pulled in. "No more fuel for the next hour or so, anyway," she said as she got out of the car. Graham hummed, squeezing his legs together and looking for the toilet. Twenty minutes later, they were on their way again, and Ginny told him about the countryside they were driving through, the animals, and the vegetation. Little did Graham know, it wasn't for his benefit but for Ginny's own. She was feeling very tired and very stressed and talking seemed to help her concentrate. Three hours later, they finally swung through Ginny's front gate.

Ginny's heart sank. She had convinced herself that Alex would be waiting. But there was only Puck to greet them. She could tell Graham was slightly frightened of the big dog, but Puck soon lost interest in the odd-smelling man.

Ginny led the way into the kitchen. "Make yourself a drink if you want one. I must see to the chooks and the horse before I do anything else. I'll show you where everything is when I come back in. Won't be long."

She was gone before Graham had a chance to answer. After putting the jug on, he hunted around and eventually found tea bags and mugs. He was feeling more and more uncomfortable. *What a fool I am, coming halfway around the world to see a woman who, as far as I can tell, isn't that pleased to see me. Why, when I met her and went to kiss her, she turned her head away. She doesn't look that well to me either—pale and tired. Why did she say that fellow's name when she woke up? That was odd too.* Graham was gripping a mug of tea as if his life depended on it when Ginny returned.

"Good, you made yourself some tea. Sorry to rush off, but I was worried about shutting the chooks up. All sorts of wildlife might get to them at night, though the biggest dangers are foxes—a bit like the UK. We also have wild dogs to worry about. Now I hope you don't mind breakfast for dinner. Scrambled eggs and bacon OK? Ten minutes and we'll have a meal. I promise to do better tomorrow."

"Of course, just let me help."

Ginny decided that was a good idea, and so Graham looked after the bacon and toast while Ginny did the eggs.

It was actually very good, and Graham felt much better afterwards, though that didn't last, as he'd assumed Ginny would let him sleep with her. After all, they had in the UK, but she showed him the spare room, gave him a large white towel, and pointed out the bathroom. She kissed his cheek and said, "Sleep well." That was that. She disappeared down the passageway and shut the kitchen door behind her.

Graham thought sleep would elude him; however, he slept very well and late too.

Ginny hardly slept at all, then the morning sickness started. She was thankful she had the en suite they had put in for Jeff. She hoped that with all the doors shut, the sound of her retching wouldn't carry through. By the time Graham emerged and came into the kitchen, she was feeling marginally better and had managed to see to the animals. Puck had picked up on her distress and growled at Graham.

"Puck, what are you thinking? You met Graham last night, you silly dog," Ginny said as Graham kissed her again on the cheek.

"What would you like for breakfast?" Ginny asked.

"Just toast and tea will do me well, thanks. Can I take you out for lunch later? My treat."

"Oh, thank you, but there is only the pub or the cafe, and neither of them do the sort of food you are used to. It's good food, don't get me wrong, but the choices are limited."

"Nevertheless, I'd like to eat out with you, see your little town, and meet the locals."

Ginny's heart sank. The gossips were bad enough regarding Alex. What would they say after seeing Graham?

"I have a better idea. Why don't I pack a picnic and take you out in the bush. There is some beautiful countryside around here. We can save going into town for when I need to do a shop. That reminds me—I hope you don't mind me asking, but how long are you planning on staying? I just want to plan ahead."

Graham sat still for a few minutes. Ginny, who was doing the toast, glanced at him. He looked worried. She was about to ask again when he cleared his throat. He hadn't thought Ginny would ask him so baldly what his plans were. He had read the whole thing wrong. He had thought he would come, make love to Ginny, share her bed and a small part of her life, then ask her to marry him. He'd been sure she would say yes. After all, she was stuck out here in this godforsaken place with no family around her, and he was well off. As time passed, she would nurse him, then she'd inherit a nice house and a good income and be near her family. In his head, it was a no-brainer. Now, he wasn't so sure. Ginny was decidedly distant, and he felt there was something very wrong, though what he couldn't imagine.

Before he had formulated an answer, the landline phone went. Ginny knew it was about hats but deep down hoped it was Alex. She rushed to answer it.

By the time she finished the conversation, Graham had thought through what he would say. He would have to hope for the best.

"Ginny, I will be honest. I came here to see you and ask you to be my wife."

Ginny gasped and sat down abruptly.

"I hadn't intended to speak of it this soon. I thought I would rekindle our relationship first, but here you are, a different person to the one I met in the UK. That doesn't mean I have changed my mind, but it does mean that maybe you feel differently, and I have made a mistake."

Ginny played with the top of the marmalade jar. She felt terrible. This man, who she was admittedly fond of, had come halfway across the world because he wanted to marry her, and there was no way that could happen. She was carrying another man's child, and she would never love Graham. There was no spark there, and she certainly didn't want to be tied to an older man who would want a nursemaid. She'd done that with Jeff.

Finally, Ginny found the words she wanted. "Graham, you are a lovely man, kind and gentle, but I don't love you. There is no spark. Yes, it was different when I was in the UK, but this is home. I don't want to live overseas. I was only twenty when I came here, so I have lived in Australia for over half my life. It's good to visit the UK, but I feel closer to Jeff here, and I have my animals and friends, and I am content. I am so sorry—I really am."

Graham watched her keenly, and the penny dropped. "You love someone else, don't you?"

Ginny's eyes flooded with sudden tears. She couldn't hold them back. She was beside herself worrying about Alex and where he was and what was happening. Why hadn't he been in touch? Unable to voice any of this to Graham, she just nodded and was spared any further reply when Jem charged into the driveway in a cloud of dust.

Ginny got to her feet and was about to let Jem in when he came barrelling through the door.

"Are you OK, darl'? I heard on the grapevine that there are a couple of dodgy blokes asking after you in town. Who are you?" He had spied Graham sitting at the table.

"It's OK, Jem. This is a friend from the UK. I picked him up yesterday."

"Where's young Alex, then? Someone said they saw him shoot through the day before yesterday. That's why I was worried. You're here alone, and I didn't like the sound of those blokes at all."

"Sit down, Jem, and I'll make us all drinks. Graham, do you want more tea, or shall I make coffee now?"

As she said this, a wave of sickness overtook her.

"Excuse me." She rushed off and only just made it to the bathroom. She hoped the men didn't hear anything as she gagged over the toilet. She'd only had a cup of tea so far, and that was in the toilet now. She felt so awful, and once she finished emptying her stomach, she sat on her bed for a few minutes, trying to pull herself together.

She returned to the kitchen and found the two men getting on quite well. Jem gave her a hard look, however, and Ginny had the uncomfortable feeling he'd guessed what was up. Graham, on the other hand, was in such an animated conversation with Jem that he hardly looked up. To Ginny's horror, he was discussing politics, and Jem's eyes seemed to be glazing over. She guessed foreign politics wasn't something that interested him. She made the men coffee and got herself some water, taking careful sips. She waited until Graham ran out of steam, then she asked Jem about the men he'd mentioned.

"As you know, I don't go into town that much, but I went to get some horse food, and Sally in the store said she saw two strangers in a big black 4WD. They were asking if you ever went into their store. Sally thought it odd, so she fobbed them off—told them she had no idea—and they left. When I drove back through town to go home, there was this big black Land Cruiser outside the cafe. It drove off as I pulled up. I only caught a glimpse, but there were two big blokes sitting in it. It had NSW number plates—that I did notice. I went into the cafe and asked June what they wanted. June said the same thing as Sally. They asked if you went in very often. June said you hadn't been in for a long time, then they left."

Ginny thought about it. There was something about the situation that made her feel very uneasy, but she put on a brave face and said, "Someone's wife wants a hat, I expect."

"Very odd way to go about it, though," Jem muttered.

Almost on cue, a black Land Cruiser drove in. Puck didn't like the look of it, and Ginny went to the door to let him out. Both Graham and Jem followed Ginny to the door. A big man dressed in black got out of the passenger side of the car. He wore dark glasses and had a shaved head. Seeing the two men behind Ginny, however, he stopped and glanced back at the driver.

"Can I help you?" Ginny asked.

"No, I think we came to the wrong place, missis." He looked at Puck, who stood by Ginny with his hackles up. "Sorry." He got back in the car, and the driver did a quick U-turn, and they were gone.

The three of them watched the car disappear. "What do you make of that?" Jem was the first to speak.

"They looked like thugs. What on earth could they want with me? I didn't like the look of them at all. I'm glad the two of you were here. I think that put them off whatever they had in mind. Maybe an unhappy customer sent them, but that would be overkill for a hat. Perhaps they want to raid the place?"

The three of them returned to the kitchen and ideas flew back and forth as to what the two men could possibly want. Ginny made more drinks and got some biscuits out. She sat and nibbled at them. Jem watched covertly. He'd guessed what was up, though Graham had yet to notice anything amiss.

"We are going to have a drive and a picnic lunch. It's getting late, so I'd better get to it, else it'll be afternoon tea," Ginny said after a little while.

Jem got to his feet. "Come out to my place tomorrow, and I'll show you and Graham round."

"Thanks, Jem. That would be great." Ginny had been wondering what she was going to do with Graham while he was visiting. She could take him out and about, but she had quite a few hat orders to get out, and now that Alex wasn't there to help, she really needed to get on with them.

She made a picnic, then she went to tidy herself up before they left. She tried Alex's mobile. Every time she had a moment away from prying eyes, she called him. His phone was still switched off. She was getting increasingly worried. When he had been in Sydney, she had still been able to ring him if she had wanted. He had always answered his phone. She had phoned him once with a question about a hat he had taken an order for when she was away, and he'd always replied to text messages too. Now, nothing. It was as if he had completely disappeared. It was stressing her out, more so as she was carrying the burden of her pregnancy and wanted so much to discuss it with him.

Despite her worries, she and Graham had a good day. He didn't push his luck with Ginny by getting too close. He had realised by now that there wasn't much likelihood of Ginny coming back to the UK with him or consenting to marrying him. He didn't think she looked well, but after asking her several times if she was OK and getting short shrift, he stopped saying anything. He had wondered about her relationship with Jem, but after watching them, he could see that friendship was all it was. She was the same with Jem as she was with him.

They had a picnic by a huge body of water that Ginny said was a dam. He'd thought it looked more like a lake until she told him it had been man-made to supply water to the nearby population. He didn't like the mossies, but Ginny sprayed him with repellent that mostly kept them away, though one bit his hand. By the time they got back, the jet lag had kicked in again, and Graham fell asleep. He only woke when Ginny told him dinner was ready. He could hardly keep his eyes open and was relieved when he could take himself off to bed.

Ginny plopped down on her bed after showering. She was too overwrought to sleep, though she was tired. She tried Alex's mobile again. It still seemed to be switched off. She sent him a text, thinking that when he switched his phone on or got a signal, he would notice it first.

She must have dozed off because she woke with a start. Her phone was ringing, but as she sleepily fumbled to answer it, the ringing stopped. Flipping on her bedside light, she looked at the caller ID. It had been withheld, and although she tried calling back, she got a recorded message saying her call was not allowed to go through. She flopped back down and let her tears flow. What on earth was Alex playing at? If he wanted to end their relationship, why not say so? Then she thought back to the last day or so. He had been as loving and kind as ever, and their passionate lovemaking had been as strong as the first time. His declaration that he adored her still rang in her ears. He wanted to marry her for God's sake. He had been upset when she wanted to step back, but his anger hadn't lasted very long. It wasn't that he was angry with her, she knew now. She resolved to ring Charles in the morning to see if he knew anything, as by now, she was sure his "accident" hadn't happened.

Unable to fall back asleep, time dragged by until she thought she could ring Charles. Graham was up and dressed when she came through. Mercifully, she hadn't been sick, though she felt nauseous.

Having settled Graham with a cup of tea, she said she had a "hat" phone call to make and withdrew into the workroom.

The phone rang for so long that she was about to hang up. A rather breathless Charles came on the other end and gasped out a greeting.

"Charles! This is Ginny."

"Ginny! How are you? It's so good to hear from you. How's that son of mine getting on? Has he done something he shouldn't? I have been wanting to come and see you again but thought I would wait until Alex went out for a bit. Margarita is one jealous woman, and I'm not sure what he'd let slip to his mother. Not that there is anything to talk about, but I am very conscious of her vicious tongue."

As Ginny had expected, Charles hadn't had any sort of accident.

"No—yes . . . no. Sorry, but Alex isn't with you?"

"He's not here." Charles spoke slowly. "I thought he was staying with you for the rest of the year. That's what his mother led me to believe when I spoke to her recently."

Ginny didn't know how to proceed. She felt caught in some family web of deception. In the end, she decided to tell Charles exactly what she knew.

"I was out for a short time the other day—actually three days ago—and when I got back, Alex was waiting for me. He had everything packed up and said you had been hurt in an accident, and he had to go to you. I haven't heard from him since. His phone seems to be switched off."

Ginny counted Charles's breaths, eager to hear his thoughts. He said, "That will be his mother playing tricks. Look, you know Margarita and I have split up, and a divorce is pending. It won't be pretty. Margarita is obsessed with Alex and smothers him. Plus, her father wants Alex to be involved with his business, such as it is.

"I fear for my son, but I can't do much to help. They are a powerful family, and I wish to God I had never met Margarita in the first place. If Alex has gone to his mother, then it's best to leave the situation alone, believe me. It sounds as if that is what has happened. Margarita didn't like you when she met you and thought Alex was too impressed by you. I worked hard to get her to agree to let Alex spend this summer and winter with you, then he'd go to college. I'm not surprised she got him away early. I'm sorry. I hope his absence hasn't left you in the lurch too much. I'll come out and see you soon. I'm rather tied up here just now."

Gathering herself, Ginny said, "No, it's fine. Thank you, and good luck." She hung up before he had the chance to answer, not wanting to let Charles know how distressed she was.

Her eyes watered, and desperation ran through her veins. The was a tap on the door even though she hadn't shut it, and Graham stood there, concern written all over his face.

"Ginny, dear Ginny, whatever it is, it can't be that bad."

Ginny groped round in her mind to find a believable answer. "Oh, it's an ongoing hat problem, and this woman was just so nasty."

Graham looked at her keenly. He didn't believe a word of it, but if she didn't want to tell him, there was nothing he could do about it.

Making a huge effort, Ginny put her tears aside as best she could, and a short time later, they headed out to Jem's place. For a while, Ginny managed to put her thoughts away. Jem took them across his property and showed them his cattle and horses. He was rightly proud in both instances. They were all magnificent beasts. Graham got very excited when a mob of kangaroos bounded away from the shade of a big gum where they had settled for the day. He was also entranced by all the different birds—the galahs especially. He had his camera with him and took many photos.

When they returned to the house, Jem fired up the barbeque. It had been a very long time since he had used it, and he'd spent quite a time cleaning it up. It gleamed in the light, ready for use. Ginny had brought salads, and they sat outside and chatted until it was dark. Jem reminisced about how the place had been when he had first bought it, then he told them about his late wife. He'd never really spoken about her before, so Ginny listened raptly.

They had wanted children, and for her, the want became greater and greater until it consumed her. She couldn't get pregnant, though doctors found no reason for this since both she and Jem were fit and healthy physically. However, she was very fragile mentally. They put their names down for IVF, and it worked. But she'd miscarried, and from then on, her mental health declined rapidly.

Jem got very emotional during the retelling, as did Ginny. She got up, came round to his side of the table, and gave him a hug. Tears ran down both of their faces. Graham looked very uncomfortable. He wasn't used to all this raw emotion. He now realised that Ginny was, in actual fact, a stranger. He had thought he knew her well—that she was easy to read. Now, he understood that wasn't the case at all. After a bit, they got themselves back to a lighthearted conversation and then Ginny said they should be going because it was getting late, and she had the animals to see to. Jem gave her an extra tight hug when they left and said quietly in her ear, "Take care. I'm here if you need a friend."

Again, Ginny had to fight her tears from forming.

She hoped against hope that Alex would be there when they got back. The driveway was empty, and she had no messages on her phone.

They only had a small snack for supper because they had eaten so well at Jem's, then Graham took a breath and said, "Can I ask you a personal question?"

"What do you want to know?" Ginny braced herself, thinking he was going to ask about Alex. "Are you in love with Jem? Is that why you are so different from the woman I met in the UK?"

Ginny burst out laughing. It sounded foreign to her own ears. "Good heavens, no. He's a mate, that is all. I promise."

"Oh." Graham blushed and stared at his hands. "But you are very different."

"You saw the holiday Ginny, not the real one."

"Am I so different on holiday, then?"

Ginny considered this for a moment. "Not so much, no. Sorry, I have a lot going on just now."

"Is it because that young bloke left you in the lurch? You're not getting the help you need. Look, if you have hat orders to see to, I am happy to laze around tomorrow, so you can get on with stuff. It's naughty of him to take off and leave you to pick up the pieces. Young people today don't seem to have any sense of responsibility."

Ginny opened her mouth to make a tart reply, then she thought better of it. She said nothing, but Graham was on a roll, eagerly talking about young people and how they didn't have a clue about real life. Everything got handed to them on a plate. Ginny abruptly got to her feet.

"I have things to do before I turn in." Without waiting for a reply, she exited the kitchen and went straight to her bedroom, shutting the door firmly behind her.

As he passed her door on the way to his room, Graham called out, "Goodnight."

She didn't respond.

CHAPTER 16

ALEX WATCHED GINNY drive off, though he had no idea where she was going. She had seemed distracted, but he assumed it was because of this bloke coming from the UK and his marriage proposal. He knew he was rushing it, but he was so sure it was the right thing to do. He loved her, for God's sake, so why wait? He had just got to the house and was making himself a drink in the kitchen when a big black Land Cruiser pulled in, and two men got out. Alex's heart sank. He'd seen them in Sydney. What the hell did they want, or rather, what did his mother and grandfather want? It wasn't going to be a nice visit, and he hoped they would be gone before Ginny got back.

Putting on a brave face, he said cheerily, "Hi, guys. Bit out of your usual spot. Can I help you with something?"

"Your mother needs you back now," the bigger man said. Alex opened his mouth to protest, but the man cut him off. "I mean now."

The urge to argue choked Alex, then he thought of Puck. Where was the dog when he needed him?

"Too bad because I'm staying here. You can tell her that," Alex stated.

Lee, one of the men, walked close to Alex and stared hard at him. "If you think anything of the bitch who lives here, you will leave, now. Rix and I will try her out for ourselves if you don't do as you are told, and it won't be pretty. Your mother knows you are fucking her, and she doesn't like it. If she had her way, the bitch would be gone from this world a.s.a.p. Do you get our drift, or should we wait and entertain ourselves with this tart?"

"No, I'm not leaving."

"Look, sonny, we mean business. This isn't a joke. I mean it. If you don't leave now, this woman will suffer. If you pack your bags and leave, we won't do anything to her. In fact, we will follow you back to Sydney. We will be waiting up the road. So if you think anything of the bitch, you will do as you are told. Get it?"

Alex did get it. He realised he had no alternative but to do as they said. Once he returned to Sydney, perhaps he could sort it out. The possibility that they would both rape Ginny was terrifying. He took the threat seriously, as he knew it wasn't an idle one. He loved Ginny with all his heart and soul. He had to do this for her, then he'd hopefully come to some agreement with his mother and grandfather.

He went back inside and heard whining. He realised he had accidently shut Puck in the kitchen when he had gone outside. Puck had been dead asleep at the time; otherwise, he would have been out of the kitchen first.

He packed his belongings. He didn't have much other than his banjo, clothes, and toiletries. Then he sat and waited. He couldn't leave without seeing Ginny, his beautiful Ginny, one more time. *Surely, I can get Mother to see reason. I love Ginny. If I fail, I'll come back and whisk her away and marry her, then Mother can't do anything. We'll elope and find a place to live and have children and a wonderful life.*

His thoughts ran on and on, then Ginny returned, and his tears ran down his face. He couldn't remember afterwards what excuse he had made about leaving. All he remembered was stumbling out to his car and driving off, scared that if he didn't hurry, the men would come back and hurt both of them.

It wasn't to be. He had switched his phone off, as he couldn't bear it if Ginny tried to ring him. He'd ring once he sorted everything out. It had been horrible when she had run after him.

But when he got to Sydney, his grandfather demanded his phone, promising he could have it back later. He winked at him, implying that he was on Alex's side against his mother. So he handed his phone over, only to find he'd been betrayed. He was watched all the time, but during the night, he managed to try and phone Ginny from the landline. She didn't pick up, and he only just managed to get back to his room before Keith, his minder, woke up. He had to let her go. He loved her too much to see her hurt. She would get over him eventually and be safe. He'd do it for her.

But first, he had to hear her voice one last time.

CHAPTER 17

GINNY ONLY SLEPT fitfully. She felt very unwell and had cried herself to sleep, which didn't help. *I've cried more over Alex than I have over Jeff. Why is that? I suppose when Jeff had his accident, I was focused on his recovery then on looking after him, and in some ways, his death was a release for him and me. This is so different. If only I knew what was going on, then maybe I could cope better.*

At five in the morning, her mobile went, startling her. It was an unknown number.

"Hello?"

"Ginny, darling Ginny, just listen, please. I haven't got long—they may hear me. Mum somehow heard about us, and she spoke to her father. They will hurt you, seriously hurt you, unless I give you up. That is why I left. Don't try to contact me. Just let me go as I must let you go. I love you too much. I don't want you to be hurt in any way. If you love me, please don't try to get in touch. Maybe one day we can be together."

Alex hung up, but not before Ginny heard the sob in his voice. She had been too numb to speak. What he'd said shattered her. But this was too far-fetched, surely? They lived in the twenty-first century not the Dark Ages. How dare Margarita rule their lives. Then Ginny remembered the two men and how they had made her feel afraid.

She gave an anguished cry and felt sick. She scrambled out of bed and only just made it to the bathroom. She retched and retched. Every time she thought it was over and made to move, the sickness returned. At last, she crept back to her bed only to feel a sharp pain in her stomach then a warm sensation on her inner thighs. She saw blood and was scared. She called out to Graham, not wanting to move more than necessary. She was fairly sure she was miscarrying but wanted to save this baby if she could. It would be all she would ever have of Alex.

Graham rushed out of his room and stood outside her door, pale and wide-eyed. "Graham, can you call Jem? He'll know what to do."

Graham finally opened the door. Ginny was lying on the bed. She was as white as a sheet and held part of her bedding between her legs tightly. There was a patch of blood on the floor by the bed and a strong smell of vomit.

It scared Graham. He'd never encountered anything like this in his life.

"How? Where's his number?" Pain took hold of Ginny, and she moaned but held out her phone to Graham who, after fumbling for a few moments, managed to get Jem on the line.

"What's up?" he asked when he answered the phone.

"It's me, Graham. Ginny seems to be bleeding and asked me to call you. I don't understand what is going on. I think she must be having a very heavy period. Shall I call the doctor?"

Jem had guessed Ginny was pregnant but hesitated, figuring Graham was already out of his depth and panicking. "I'll be there in about twenty minutes. If she gets worse before I get there, call the doctor." He hung up.

Graham worried about what he might find if he opened the door to Ginny's room again. He had shut it to speak to Jem. Ginny had moved to the bathroom, leaving a trail of blood in her wake. Graham didn't know what to do, so he called out and told her that Jem was on his way. He couldn't bring himself to go and see what was happening. He prayed Ginny would be all right. She didn't answer him, so he retreated to wait for Jem by the outside door.

He heard nothing coming from Ginny and hoped she was OK. Truth was, he didn't cope well with any sort of medical drama or anything confrontational, and the little he had seen of Ginny's condition was already burnt into his mind like a wound.

It seemed a long twenty minutes, and he had just decided to ring the doctor when Jem barrelled up in his ute. "How is she?"

"I don't know. She's in her bathroom. I haven't seen her since I rang you."

"What! Jesus, man." Jem barged by him and disappeared into Ginny's bathroom. He emerged in moments and dialled a number on his phone.

He gave the address then said, "Her name is Ginny Harrison. She is miscarrying and haemorrhaging badly. Sure, yes, I'll do what I can."

Ignoring Graham, Jem went back into the bathroom. Graham realised he had better do something, so he cautiously approached the bathroom. Jem was helping Ginny lay flat, as she had been curled up, partly due to intense pain. He had fetched a pillow from the bed and covered her up with a blanket. Ginny's eyes were shut, and she shivered violently.

Jem stroked her hair back from her face gently. "It's OK. Help will be here soon. It's OK."

Tears oozed from Ginny's closed eyes, but she didn't answer. "Get her some water, Graham."

Graham shakily went and filled a beaker with water and passed it to Jem. He supported Ginny's head and shoulders and managed to get her to have a sip or two.

Graham stood in the doorway. He didn't know what to do. Jem ignored him. Not long after phoning for help, an ambulance turned up, and Ginny was whisked away to the local hospital.

Jem turned to Graham angrily. "You weren't much help."

"I-I'm sorry. I didn't know what to do."

Jem relented a bit. "I suppose not. I'm used to dealing with animals, and humans aren't much different at the end of the day. Then there was Mary . . ."

"But I don't understand. How is Ginny pregnant? Who—"

"Don't look at me! It's Alex's baby, and it seems he has shot through, the bugger. I expect Ginny told him, and he couldn't hack it. I'll take the bugger to task if I get the chance."

"The young bloke who was looking after everything?"

"Yep."

"Good God, what—how did that happen? Surely Ginny, well, I don't know what to say. Did he compel her to have sex with him? What happened?"

Jem took a deep breath. He wasn't comfortable talking to this silly pommy bastard, but he felt compelled to stick up for Ginny and Alex. He had seen how much Ginny loved him and had thought Alex felt the same even though he was very young. He was very surprised he had taken off, but maybe it was temporary. He hoped so for Ginny's sake. She was going to need a lot of support now.

"Age means nothing if you love someone. You love them no matter what. After seeing them together, I knew they were in love. I just hope Alex returns and supports Ginny through all this. She is going to need him."

"And to think I was going to ask her to marry me! I'll see what flights I can get and go home. This trip has been a complete waste of time."

"You do that. I'll drive you to the airport." Jem broke off before he said good riddance.

Graham went off to see what he could arrange. Jem let the chooks out and saw to Millie. Puck followed him about, looking lost. "Would you like to come home with me?" Jem asked him, rubbing behind his ears. Puck pushed his head into Jem's hand. He had been one very distressed dog throughout the morning drama, but no one had even noticed him.

"Graham," Jem called. "Come and help me clear up this mess, will you?"

Graham looked anything but pleased when he found out Jem was referring to Ginny's room and bathroom. However, he helped Jem strip the bed and clean up the blood. Jem, after hunting around, found clean bedlinen, and they remade the bed. Jem announced he was going to burn the worst of the stained bedding and took it down to the paddock and started a small fire. Luckily it had rained in recent days, so he could safely do that.

When he got back to the house, Graham announced he couldn't get a flight for three days, but he asked Jem to drive him to Brisbane anyway. He'd rather stay at a hotel than at Ginny's place.

Jem looked at the time. "Sorry, mate, I have animals to see to, and it's midmorning. I'll take you tomorrow. Later this arvo, I'm going to the hospital to see Ginny. Do you want to come?"

"No, um, yes . . . I don't know. I feel as if she is a stranger, but on the other hand . . . I really don't know."

"Well, make up your mind. I'm off, and I need to know."

Graham mentally struggled with himself then said, "OK, I'll come. I owe

Ginny that much and then I can report to her family once I am back in the UK."

"I'll pick you up about two thirty." Jem got in his ute with Puck and drove off without another word.

Graham looked around. It was very strange to be in such an isolated place on his own. He didn't like the feeling much. Not that it was completely isolated, as the town was only five kilometres away, but there were no near neighbours, and it felt lonely to him. Although he lived in rural Suffolk, this was almost an alien landscape to him. He was a businessman through and through, and he never got his hands dirty. He had a gardener and a cleaner who came three times a week. He was capable of cooking food but ate out a lot. Being left like this in a strange place was very unsettling. He sighed and went back to his room. He had a shower then got himself some toast. Ginny had a coffee machine, an old one that was temperamental, so he made himself tea, though he would have preferred coffee.

He had just finished and was putting the dirty dishes in the sink when he heard a car. Going through to Ginny's workroom, he looked out to see a tall, dark-haired man striding towards the workroom door. He opened it as the man got to it.

The man stared at him. "Who are you?"

"I was about to ask the same question," Graham said, feeling pleased to see someone. He held out his hand to shake the visitor's. The stranger hesitated before taking Graham's hand, then they both spoke at once.

Graham said, "I'm visiting from the UK. Graham—"

The man said, "I'm Charles Unwin. Alex is my son. I gathered from Ginny that he isn't here. Where is Ginny?" Charles seemed agitated. He had spoken over Graham.

"She's—" Graham swallowed. "She's in hospital." Graham wondered what on earth he should say. Did this man know about the relationship between Ginny and Alex? He looked stressed and worried. But Jem had led Graham to believe that no one else knew about the relationship or at least that Ginny was pregnant. "Come in. I'll make you something to drink. Coffee or tea?"

Charles didn't reply, but he followed Graham through. Graham busied himself putting the coffee-maker on. He wasn't quite sure how it worked but thought he could figure it out.

Charles sat down at the table. "Ginny rang me. I could tell she was desperate to speak to Alex, so I took the bull by the horns and phoned his mother. She claims Ginny and Alex are lovers, but I'm having a hard time coming to terms with it. Ginny seemed far too sensible, and I trusted her. Alex is twenty-one. What could he possibly see in Ginny? She's much, much older. It must be all her fault. She somehow seduced him. I know he had a wild time when he was in Sydney, but this is—this is . . ." Charles trailed off.

Graham, for all his disapproval, didn't like the fact that Ginny was being blamed. He thought he had better refrain from telling Charles why Ginny was in hospital.

"Ginny is an extremely desirable woman, and it takes two to tango. I think it's unfair to blame her. Maybe your son really likes her."

Charles grunted into the coffee that Graham had set before him. "Why is she in hospital?"

Graham regretted saying where she was. "Oh, just a minor mishap. I expect she will be back soon."

Nothing more was said for a few minutes since neither man knew what to say. Graham didn't want to make matters worse, and Charles focused on his need to visit Ginny. Had she done something silly? Although Charles disapproved of her relationship with Alex, he had liked her. He'd thought of having a serious relationship with her but was worried for her now. He had picked up on the desperation in her voice on the phone but decided not to ask this rather odd man about her. Instead, he'd visit Ginny and talk to her in person.

"Why are you here? Are you a relative or something?" Charles suddenly broke the silence.

"Yes, no—a distant relative. Thought I'd find out what Australia's like, so here I am. Only here a day or two, then I'm moving on." Graham wondered why he had told a fib but then thought it was none of this man's business anyway.

Charles, however, was distracted. He got to his feet. "Thanks for the coffee." He strode to the door.

Graham followed him. "I'll tell Ginny you called when she comes back."

"You do that." Charles got into his big 4WD and drove off at speed. Graham shook his head. What a strange bunch of people.

CHAPTER 18

CHARLES DROVE STRAIGHT to the hospital and walked into reception, demanding to see Ginny. Since it was only a small cottage hospital, everyone knew everyone, and the gossips had been busy. Everyone knew Ginny had suffered a miscarriage and who the father was. After all, they had been busy gossiping for some weeks about Alex and Ginny.

"Of course, Mr Unwin. She's out of theatre now. I'll just check to see if she can have visitors," the receptionist told him.

"Theatre?"

"Yes. I'm so sorry for your loss. That would have been your first grandchild, right?"

Charles stood stock-still, staring at the woman.

"What did you say?" he roared.

Maisie, the receptionist, realised she had spoken out of turn, but it was too late to take the words back.

"Um, s-she had a, um, a miscarriage. I'm sorry." Maisie wasn't sure if she was apologising for saying something she shouldn't have or for the fact Ginny had lost the baby.

Charles turned on his heel and left. He drove off at top speed. Anger had completely taken over. He would ring Margarita and tell her. But as he drove, he was aware that part of his anger was jealousy. He had really liked Ginny. He envied Alex for having the courage to start a relationship with her. He knew his son well enough to know it must be more than a fling or a brief affair. After all, he had wanted Ginny himself, so he also felt betrayed, though he wasn't sure whose betrayal hurt worse.

He also knew it was Margarita's father who would have encouraged Alex to play the field when he was in Sydney. He was a larger-than-life character and had narrowly escaped jail on numerous occasions. Charles had met him through his property development business. Charles himself had sailed a bit close to the wind a few times, and Marcus knew this. He'd introduced Charles to Margarita, thinking he was the sort of son-in-law that would fit in with his business. However, Charles had proved more independent than Marcus had bargained for, and Marcus was even less happy when Charles sold his business and went off to the outback and bought a cattle property. It hadn't been long before Margarita ran back to "Daddy." Marcus's wife had bailed out of their marriage when Margarita was small, so father and daughter were very close. Margarita could do no wrong, and the same had been true for Alex as he was growing up, but Marcus was appalled by Alex's career choice and told Margarita so. They had both tried to pull Alex into line. Two of Marcus's men had gone up to Queensland to suss out the situation. Marcus and Margarita had been unprepared for the news the men had reported back. Marcus had instructed his men to remain in case Alex had to be pressured in the future.

Marcus had then given his grandson an ultimatum: "Come back to Sydney and leave that woman. If you don't, it will be worse for her. Lee and Rix are there to make sure you don't do anything silly. You understand me? One day, my business will be yours. I don't want you distracted by stupid older women or stupid career choices. Do I make myself clear?"

Alex had hung up. He knew Marcus didn't make idle threats, and he also knew that if he loved Ginny, he had to leave her. However, Marcus had then told Lee and Rix to go round Ginny's place and make sure Alex left. "I don't want him hurt, but you can scare him any way you like," Marcus said. "As for the woman, well, that is up to you." At that time, no one had known about Ginny's pregnancy.

Charles drove straight home, and when he got there, he immediately phoned Margarita. "Is Alex there?"

"Not at this precise moment. He is with my father. They took the boat out. Dad wanted to talk to Alex without interruptions. Why? It's none of your business."

"I'm calling about Ginny, the hat woman."

"Don't worry about her. Dad put a stop to it. Silly boy, but I suppose there is no harm done. He'll get over it."

"She's pregnant—or rather was pregnant. She lost the baby."

"What! No way—my God. Lost it, you say? Just as well. What were they thinking, or rather, what was she thinking. Alex wouldn't do anything so stupid." Anger and jealousy coursed through Margarita's veins. Alex had told her he loved Ginny but hated her, which was why her father had taken Alex out in the boat to get them apart because their quarrels were bitter and uncompromising.

"I'll make her pay for this, believe me. I'm not going to let this pass by. Because of her, Alex and I are arguing. I'll make sure she never thinks of getting close to him again."

"I don't imagine she wants to, anyway," Charles said dryly, suddenly feeling sorry for Ginny. If Margarita was intent on revenge, then God help Ginny. Margarita was one very vindictive woman, as Charles well knew. He almost felt sorry for her but quashed those feelings quickly. Best he didn't get involved.

"Will you tell Alex?" he asked.

"Are you mad? Of course not. He's in such a state over this bloody woman as it is. He'll never know if I have my way."

Charles hung up. He'd keep the secret for now, but later, well, he'd see.

CHAPTER 19

Jem was on time picking Graham up. The pommy was bursting to tell him about Charles turning up. Jem took the news grimly. "You didn't tell him that Ginny had been expecting, did you?"

"No. I was tempted, but then he drove off before I got the chance."

"Just as well. They are a strange family. Alex seems like the most normal one. If Alex doesn't know about the pregnancy, then it's best to keep it quiet. If Alex comes back, Ginny can tell him herself. If it wasn't the baby that scared him off, I can't think why he shot through. They seemed so happy."

"His father heard about how involved Ginny and Alex are. He seemed very angry when we talked about it," Graham admitted. "Oh dear, did I make matters worse?"

"It's too late to worry now. Let's hope Ginny is on the mend."

The two men got some strange looks when they got to the hospital, and it took a while to convince the nurses that Graham should be allowed in too. Since they knew Jem, he didn't have a problem. They were both shocked when they got to her bedside. She was deathly pale, her eyes were red-rimmed, and she seemed to have shrunk and looked small in the bed. Graham had brought her a clean nightdress, a hairbrush, and wash things. He wouldn't have thought of it if Jem hadn't mentioned it, and he was embarrassed when Ginny thanked him. Her voice was barely a whisper, and it was plain she didn't feel like talking. They had agreed not to say anything about Charles's visit, and after telling her all her animals were OK, they ran out of things to say. They didn't want to refer to the miscarriage unless Ginny brought it up, so after a few minutes, silence reigned.

Ginny turned eyes swimming with tears to Jem. "I lost the baby. I didn't know I wanted her until I lost her, and I lost Alex too. He is gone forever. How can I still live and breathe without him?"

"Come on, old girl. You don't know he's gone for good. It might be he's just—"

Ginny made an impatient movement with her hand. "Alex phoned me. He didn't give me the chance to say anything. It was very brief. But his mother and grandfather got to hear about us. He said—he said they would hurt me. He's gone. He's really gone. What will I do?"

Ginny started to sob uncontrollably.

The two men didn't know what to do and were thankful when a nurse appeared. They got to their feet. Then Graham said quietly, "I'm going home, but why don't I wait and you come with me. You can stay with your folks for a bit. It might help."

Ginny was now crying hard and just shook her head. The nurse ushered them out.

"Will she be all right?" Jem asked anxiously.

"She will in time," the nurse said. "It's early days yet. Time will help her."

The two men didn't speak until they got back to Ginny's. "Look, Graham, I can see you are shocked at their age difference, but to me, they were great together," Jem said. "I don't know if it would have lasted, but I do know that Ginny is going to be very vulnerable for a long time to come. It seems Alex's family have stepped in. I don't think you will persuade her to come to the UK straight away, but I will do my best to persuade her later. She needs to recover first, in any case, but her family is what she needs. She has no one here. She isn't close with Jeff's family, and after this, well . . ." Jem shrugged. "Who knows what'll happen. I think you should go ahead and go home. I'll run you to the airport tomorrow as we arranged."

"OK." Graham didn't feel like arguing. He felt exhausted and disappointed by the whole episode. The trip had been a disaster, and home was the only place he wanted to be right now.

The next day, after a restless night, Graham was more than happy for

Jem to drive him to the airport. He had another day and a half before his flight but appeared eager to get away from Ginny's house.

Jem had seen to the chooks and horse before he took Graham, and when he got back, it was very, very late, though he still went to Ginny's to check on the animals. All seemed OK, and when he finally climbed into his own bed, he was exhausted. However, something niggled at the back of his mind.

CHAPTER 20

JEM WOKE THE next morning and knew what had bothered him the night before. Millie hadn't been shut in her paddock. The gate had been open. She had been in there, but she could have been anywhere else she pleased. The front gate had been shut, and Jem couldn't imagine leaving the paddock gate open, but on reflection, he must have done so.

He got up and saw to his animals, then, with Puck's head hanging out of the window, he drove to Ginny's. Everything seemed to be in order. No open gates and every animal was accounted for. However, he looked in the veggie garden, and sure enough, he found evidence that Millie had experienced a high old time in there. Hoof prints and trampled veggies abounded. Some, she had eaten. The same carnage marred the flower garden too. *Oh hell. I must not have fastened the gate properly. What an idiot. Too much on my mind. I'll have to repair this damage as much as I can before Ginny gets back. I'll ring the hospital now.*

The hospital told Jem that Ginny could come home the next day, provided everything was still all right with her, and she hadn't developed any problems. Jem decided he'd pop in to see her later.

He set about trying to make the garden look presentable again and generally tidying up. Then a thought struck him. Ginny would need someone around when she got back, so he resolved to talk to Jo. She and Ginny had been friends once, and they had only fallen out because of Alex. Jem was nervous doing this, as Jo had gossiped about him abusing his wife, though to be fair, she had stuck up for him after the truth came out.

He wasn't sure she would be home, as she had a part-time job at the supermarket, but she was. As Jem had suspected, news had spread about Ginny having a miscarriage.

"Jem, I haven't seen you here before. What's up?"

"Hi, Jo. Look, I know I was rude in the past, and you don't like me much. Don't blame you, really, but I'm not here for me. I'm here for Ginny. You know what happened to her. She's going to want a good mate when she comes home tomorrow. I wondered if you could bring yourself to be that person."

Jem watched emotions flit across Jo's face. "I don't know. We rather fell out. Actually, I made Ginny cross. I was so surprised when I heard about her and Alex, though I have to say she was right. Old men marry young girls, and on the whole, people accept it, but when it's the other way round, they don't. It does seem silly, really. So it's true. Ginny had a miscarriage and Alex shot through?"

Jem nodded.

"The bastard, but I suppose it was to be expected. If Ginny is OK with me helping her, I'll do whatever I can."

"Good. She is coming home tomorrow, I hope. She lost a lot of blood, so she'll feel weak, but it's the emotional part of it that's going to be hard. I know!"

"I'm sorry that we all misjudged you. The way you are looking out for Ginny proves what a great guy you are."

Jem was highly embarrassed and blushed. It was the nicest thing anyone had said to him in a long time, apart from Ginny's endorsement.

When Jem got to the hospital, Ginny made a big effort to be more upbeat, but Jem saw through it. He didn't say anything and indulged her. He even managed to make her laugh a few times by talking about Graham and some of the things he had said on the way to the airport. For herself, Ginny was relieved that Graham was returning to the UK. She had enjoyed his company well enough when over there, but everything had been different then. She hadn't acknowledged her feelings for Alex, nor had she realised where all that would lead. If she had, what would she have done differently?

She'd change only one thing; she'd make sure she didn't get pregnant. She had begun to come to terms with the fact that Alex had gone under pressure but gone none the less. In her heart, she'd known he would leave her at some point, as he had his whole life ahead of him, but it was as if he had been torn from her arms. If she hadn't lost the baby, she would have had something of him to hold onto. She knew she would never love another. He was her one and only. She was grateful she'd had him in her life for a short time. Her heart was broken, but there was no way she was going to let it defeat her. She looked forward to returning home the next day.

"By the way, I spoke to Jo. She is going to help you for a few days. I hope that is all right." Jem's voice broke into her thoughts.

"Not Jo. We had words!"

"I know. Jo mentioned that, but she regrets them now, and she wants to be friends again. Give it a go, please."

Ginny nodded slowly. She knew she was feeling lost and vulnerable just now. Maybe another woman would be good to talk to.

Jem chatted some more then got up to leave. He stopped on his way out. The red-headed nurse he had seen during his previous visit walked towards him. She was pretty. The new Jem was once more taking an interest in women.

"Hi," he said. "Just coming on duty?"

She stopped and smiled at him. "No. Been on a short break, though. You been visiting your girlfriend? I'm sorry about the baby."

Jem was rather horrified. "Jesus, no. She's just a friend. The baby has nothing to do with me!" He looked at her curiously. "You must be new around here."

"I moved here from Townsville, and this is only my third day. I haven't got to grips with who is who yet. Sorry, I assumed you were the younger lover everyone is talking about, but I have to say, you don't look that young."

Jem burst out laughing. Not so long ago, he'd have been very angry, but he had changed a lot lately.

"That's a backhanded compliment if ever I heard one. I'm Jem, the local, nasty, badtempered bugger." He held out his hand.

The redhead took it. Now that he was closer, he realised she was quite a lot older than she had first appeared. "Helen, but everyone calls me *Red*."

"I wonder why?" They both burst out laughing. "I'm picking Ginny up tomorrow. Maybe I'll see you then."

"I expect so. Nice to meet you, Jem."

Jem almost danced to his ute. He reckoned she must be somewhere in her thirties, and what a looker. It was the first time he had been attracted to a woman since Mary had passed away, and it was an exhilarating feeling. He had forgotten how good it was. When he tended to Ginny's animals and his own, he did so in a kind of trance. Was it love at first sight? Did that actually happen? He didn't know, but it certainly felt pretty good.

CHAPTER 21

THERE WAS AN air of suppressed excitement around Jem as he drove to the hospital the next morning. He worried that fate would intervene, and he wouldn't see Red. But he told himself he was being very silly because even if he did see her, she was quite possibly married or with someone. By the time he parked, he had become a bundle of nerves. However, he was in luck. Red was actually helping Ginny get ready for discharge.

"Hi," was all he could think to say when he got there and saw the two of them: Red, vibrant and smiling, and Ginny, gaunt and weighed down with misery.

"Hi," both women replied, then there was a slightly awkward pause.

"Ginny is just about ready," Red said, smiling at Jem. Her smile lit up her whole face, and though she was not pretty in a standard way, when she smiled, it was as if there were moonbeams dancing over his senses.

He was even more befuddled now. He'd never felt like this even when young with Mary.

Ginny looked from one to the other. They both had silly grins on their faces, and a stab of jealousy shot through her. She quickly tamped it down. Jem deserved to find someone, and it was plain there was attraction brewing. She moved towards the toilet.

"Be with you in a jiffy, Jem," she said.

Jem cleared his throat. It was now or never. "Would you like to have coffee with me sometime?"

Red looked uncertain for a few seconds, then she said, "I can have coffee tomorrow at eleven if that suits you? The cafe in town?"

Jem grinned from ear to ear. "Sounds like a plan. I mean good, um, yes."

Ginny reappeared, and without further ado, they sorted themselves out, and Jem took Ginny out to his vehicle. Once settled, they set off. It was only a twenty-minute drive, and for the first few minutes, Ginny was quiet, then she said, "You like the look of that nurse, don't you?"

He shifted in his seat. "She seems like a nice person."

"She is. She is divorced, and her teenage son lives with her. They are renting at the moment because she is waiting on money from the divorce settlement, then she is hoping to buy something. Her husband sounds like a real bastard."

Ginny didn't tell Jem that she had gleaned all this from Red after she had clocked them talking together in the passageway the day before. She had been on her way to the little room where the TV was. It was the first time she had ventured out, and she'd been surprised to see Jem in a conversation with the nurse.

When they got to her house, Jem fussed around so much that Ginny got impatient with him. "I can manage. I can't lift anything heavy, and I've been told not to ride for a bit, but it's OK. I can do most things, really. Just go and bring Puck back, and I will be fine. Also, thank you for clearing up the bedroom and bathroom. I think you did a great job."

"Graham helped too. His flight out is this evening."

"I know. I will give him a ring before he leaves."

Jem went back to his home and saw to his animals, then he returned to Ginny's with Puck. He brought a casserole that he insisted Ginny share with him.

"You're a good mate. I didn't think much of you when I asked you to help me catch Millie."

"Yea, well, I wasn't in a good place then, but you have been a great help in getting me back to some sort of normality. All that shit went on too long, and even after Mary's mother put people straight, I just didn't trust anyone. Thanks." Jem gave Ginny a brief hug.

Later, after Jem left, Ginny phoned Graham on his mobile.

"I'll be boarding soon," he said. "How are you?"

"Coping. Thank you for helping me that day."

"Once you are feeling better, why not come back to the UK? You can move fully or have an extended stay. You have friends in Australia, I know, but there is nothing like family."

"I will think about it."

They talked a little more, but it was a stilted conversation. Ginny sensed that Graham was having trouble processing what had happened. Ginny was relieved when Graham said he had to board his flight.

Meanwhile, while Jem drove home in the dark, he saw a big 4WD parked on the side of the road about five kilometres from Ginny's house. It worried him, so he turned round and drove back, but there was no sign of it. As there were several gravel roads nearby that the driver could have taken, he decided to leave, but his worry refused to fade. The situation reminded him of the two blokes they had encountered before.

CHAPTER 22

GINNY GOT HERSELF ready for bed slowly. She was so very tired—even undressing was a chore. Finally, she got into the shower and let the hot water cascade over her. She tried not to think. She longed to do her nightly preparations with a blank mind. While she rinsed her hair, Puck let out a deep growl. He sometimes growled at kangaroos if they came close to the house and if he heard unexplained noises, but this was different. He was plainly worried by something or someone. Stepping out of the shower and wrapping herself in a large towel, Ginny went to the back door to let Puck out, but some instinct stopped her. She decided she wanted Puck in the house with her not charging around outside in the dark. "Quiet, boy. Sit."

Puck sat reluctantly, still growling and looking towards the door. Ginny listened but couldn't hear anything except her own heart thumping away rapidly, as if she had run a marathon.

After what seemed like a lifetime, Puck relaxed a little and stopped growling, though he was still on high alert. In the distance, she thought she heard the deep, throaty roar of an engine, but it was very faint, and she wasn't sure. She eventually plucked up the courage to open the door a crack. Puck decided enough was enough and pushed by Ginny, squeezing through the gap and nearly taking the sliding door off its runners. He tore away into the darkness.

Ginny shut the door again. She was shivering. Early winter wasn't the best time to stand at an open door in only a towel. She went and put on an old T-shirt she wore in bed and found her dressing gown, then she went back to the door and waited for Puck to return. He was gone much longer than normal for any night-time adventures. His typical evening jaunts involved chasing any roos out of the garden and yard, having a general snuffle round, then coming back in looking very pleased with himself. In the end, Ginny put the outside light on and called and called him.

At last, he returned but from the front of the house, which wasn't the direction she had thought he had gone at all.

"Come on, Puck. What was that all about, hey? Didn't hear you barking out there. Come on, time for bed."

Puck was allowed the run of the house at night, but tonight, Ginny wanted him in her room, so she made sure she shut him in with her. She had done this sometimes after Jeff had passed away, but she had not invited Puck inside since she had taken Alex to her bed. Now she needed the comfort of knowing Puck was nearby.

She didn't sleep, only catnapped. The hospital had given her sleeping tablets, but she didn't want to get into that. While she was wide awake, she could make herself think of random things, but when she was dozing, Alex was there, laughing at some silly joke, regarding her with his beautiful eyes, stroking her, kissing her, and loving her. Each time, she would jerk herself awake, and tears of anguish would flow.

She got up in the cold grey dawn, unable to stay in bed any longer, and went through to the hat room and tried to concentrate on the hat she had been working on. Only a few days had passed since she'd last worked on it, but it felt like a lifetime ago. It could have been years based on the way she was now feeling.

She fiddled with the hat, but her heart wasn't in it. When Jeff was alive, she'd wondered if their imaginary children would follow in her or Jeff's footsteps. If she'd had Alex's baby, what would she have been like? Would she have been tall, dark, and handsome like Alex, or would she have had light-brown hair and grey eyes like her? The tears started to flow again.

Getting up to find the box of tissues she kept nearby, she saw a note that had been pushed under the door. Sighing, she picked it up. *Some woman wanting a hat yesterday, I'll bet. Well, she'll have to wait. Oh my God!* She flinched and nearly dropped the note but finished reading it while holding her breath.

"This is just the start, you child molester, you paedophile, you bitch."

She stared at the note in horror. To start with, the words made no sense. What on earth? Who would think or say such a thing? Then she remembered Alex's frantic phone call. *My God, this must be Margarita's doing, and it must be those men. But what does it mean? What have they done?*

She looked outside but could see nothing alarming. Now she understood Puck's behaviour last night. All seemed fine at the front of the house, so she went out the back and soon saw what had happened. The chook run had been pulled up, and the hut door was swinging open. Some of the chooks were scratching about in her garden but many remained out of sight. It wasn't that bad, but it was frightening to think someone had been creeping round her house while she'd been in the shower. She thought about ringing Jem, but what could he do? She squared her shoulders. She was being pathetic. It was time to stop being a weak woman and get on with her life and everything in it. Alex was gone, and she had to live with that. His mum and grandfather were just trying to make a point. Alex was back with them, so what more did they want? Suddenly, she remembered it was Alex's birthday the next day, and she had been planning to make it special. Again, tears threatened.

CHAPTER 23

RIX AND LEE were fed up with this strange job the boss had given them. Normally their jobs involved making sure businesses paid their "insurance" money on time and ensuring the lower end of the boss's drug scene behaved itself. Lee was especially unhappy.

"I didn't sign up for frightening women, especially women like her. She's all right," Lee grumbled to Rix the next morning.

The two men were camped out in an isolated spot on the Unwin property. Charles was unaware they were there, but one of the men on his payroll was working for his father-in-law. He'd been put there at Margarita's request.

"I don't like being out here in the bush either," said Rix. "We've snakes, spiders, and mossies to deal with, then there are bloody dingoes making a racket at night. Never been one for camping. My old man used to take us kids. I always hated it."

"Why don't we just leg it back? Tell the boss we've frightened her well and done what he asked. I don't get it. Why are we doing this? Do you know?" Lee asked.

"Apparently, the boss's grandson had a fling with that woman. Didn't you read the note I gave you?"

"No. By the time I let the chooks out, I was getting jumpy. I was worried about that big dog."

"Anyway, the old man's daughter is some sort of control freak and hates the woman we're here to scare. She had an affair with the young bloke, Alex, and when the boss phoned yesterday, he was off his nut with anger. I didn't get it, really. I think we head back tomorrow and tell the boss we've done as he asked. I don't like this job either. He can find someone else if he still wants to put the frighteners on her."

The next morning, they started to pack up when Rix's mobile went. The signal was very weak, and he had to walk away from their camp to hear what the boss had to say.

When he returned, he didn't look happy. "Bloody woman. Boss's daughter wants us to do more. She wants this lady to suffer. We'll have to think of something else, then we leg it before the boss has the chance to come up with more."

"We let the horse loose and the chooks, not that either did much. We could do something to her car. I don't fancy tackling the dog, but we could do something to him. I hate dogs."

Rix grinned. "They don't like you much either, mate, but you've given me an idea. Chocolate is poisonous to dogs. Let's feed that dog chocolate, then he'll be done for, but he'll die happy. What do you think?"

"It's a thought. Not sure how we'd do it, though. I don't want to get near the brute. Anyway, how do you know the chocolate thing is true?"

"I saw some advert for a vet practice or something, I dunno. Maybe I read it."

"We wouldn't have to get near him. We can just unwrap a bar and leave it near the house somewhere."

"Take more than one bar."

"Two or three, then."

"OK, if we don't think of anything better, we'll do that."

Happy with their plan, the two men settled down to wait for later in the day.

CHAPTER 24

GINNY FORCED HERSELF to get on with the hat she had been working on, but it didn't distract her enough, and her mind was in turmoil. Every little while, tears leaked out of her eyes and ran down her cheeks. Sometimes she wasn't even aware she was crying. It was as if a tap had been turned on inside her, and she couldn't turn it off. She was weeping over losing Alex and her baby. She had never felt maternal urges and had been quite happy when Jeff had said he didn't want children. Now, she regretted it more than she'd thought possible. *If only we'd had children. If only I hadn't lost Alex's baby. If only, if only.* She was wallowing, she knew, but she couldn't seem to stop.

Then Jo was there. Ginny hadn't heard her arrive, and she walked straight into the workroom. "I did knock—oh, Ginny, you poor thing." Jo wrapped her arms around Ginny, who then started to sob.

Jo guided her into the kitchen and put coffee on. Ginny made a supreme effort to pull herself together. Jo, having got them both a steaming coffee, sat down. "You need to talk to me. If not me then to someone. This is awful. I hate seeing you like this. You were very stoic when Jeff passed away. I am guessing this is harder."

With a box of tissues by her side, Ginny let it all out. She told Joe that she had loved Alex for some time—not just his good looks but his personality, his kindness, his connection with animals, his sense of humour, and his zest for life. She admitted to fighting her feelings, then without details, she told Jo how Alex made it impossible for her to resist any more.

"I knew it wouldn't last, that he would find someone near his own age, but I thought I should take happiness while I could. I never expected him to be torn from my arms like this."

"What do you mean?"

Ginny carried on with her story, and in the end, Jo was in tears too.

"Oh, Ginny, to lose his baby makes it even harder, I can see that, but you are a strong woman, and maybe one day, you'll find someone else."

Then Ginny told her about Graham. "I think he wanted someone to look after him in his old age. I wasn't up for that. I don't want to be a caretaker any more—not after Jeff. I think, in some ways, Jeff's death was a relief to both of us. A strange thing to say but true. He hated who he had become, and he knew he was a burden even though I never let him see how hard it was sometimes."

Jo looked at the clock. "I'll make us lunch. Did you have breakfast?"

"No, and I don't feel like eating."

"Rubbish. You need to eat."

Jo bustled about, and under Ginny's directions, she got some food on the table. The fridge contained salad and cold meat but not a lot else. "I'll do a shop for you," Jo said. "Look, I know I wasn't very understanding when I first heard about you and Alex, but I understand now. Are we OK?"

Ginny's throat closed up once more. She nodded.

Later, when Jo had gone, Ginny realised that talking to her had helped, and she felt more able to cope with the day.

Jem turned up near sunset. Ginny had been feeling reluctant about going out to see to the chooks. After reading the note that morning, she'd had to force herself to see to the horse and chickens, but leaving the house seemed worse now. She was in two minds about showing him the note. In the end, she decided against it. It would worry him, and he had his own life to get on with. He looked like the cat that had swallowed the cream when he walked in.

He walked straight up to Ginny and gave her a hug. "How are you, darl'?"

"I'm OK." Not true, but Ginny wasn't going to let on. "You look—you look different." Then the penny dropped. Red. He was meeting her. Had it happened today?

"Would a certain redhead have anything to do with this new Jem by any chance?"

Jem looked embarrassed. "We only met for coffee, but we got on so well. I can't believe that she is interested in me. Me! But she seems to be. She's coming out to the farm on the weekend with her son. We'll see how we go."

"I'm so pleased for you. You deserve some happiness."

"Thanks, mate. Are you sure you're OK?"

Ginny touched her cheek self-consciously. Her eyes were red and her skin too pale. She must look a fright.

"Yea, I'm fine. Jo came today. She's doing a shop for me. She'll bring it round tomorrow."

Jem was worried Ginny wouldn't eat. He remembered Mary. "What are you having for your dinner?"

"Eggs. Don't worry, I'm fine, really."

Jem didn't believe her, but he soon departed, as he had got behind with his chores and daylight was dimming. He still had jobs to do.

Ginny was very jumpy that evening, and the slightest sound had her on the edge of her seat. She thought she heard a vehicle at one point, but though Puck raised his head, he didn't seem that worried, so Ginny relaxed.

She slept better that night, which was largely due to exhaustion.

When she woke, it was with the realisation that today was Alex's birthday. Ten days ago, she had been planning all sorts of things, but now her life was empty. She decided to send a message to his mobile and hope that he would get it at some point. She was aware he may not have it any more but decided to take the risk.

Her fingers shook against her phone screen. "Happy birthday, my love. I hope you get this and have a wonderful day. Love you forever."

After she sent it, she got up and let Puck out, then she had a quick shower, made a coffee, and sat down to work. She refused to let her mind drift to Alex.

Puck came in. He had a sheepish expression on his face and something dark around his mouth.

Ginny, trying hard to concentrate on her work, spoke to him but didn't get close.

"Good boy. What have you been up to? Lay down. I'm working."

Puck did as he was told. For the next hour or so, Ginny worked on the hat while Puck kept getting up and down. At one point, Ginny told him off because he was so restless. Soon afterwards, Jo appeared with the groceries, and the two women sorted out payments, and Ginny started to put the food away. Jo put the coffee machine on again.

"Have you eaten breakfast?" Jo asked.

Ginny opened her mouth to speak when Puck, who had followed them into the kitchen, suddenly shot for the door, but as he ran, he was sick. Not normal doggy sick but horrendous projectile vomit. Dark-brown chunks splattered against the kitchen floor and cabinets. Ginny had never seen anything like it. It didn't stop, and the dog shook and whimpered.

"Oh my God, he's been poisoned." Ginny knew instinctively that Puck's illness wasn't natural, though she had no clue what he'd been poisoned with.

The two women looked at each other. He was such a big dog, and in this state, they wouldn't be able to carry him to the car by themselves. Ginny rang the vet immediately. Without saying anything, Jo went to Puck and stroked his back. He had not stopped vomiting, and now his bowels had given in to the poison too, and watery poo shot out of him. He was in a terrible state.

Bill, the local vet, knew Ginny since he sometimes came out to see to Millie and give Puck his yearly vaccinations so Ginny didn't have to lug them into the surgery. That had been because of Jeff. Bill knew how difficult things were for her then.

Ginny rapidly explained Puck's symptoms.

"I'll be there shortly," Bill said. "Luckily, I'm not too busy."

Twenty minutes later, Bill rolled up. "What did he ingest? Do you know?"

"Early this morning, he came back in looking as if he had done something he shouldn't have, and he had something brown around his mouth. His vomit smells funny, a bit like chocolate, but how would he get any?"

Bill took Puck's vitals. "The symptoms are certainly like chocolate poisoning. Help me get him into the back of my ute, and I'll take him back to the surgery. He's going to need fluid and medication. I have to warn you that he may not survive. It depends on how much he's had, but the next seventeen hours will be crucial."

"Oh my God, I can't lose Puck too, I just can't." Ginny was nearing hysteria.

Bill shook her gently. "Come on, old girl. Help me get him into my car. He'll be all right, I'm sure."

With a huge effort, they got the almost comatose dog into Bill's ute. With a wave of his hand and a promise to keep Ginny updated, he drove off.

"He's a lovely man," Jo observed as he disappeared out of the gate.

Ginny, who was trying hard to hold herself together, nodded. "He seems timeless, somehow. He's been here forever, I understand."

"He has, and he is a very good vet. We are lucky to have him here. If anyone can save Puck, it's Bill."

CHAPTER 25

JO STAYED UNTIL nearly lunchtime, then she left as she had things to do. A little later, Jem popped in and was appalled to hear about Puck. Bill was as good as his word and phoned Ginny every two hours.

Jem and Ginny searched around to see if they could see where Puck had picked up the chocolate and concluded it had been thrown over the front fence from the road, and Puck had found it. How much he'd eaten, they didn't know, but Ginny hoped against hope that it hadn't been too much. She then told Jem about someone interfering with the hen house and letting them out at night. Jem then told her about Millie being free.

"Come and stay at my place tonight," Jem suggested. "Without Puck, you'll be even more vulnerable and alone."

Ginny stood straighter. "It's very kind of you to offer, but I'm staying, and that is that. If Puck's poisoning is connected to Alex's mother, then I'm not letting that horrible woman think she can frighten me. I don't think Charles is in on this. He seems a nice man. But as for Margarita and her father, well, what can I say?"

"Are you sure? I worry about you. Red and her son are coming on Saturday. Did I tell you?"

"Yes, you did, several times. I am pleased for you."

Jem looked shamefaced. "Sorry, I keep repeating myself. It's just amazing, but I'm a little worried about meeting her son. What will he think of me? Suppose he doesn't like me. What'll I do then?"

"Jem, you may not like him. Just because you like Red doesn't mean you'll like her son, and from what I saw when I was in the UK last year, teenagers can be very tricky."

"Oh, well, I suppose you are right. I hadn't thought of it like that. I assumed, being Red's son, he'd be OK. Gosh, I'm even more worried now."

"Don't be. What's meant to be is meant to be. Take it as it comes. That was how I got through looking after Jeff. I haven't been so good at it lately, mind, but I'll get there."

Jem gave her a hug. "Thanks, you are right. If it's meant to be, it will be. You are such a strong person. I do admire you."

"If I was as strong as I should have been, I wouldn't have let Alex—" Her eyes flooded with tears. Taking a breath, she said, "I wouldn't have let him make love to me."

After Jem had gone, Ginny sat in her workroom, looking at some of the unfinished hats that were waiting to be done. A thought came to her. She didn't want to make hats any more. But what on earth though could she do instead? Deep down, she suspected her change of heart was because millinery was something she and Alex had done together these last few months, and not having him beside her was too hard. It made her think of him more when she was desperately trying not to.

She was dog-tired when she finally climbed into bed. Bill had rung her to say that he thought Puck would pull through but not to hold her breath. He was an old dog, and the only reason he had survived was because he was a big dog, and the amount of chocolate he had ingested may not have been a huge amount. Bill admitted that it was speculation on his part, though. Ginny had felt more hopeful after this and got ready for bed early. She was so tired she thought she may sleep.

She was in a deep sleep when her mobile went. Groggily, she answered it, thinking it may be Bill.

"You bitch. You worm. Molesting my son—my son! I read your message. Thought he'd get it, did you? Well, I did. You'll pay. My God, you'll pay."

Click. Margarita had hung up.

Ginny sat, frozen with distress. The woman was a monster. What would she get those men to do next? Ginny felt very fearful, and her heart thumped away in her chest, almost as if it would burst out. Sleep would be impossible.

She looked at the clock. It was only eleven. Wearily, she climbed out of bed. Upset though she was, she didn't cry. She had cried enough tears to fill a dam. It was time to stand up and not be a victim.

She made herself a hot chocolate and sat up in bed drinking it. Many thoughts swirled round in her head, and finally she decided to go to the police and tell them she was being threatened and also tell them about Puck. She lay down and managed to sleep, even though it was fitful.

CHAPTER 26

AFTER THEY THREW the big bar of cooking chocolate over the front fence of Ginny's house, the two men set off back to Sydney, having already packed up their camp.

They drove straight across to the coast and decided to take their time returning. "The boss owes us a little holiday," Rix said, grinning.

They both turned their phones off, as they knew Marcus would call them if they didn't and demand they return. Since their job was complete, they indulged in drugs, alcohol, and women. They were both in quite a state driving back to Sydney.

Lee was driving since Rix was in a worse state than him. He suddenly put his foot hard on the brake. "Shit. Cops. We'll fail an RBT. Shit." He made to turn round.

Rix stopped him, putting his hand on his arm. "The buggers will come after us if we make a run for it. You might be OK. It's been a while since you had that weed."

Lee nodded. That was why he was driving. He wasn't as hung-over as Rix.

The young policeman took his time looking at Lee's licence, then he gave him a breath test, which was negative. Not so the drug test.

"How long ago, mate?" The policeman asked when Lee admitted he'd had a joint. The officer handed him a plastic paddle to scrape down his tongue.

"Last night, not sure of the time."

A few minutes later, Lee found himself having a second drug test, which was positive.

"I'm afraid you can't drive, sir. You'll have to leave your car. Is there anyone who can pick you and your mate up? We will park it for you over there." He indicated a small car park across the road.

Rix and Lee looked at each other. Neither of them were game to tell Marcus what had happened. He might be a drug runner and supplier, but he didn't tolerate those on his payroll getting on the wrong side of the law and getting caught as they had. On the other hand, it also meant they were going to be even later getting back.

"We could phone Luke?" Rix said quietly.

Lee looked at the police officer and said, "We'll phone a mate."

Rix was relieved that it was Lee who had been driving since his licence was fairly clean whereas Rix had priors. Also, he had the bigger criminal record. Luke's was the worst, though none of them were big players.

It was several days after poisoning the dog that they faced Marcus.

"What the bloody hell were you playing at? From what you told me, you didn't give this woman that much grief, but now I understand she had a miscarriage. Did you know?"

"No—yes. Well, we knew she was in hospital, but we weren't sure why."

"My daughter is even angrier now. She wants to make this woman regret ever going near Alex. You'll be going back shortly."

Lee didn't usually stand up to Marcus, but he did now.

"Boss, why? We frightened her, and your grandson is safely back in Sydney. Why do more? It's way out of your area up there in Queensland. They had sex—so what. I . . ." He trailed off as Marcus looked angry.

"Alex needs to understand. He has to forget this woman. He is very stubborn, and I think he is letting the dust settle, then he will take up with her again. He told me, though not his mother, that he wants to marry her. I'm not sure if she is some sort of gold-digger or what. I want her eliminated. It's the only way Margarita will be satisfied, and the only way young Alex will give up wanting her."

Rix and Lee looked at each other. They both knew what the other was thinking. While they were happy to rough people up on Marcus's orders, they had never eliminated anyone. He'd never asked them to. Though he was a big player, he was also a very careful one. Prison wasn't on his agenda. They both looked at him. He shrugged. "I want to keep my daughter happy. She can be very difficult. It's a long way to Queensland. Rest a little, then head back in a few hours."

"What about your grandson? He'll be suspicious. Won't he guess what's going on?"

"I have a plan to make her death look like an accident. I'll tell you what to do."

CHAPTER 27

TIME PASSED SLOWLY for Ginny. After a few days, she had Puck back. He was weak and had lost a lot of weight. Always a rangy type of dog, he now looked like a walking skeleton.

When she'd left the surgery, Bill had said, "Just feed him small amounts of food—little and often. Give him fish and chicken for the first week or so, then gradually go back to his normal diet. Introduce it bit by bit. His body has taken a hammering, but he'll pull through. I'm sorry, my dear, but the bill will be rather large."

It had been. Ginny sucked in her breath at the memory. She wouldn't give up hats just yet. She wanted to, but since she couldn't decide what else to do, she was stuck. Orders seemed to have dwindled too, and she was suspicious that some of that was due to a few rather uncomplimentary posts she had seen on social media. Nothing too blatant but enough to make people cautious. She didn't know who was behind it but suspected Margarita or someone close to her.

Jem came after the visit with Red and her son. "How was it?" Ginny asked, though she could see the answer in his eyes.

"It was good, very good. The lad didn't want to engage with me to start with, but once we went across and looked at the cattle and horses, everything changed. Apparently, he's always wanted to ride, so I gave him his first lesson. He's a natural—took to it like a duck to water. They are staying over next weekend."

Jem looked a bit worried after he said that. Ginny guessed he was worried about sleeping arrangements and if it would be difficult with Red's son. It was one thing for the boy to accept Jem as a casual friend who happened to have horses, but it was quite another to accept his mother sleeping with said man.

"It will be fine. Just play it by ear. Red knows her son and what his expectations are. Trust her."

"Thanks for your words of wisdom."

"Pity I didn't use such wisdom before I got involved with Alex."

"Could you have?"

Ginny thought long and hard for a minute. "I had this compulsion, this need, and in the end, I couldn't resist it. I never expected to love anyone again after Jeff, but this is greater. This feeling I have—it's all-consuming." Her eyes misted with tears, and she brushed them angrily away. "I feel weak and lost, and I've never felt like this before. I can't see a future or any happiness ahead. It's too hard. Where do I go from here? What do I do?"

Jem put his arms around her awkwardly. "Give it time, like I did after Mary. Time is a healer."

Ginny stepped away from him and shook her head. "I know what you are saying, but I also know my own mind. I may stop crying and being miserable, but I also know that even if I meet someone else, I will never love anyone like I love Alex. I knew he would find someone his own age in the long run, but to me, age is irrelevant. Once I gave in and realised he loved me too, it stopped mattering. I was content with knowing I'd have him for a time, but it's as if he has been torn from my arms, and the baby . . ." Ginny started to cry again in earnest.

"Oh, Ginny, I'm sorry. I should have kept my big mouth shut. I am so sorry."

Taking a big breath, Ginny shook her head. "It's not your fault. It helps to talk. Jo isn't much of a listener, so thanks for this. I told her not to come today; I'm all right, and I need to get on with some work."

Ginny was actually slightly worried about her finances. Most of the money she and Jeff had got when they sold their cattle property had been taken up making the house wheelchair and disability friendly. It hadn't come cheap. Jeff had an insurance policy, but it wasn't that big, and her holiday to the UK had been more expensive than she had bargained for. She had been rather generous treating her family to things, but now she wished she had been more frugal, especially since her business wasn't doing well.

When she went out to see to the animals a couple mornings later, Millie was lying down and had been rolling. It looked like she had colic. Ginny ran back to the house and called Bill. Jean, his wife, answered the phone. "Bill was called out to the Smith property—something about their prize bull hurting himself. I'm not sure how long he'll be. I'll ring him and see what he says."

Taking her mobile with her, Ginny ran back to Millie. She was standing again but bathed in sweat. Just as she got to her, Jean rang her back.

"Bill says he will be at least a couple of hours. Try ringing that young vet who just moved into the area. I'll give you his number."

Ginny called the new vet, whose name was Gareth, and he told her he would be with her in twenty minutes. While she waited, he advised her to walk Millie round and not let her roll. *It's a wonder I didn't ask him if he tells his grandmother how to suck eggs.*

Millie wanted to get down and roll several times, and with difficulty, Ginny managed to keep her walking. She was thankful Millie wasn't a huge horse; otherwise, preventing her from rolling would have been impossible.

After thirty minutes, Gareth finally turned up. He looked a little flustered but didn't say anything. He made a big show of checking that it was colic and nothing else, which annoyed Ginny. She had been around horses long enough to know when a horse had colic and nearly said so. When he had appeared, she had thought, *My God, he looks about twelve. Why didn't I ever think that with Alex?* Gareth was of medium height with sandy hair, a lock of which kept falling in his eyes. He gave Millie an injection and said he would wait and see if it worked. Shortly afterwards, Millie started to release wind, then she pooed and pooed.

"I think she is going to be all right now, Mrs Harrison," he said.

"Ginny, please. Thank you for your help. You'll send me the bill?"

"I can give it to you now, and to make it easier, I am happy to accept a bank transfer."

"Oh, OK. I can do that."

He went to his car and came back a few minutes later with the bill. Ginny took it and nearly dropped Millie's lead rein.

"This is a bit more than I thought it would be—more than Bill would have charged," she said. "Sorry to be frank, but it is."

Gareth didn't seem fazed by this remark. He shrugged his shoulders and said, "When did he last come out here to see the horse?"

"Quite a while ago. Millie is pretty healthy, but she's getting on in years now."

"Prices do go up, you know, and I have a very modern and up-to-date practice with all the latest equipment."

Ginny decided she didn't like him much; she thought he was full of his own importance. He wouldn't last long in their small community.

When she got back into the house, she had to make a transfer from her savings account, something she didn't like doing. Interest rates were so low that she never seemed to get ahead. Money worries on top of everything else were not helping her feel more positive at all.

The weekend loomed in front of her again. Ginny found them the hardest, though she didn't know why. *Maybe it's because weekends are a time for families to do things together. I feel somehow left out.* The little voice in her head spoke too honestly. She wondered how Jem was getting on. She was already feeling his absence. He didn't call in so often now that he'd found Red. Tears of self-pity pricked her eyes. She shook her head at herself and got on with the hat she was making.

CHAPTER 28

THE FOLLOWING FRIDAY, Jem asked Ginny to come out to the farm that weekend. But he did not ask her in person. Instead, he texted her the invitation, which she politely declined. She didn't want to see his happiness, and he hadn't been to see her in nearly a fortnight. She just wanted to be left alone. No one cared, so why should she?

Two hours later, Jem came flying into her drive as he always had. He looked cross when he stalked towards the house.

"Hello, Jem. What brings you out here?" Ginny asked while sitting at her workbench.

"You did. What do you mean by that text: 'Thanks, but no thanks.' What have you got to do that you can't spare an hour or two with friends?"

Ginny mentally wriggled. She knew she was being selfish and silly but somehow couldn't help it. "I didn't want to get in the way," she said lamely.

"Jesus, woman, listen to yourself. You are talking complete rubbish, and you know it. I thought we were mates. If I didn't know you better, I'd say you were jealous."

Silence reigned for a few minutes. Ginny fiddled with the hat she had been stitching, trying to hide the tears that were threatening. Taking a big breath, she finally said, "You are right. I am jealous. I'm jealous of your happiness and that makes me a very bad person since you have had such a hard time. On the one hand I am—I really am—so pleased for you, but I don't know if I can see you with Red and cope. I still feel so lost."

Jem came round the workbench and pulled her into his arms. "Hell, Ginny, I do understand, as that was me not so long ago. But believe me, if you give in to it, it will get worse. Come on, dry those tears and say you'll come. I'm going to make myself a cuppa since you haven't offered. What do you want to drink?"

Ginny smiled through her tears. Who would have thought that the grumpy farmer who wouldn't help her catch Millie could be such a good friend.

"It's been nearly a year. Do you realise?" she asked a little later when they had finished their drinks.

"What are you talking about?"

"When I asked you to help me catch Millie."

"I'm sorry. I was a bit of a bastard that day, wasn't I? I was clearing out some of Mary's stuff. It had been sitting there so long, and the day I met you was the day I finally got round to moving it. I was taking some if it down to the Salvos when I saw you. I wasn't very happy, and I took it out on you."

Ginny smiled. "Millie did me a favour. If she hadn't acted up, I may not have met you, and we may not have become friends, good friends. And yes, I will come out to your place. I'm sorry about before. I was being silly."

"You weren't. I do understand how you feel. Maybe it's unkind to ask you, but we both want you to come."

"In that case, I certainly will. Thanks, Jem." As she said the words, her heart told her she wasn't looking forward to it.

On Saturday morning, she drove out to Jem's. A big black Land Cruiser was parked almost out of sight further up the gravel road.

"She's going somewhere, which is good. Gives us a clear run." The two men made for Ginny's house.

They drove into her driveway, quite confident, and Rix started to get out. Lee was driving. The next second, Puck came charging round the corner of the house, and Rix only just managed to scramble back into the car in time.

"Bloody hell, I thought we'd fixed him up," Rix said. Lee was having a job keeping a straight face. Rix had looked so scared.

"Seems not."

"What do we do now? I'm not game to get bitten by that brute. We need to think of something else."

"Night-time would be good."

"Yes, but she'll be back by then, and I don't like that idea."

They drove off, trying to work out a plan.

CHAPTER 29

GINNY FELT NERVOUS as she approached Jem's place, which was silly. Lately, she didn't understand her own feelings.

As she drew up, Jem, who must have been looking out for her, came down the verandah steps and hugged her as she got out of the car, then Red was hugging her, and suddenly she knew it would be all right and she need not have worried.

A rather spotty teenage boy stood behind Red. "This is Jackson," Red said rather unnecessarily. Jackson stepped forward and shook Ginny's outstretched hand. His grip was strong, and Ginny took a closer look at him. He had a strong jaw and very clear blue eyes. He was tall too, and his hair was strawberry blond.

"I hear you like horses," Ginny said as they settled themselves down to have coffee a few minutes later.

Jackson looked embarrassed as only teenagers could. "Jem is teaching me to ride," he mumbled.

"So I hear. You can come and ride Millie, my horse, any time you like. I don't ride her half as much as I should."

"Why is that?" Red asked. "You should be good to ride again now."

This was true. Ginny had been signed off by the doctor who'd told her she could resume leading a normal life. Ginny had wondered at the time what "normal" was.

She said, "Well, I need to get on with making hats. I seem to have got behind lately, so I haven't had the time."

In truth, Ginny hadn't felt like riding. When she had been depressed about Jeff, it had been a solution and then she had met Jem. Now, riding was something she didn't want to do.

Jem was looking at her keenly. He'd got to know her well, and she was always pretty much an open book to him. He could read her mind quite easily.

However, he let it pass.

"Why don't we all ride out to the dam in the far paddock?" he suggested. "I've enough horses and saddles for everyone. Always wondered why I kept it all, and now I know!"

Red looked alarmed. "I haven't been on a horse in twenty years. I told you that the other weekend."

He put his arm around her waist and gave her a squeeze. "I'll put you on old Bib, and we'll take it real slow."

"But I ride Bib," Jackson piped up.

"You can ride Jazz."

"Really! Wow, thanks." Jackson's eyes sparkled.

It took some time to get the horses saddled and everyone comfortable, but once they got going, Ginny noticed Red was quite relaxed. She, like her son, was a natural on a horse.

It was a beautiful late-winter day. The grass was rather dead as there had been no rain since the autumn, but the black Brangus cattle were fat and happy. Cows and calves hardly bothered to lift their heads as they rode by. The distant hills were hazy mauve and purple. The air was fresh but not cold. Ginny sighed. She loved this part of Queensland.

They rode out to the dam, and Ginny was amazed by the number of pelicans and cormorants and other water birds that were there. As they were going into a drought, she was also surprised by the amount of water in the dam, which nestled at the foot of some small hills. The water was so calm and clear that it was like a huge mirror—everything was reflected in it. It was so beautiful it brought a lump to Ginny's throat. Looking around, she realised they hadn't explored this far when Graham had visited.

"You didn't bring us this far when Graham was here, Jem," she commented.

"Nah, I could see his eyes were beginning to glaze over. My place actually goes as far as the other side of the hill."

Ginny was surprised again. She'd had no idea Jem owned such a large place.

As if reading her mind, he explained that the dam was fed by a spring. "When I bought this place, everything was lush and green, especially here. I found this spring and thought it would be good to have a dam here for when we have a drought. Seems I was right to build it. Mary told me I was mad. The cattle like it up here. That is why most of the stock are in this area."

"You're lucky. Jeff and I had problems in drought season."

For the next ten minutes, Ginny and Jem talked cattle, farming, and the pros and cons of the weather and drought. Suddenly, Ginny said, "Oh my word, Red, I'm sorry. You must be bored, you too Jackson, with us ranting on."

Red grinned at her. "Not at all. I learned a lot in the last ten minutes. It's good to know."

They had got off the horses when they reached the dam, and Jem had brought out a flask of coffee that they had consumed as they talked. Since their drinks were gone, Jem said they had better get back, so he could fire up the barbeque.

"We might not get to eat outside, anyway," observed Jackson. "Look." He pointed west, where very dark, menacing clouds gathered. It had been a beautiful late-winter day until then.

Ginny shivered. A strange feeling of impending doom passed over her, and it wasn't just the gathering clouds. She shook herself. She was getting fanciful.

The rest of the day passed happily enough, though Ginny still had a feeling of foreboding. There was a storm, so they ended up eating indoors since it turned cold, though Jem still used the barbeque to cook.

It was dark and dreary when Ginny returned home. Puck was very pleased to see her. "Had a quiet day, have you, mate?" Ginny said, patting his head. Puck wagged his tail. He'd tell her if he could.

CHAPTER 30

OVER THE NEXT few days, Ginny didn't stray far from her home. She had no need. But on the following Wednesday, she had some hats to dispatch interstate. She set off for the post office, unaware she was being watched. As soon as she disappeared down the road, Lee and Rix made a beeline for her house. They had a joint of lamb they thought would keep Puck out of the way while they put their plan into action. They had just stopped their car when Ginny drew in behind them.

"What the fuck?" Rix burst out. Ginny had forgotten her purse and, with much cursing, had turned round and followed them in. They had been so focused on what they were doing that they hadn't noticed her. There was a big turning circle in front of the house, and they made use of it now, driving away before Ginny had hardly got out of her car.

She watched them go. She knew they were the same guys as before. What did they want now? She was scared. She thought about phoning the local police. She had never got round to it. Now, as then, she wondered what she could say. She was fairly sure the two men had poisoned Puck but had no proof, and Puck's attack was now some weeks ago. Why the gap, and why had they returned now? What did they intend to do? They hadn't confronted her. Maybe Puck had scared them, but she really didn't know what to make of it all. Puzzling it over in her mind, she got her purse and wondered if she dared go to the post office, but she really had to get the hats posted, so she set off once more.

Meanwhile, Rix and Lee had retreated some distance away. "We have to get her away. I don't fancy carrying out Marcus's plan with her there," Lee said.

"We might not have a choice if the silly bitch doesn't leave."

"If we take the dog, she will have to look for him."

"How the hell do you propose we do that? Bugger, he looks like he'd eat us alive."

"I was thinking our joint of meat needs a sedative in it. If we can knock him out, it will give us time, and better still, why don't we—"

Rix's phone went. It was Marcus wanting to know how they were doing. He wasn't best pleased and told them to stop farting around and get on with it. Rix came off the phone, and Lee outlined his plan.

"We'll give it a shot," said Rix.

Ginny had been well and truly spooked by the two thugs in the car. She had only really seen the one who had approached the house before, but she was guessing the other one wasn't much better. She considered phoning Jem, but she knew he was extra busy right now with some of his cattle. He'd even needed to draft in extra help, so she decided to leave him alone. Maybe she would tell him tomorrow or when he got his cattle sorted. She had already discounted phoning the local police. She had nothing of real substance to report; she would wait and see if the thugs turned up again.

Going to bed that night, she was very jumpy, but Puck seemed as relaxed as usual, and she finally got some sleep, though it was fitful. Consequently, she entered a deep sleep towards dawn then overslept. She felt fearful again when she went to do Millie and the chooks, not that there were many left after the previous episode. She resolved to get some new ones. These old hens were getting too old to lay much, in any case.

The day passed slowly but normally. No one came, and the phone only rang twice—both with hat enquiries. Later in the afternoon, she fell asleep. She had been struggling to keep her eyes open as it was. Next thing she knew, it was pitch dark, and she hadn't shut the chooks up or fed Millie. Puck came with her to do the jobs, which pleased her, as she was still feeling nervous. When she finished, she found he had disappeared, though he often did, and she wasn't worried. He'd tell her if someone was about.

Hurrying back inside, she turned on the light in her workroom, ready to tidy the bench as she did every night, and saw a note had been pushed under the door. It must have got there when she was down the back, else Puck would have barked. She shivered. She was being watched, it seemed.

She read the note then read it again, her heart in her throat. In a panic, she went to the door and called and called for Puck, but he didn't appear. She got a torch and, with her heart beating as if it would pop out of her chest, she searched everywhere. He was nowhere to be found.

Hands shaking, she went back indoors and read the note again. It was written in capital letters.

"IF YOU WANT YOUR MUTT ALIVE, COME TO THE OLD QUARRY ON STERN ROAD. YOU WILL FIND HIM TIED TO THE OLD HUT THERE. COME ALONE AND TELL NO ONE. IF YOU DON'T COME ALONE, IT WILL BE WORSE FOR THE DOG."

She sat and stared at the note. What possible reason could they have for taking Puck out there? Then it hit her. They wanted her. That was why she had to go alone. But should she phone Jem? No. Jem would try to dissuade her. She loved Puck. He was the only thing that mattered at that moment. He had been there for her through thick and thin, especially these last few months.

Shaking uncontrollably, she went out to her car and got in. She took some deep breaths and tried to calm herself. What would they do to her? Rough her up? Rape her? What? But she didn't really care about herself. If they killed her, at least she would be free from the continuous torment of missing Alex. Death might be a relief!

Oh God, what happened to me to make me feel like this? I never got so down when Jeff passed away or when he was ill. If I get Puck back, I will make a real effort to pull myself together. Alex would have tired of me in the end, anyway. But if I hadn't lost the baby, I would still have part of him and a connection to him. As she drove, her thoughts ran round and round in circles. She knew the turn off to the old road but had never been down it, as it led only to the old quarry.

The road, which was little more than a track, was getting rougher and rougher. Suddenly, a big black dog appeared in front of her. She was going slowly, so it wasn't hard to stop. The dog stared at the headlights. Its eyes glittered and looked almost unreal. "Oh God, Black Shuck!" she said aloud.

It seemed like the dog stood there for minutes, but in reality, it was only seconds. Ginny, already scared and upset, was even more frightened now. Part of her wanted to believe it was only a dark-coloured dingo, but the other fanciful part of her insisted it was the mythical beast famous in Suffolk. The harbinger of death and destruction. The devil in the form of a dog.

The dog turned and disappeared into the bush, and Ginny let out the breath she had been holding. It was a dark night: overcast, no stars or moon, and the bush that she had always loved seemed menacing and dangerous. She was suddenly aware she was out here in the middle of a vast area, and no one knew where she was. She didn't think she had ever felt so alone or scared. Before easing forward again, she fumbled for her phone, but after looking at it, she caught her breath. No signal. The track was too narrow to turn around without damaging her car. She had to go on, and anyway, she was now even more desperate to find Puck. But maybe something atrocious awaited her. Then another thought struck her. There was no evidence that a vehicle had been down the track lately. Even if that was the case, she still had to go on.

Without warning, the track suddenly dipped down steeply out of sight, and if she hadn't been going slowly, she might have come to grief. She eased down the incline, which was quite steep, and found herself in the bowl of the quarry. Carefully, she turned the car round in a circle, looking for the hut or anything else. Maybe the men were hiding somewhere, though she was convinced it was a wild-goose chase. She could see the hut. It looked very decrepit. She drove as close as she dared, then she climbed out of the car, holding her torch in front of her like a weapon.

The old wooden door was half open and hanging on one hinge. She tried to open it then changed her mind. Instead, she peered in around it, shining her torch as best she could. It was empty apart from an old table and a couple of broken chairs. Cobwebs and dust were plentiful; it was plain no one had been there for some time.

The silence and darkness seemed even more intense, if that were possible, and with a little moan of fear, she turned back and scrambled into her car, slamming the door shut behind her. Her breathing was ragged, and she was trembling with fear, though of what she wasn't sure. The whole place was eerie and menacing. Then she heard a dog howling, but it was some way off, or was it? It echoed around the walls of the quarry, and the hairs stood up on the back of her neck. It was a ghostly, unearthly sound—like some poor soul in torment. It didn't sound like Puck, however. She was sure it was another dingo. Nevertheless, she started her car and drove a little further into the quarry. It actually wasn't very big. It had been abandoned years before after the stone proved to be poor quality, and the whole place hadn't been viable.

A moment later, she saw a dingo in her headlights, though this one didn't stop to stare and ran out of the beam. She reckoned it was the one she had heard.

By now, she was too stressed to think straight and decided to head back. She headed towards the steep slope out, and to her horror, the loose stones made her car slip and slither, and she stalled the engine as the wheels spun.

She did the only thing she could. She reversed then put the pedal to the floor. She was nearly at the top when the vehicle slowed and almost stopped, the engine straining, then the front wheels gripped solid ground, and she lurched over the brow. She stopped and rested her head on the steering wheel for a few moments. She gave way to tears of frustration and fear. Gathering herself together, she started the torturous journey back along the track to the road. It didn't seem so far as it had before, and she was almost surprised when she got to the bitumen. Something made her look at her fuel gauge; it was low, very low.

Please let me make it home, and please let me find Puck. Why was I so stupid to drive off and not check the fuel and look round for Puck more at home? Why did I come here? But in her heart, she knew the answer. Puck was her sole companion, and she needed him to protect her and love her as she did him.

Looking ahead, there seemed to be a glow in the sky. Was it the moon breaking through the clouds, or was it nearly morning? She glanced at the time on the dashboard—just gone midnight, so it couldn't be the sun. After driving a few kilometres, she knew it was a fire, a big fire. As she travelled down familiar roads, she realised it was her house.

CHAPTER 31

DAWN FOUND GINNY in her car, sipping water from a bottle a kind fireman had given her. They were still hosing down what little remained of her house. It was like a bad dream. She had driven the last few kilometres knowing the fire was at her place, but part of her brain had been in denial. Her home had been well alight when she got there, and as she had tried, with shaking hands, to ring the fire brigade, they'd turned up. Someone had alerted them to the fire. It had been a truck driver, and he had stayed for a bit to talk to Ginny, who was in complete shock. She'd heard him speaking and herself replying but later couldn't remember a single word. She just sat and sat, unable to do anything. Her whole body was leaden, and her brain was numb. The police had come too, and one of them approached her now.

"Mrs Harrison, there will be an investigation. You realise that?"

Ginny nodded. Her mouth was too dry, and her throat was closed up. She could not speak.

"Where were you before the fire started?"

Making a huge effort, Ginny croaked, "I was out searching for my dog."

"Did you find him? Where were you searching?"

Sudden hysteria took over, and Ginny screamed, "I couldn't find him! They took him. They took him. Where is he? Where—" Ragged sobs shook her body, and the young policeman instinctively stepped back. He looked worriedly over to the other officer who spoke into his radio.

Ginny scrambled out of the car. It was the first time she had moved since she had arrived back home. She ran around the smouldering remains of her house to the paddock at the back. Millie was standing in the field shelter looking more interested than worried. The three remaining chooks were safely in their hut. Everything there was normal, or as normal as it could be. She had a small dam at the far end of the paddock which had been low and was now nearly empty. The fire brigade had used some of that water when their tanks had got low. Not that they could have done much. The whole place had been well alight when they arrived.

"Oh, Millie, what shall I do? I've lost Puck now too. Please don't leave me. Please." She babbled this mantra over and over.

Then a gentle voice said, "Come on, old girl. This won't do. Come on." Gentle arms were holding her, and her tears were being wiped from her cheeks. She buried her head in Jem's shoulder. Her legs were weak, and she almost slid to the ground. Jem picked her up and carried her back to where his vehicle was parked behind hers. He spoke to the policemen and then, after locking Ginny's car, he slid into the driver's seat. "You're coming home with me. I'll come back later and see to Millie. She will be fine for now."

On the way back, he phoned Red. He had Bluetooth, so he could do it safely. Ginny had reverted back to numb silence and sat like a ghost in the seat.

When they got to his house, Ginny sat without moving or speaking. Jem ended up picking her up and carrying her indoors. He sat her at the kitchen table and set about making some strong sweet tea.

A few minutes later, Red turned up. "I can't stay long, Jem. My shift . . ." She trailed off when she saw Ginny, who was like a zombie.

"What happened? Jem, you just said you needed my help. Ginny?"

"Her dog disappeared, and her house burnt to the ground. That's all I know. Jamie, one of the firemen, knows I'm a mate of Ginny's, and he rang me to tell me. They were worried about her."

Red sat down next to Ginny and took her hand. "Ginny, love, can you hear me?"

Ginny turned tormented eyes to Red and nodded.

"When you are ready, can you tell us what happened?"

Ginny nodded again, then more tears started leaking out of her already swollen eyes. Her hands shook so much that she couldn't hold the mug of tea Jem put in front of her, and Red had to hold it for her. Slowly, she sipped the tea, and the tears stopped.

Then she whispered, "Puck. Puck is missing."

"We'll find him, love. Don't worry," Jem said.

Red got to her feet and pulled Ginny up with her. "Come on, you need a nice hot shower then sleep." She signalled to Jem, who leaped into action. As Red took Ginny into the bathroom, he passed a big towel in then made up the bed in the spare room. He had some old sleeping pills, but when he told Red this, she shook her head.

"They are old, and I think she will sleep fine on her own."

By this time, Ginny was wearing an old T-shirt of Jem's, and Red had tucked her up in bed. Sure enough, Ginny's eyes were closed before they exited the room.

Jem had promised Ginny he would go and see to Millie, so after she fell asleep, he headed back to her house. Red rang in and spoke to her supervisor and explained the situation. They gave her the day off, for which she was grateful. While Jem was gone, she made a cake. She knew her way round Jem's kitchen. She was very fond of him, and he continually surprised her with his compassion. The first time she'd gone out for coffee with him, a busybody had warned her that he wasn't the nicest person around, but she had gone with her instincts. She'd seen how caring he had been with Ginny when she lost the baby, so she hadn't trusted the busybody. While she decorated the cake, it occurred to her that she actually loved Jem. The way he had been so kind to Ginny this morning made her realise what a special person he was. *Maybe I can learn to be a farmer's wife,* she thought to herself.

When Jem came back, he smelt the cake and asked if he could have some. "You silly man. It's still in the oven. It's a rich fruit cake, so it won't be ready yet," Red said.

Jem caught her around the waist and sat down, pulling her onto his lap. His hands lifted her top and bra, and he started to fondle her nipples, though what he said distracted her from the excitement he was generating in her body.

"I know we haven't known each other long, but I'd like you to move in with me. I'd like, um, I'd like you to be my wife."

Red had been sitting on his lap with her back to him, but now she wriggled round, making him let go of her. She looked into his eyes. "Are you sure?"

"I have never been more sure of anything. We're not old, but we're not young either, at least I'm not. I don't want to waste more time. My life was pretty shitty until I met Ginny, and she believed in me and then I met you. I love you, Red. I'm sure about that. All this rubbish that Ginny went through made me realise our time on this earth is short. Let's not waste it. What do you think? Can you put up with me?"

"Oh yes, Jem, yes! I was just thinking about how I'd really like to marry you. I know nothing about being a farmer's wife, though." Red suddenly looked worried.

Jem laughed. "It doesn't matter. Nothing matters. We'll work it out."

They kissed long and deep. Then Red jumped off Jem's lap. "The cake!" she exclaimed.

Ginny slept deeply for four hours, then she woke with a start. For a few moments, she couldn't remember where she was, but the memories came rushing back, and she let out a small mewl of horror. She lay still for a bit, her heart racing, then threw back the covers and scrambled out of bed. Where were her clothes? There was no sign of them. Putting the bed cover around herself for modesty, she made for the kitchen. Jem had seen most parts of her body when she miscarried, but this was different. Red was in the kitchen washing up the plates they had used for lunch. When she saw Ginny, she went straight to her and put her arm across her shoulders.

"How are you feeling now, love?" she asked.

At these words, Ginny nearly started to cry again, but she swallowed the tears down and said in a very croaky voice, "I need my clothes, then I want to search for Puck."

"Your clothes are in the drier. I washed them all and—" Before Red had finished speaking, the door flew open, and a big brown-and-black shape launched itself at Ginny.

"Puck! Oh, Puck, where have you been?" Ginny wrapped her arms around the dog while he desperately tried to lick any part of her that he could. Jem walked in behind Puck.

"Police rang your mobile. It was on the table here, so I answered it. They had Puck. He was found wandering around town early this morning. So I went and collected him. You didn't tell her, Red?"

"I was about to, but Puck thought he'd tell her himself." Red smiled. "I'm glad I didn't. It was lovelier this way. Ginny only just got up."

Red went to the laundry and came back with Ginny's clothes. "I think you'll find they are cleaner now, and Jem scrubbed your boots. They are by the door." Ginny cried again, but they were tears of joy. Puck tried to lick them up.

She went back to the bedroom and put her clothes on. After finding a hairbrush in the bathroom, she brushed her hair. Puck, who had followed her, watched her, looking very pleased with himself.

She now felt more able to face what would come next now that Puck was back.

Going back into the kitchen, she started to thank Jem and Red, but he cut her short. "It's unnecessary to thank us. Also, you can stay as long as you like. Not ideal with your horse over there, I know, but quite frankly, there is nothing of your house left, so be prepared."

"I know. I got back the same time as the fire brigade showed up. I sat and watched. It was unbelievably horrible to witness so many memories going up in flames. Things I cherished, things I always wanted to keep. I don't know how it happened. I am sure I left nothing on, but maybe I did. I was worried about Puck. He'd been gone a long time, then there was the note."

"What note?"

"That if I wanted Puck back, I would find him at the old quarry. I can't believe how stupid I was. I should have guessed it was a ploy to get me away."

"Hindsight is a wonderful thing. We can all say we've done silly things, and looking back, we wonder why we did them," Red said.

"I agree." Jem nodded. "I doubted my actions often, especially when Mary died."

"I was so scared about what I might find, then when I went down the track, the sides of my car were being brushed by bushes, and some branches broke as the track got worse and worse. At that point, I guessed the note was a lie, though part of me still wanted to find Puck, so I carried on. It was too narrow and overgrown to turn around, in any case. I nearly lost the car when the track dipped down. I found the hut, but there was no one, human or dog, there. There were some dingoes about. One of them reminded me of Black Shuck, which made me even more jumpy."

"Who's Black Shuck?" Red and Jem both asked at once.

"A big black dog who is supposed to roam the coastal area of Suffolk and maybe parts of Norfolk. They say he's the devil in disguise. If you see him, I think it means your number may be up. There is a church up that way that supposedly has his claw marks on the door. Silly, but the dog stood and stared at my car. It made me even more frightened. Deep down, I knew it was a dingo but—" Ginny shivered.

"Anyway, Black Shuck is bad news, and I was frightened enough as it was, then I heard a dog howling, but I kind of knew it wasn't Puck, and by that time, I was so scared I couldn't get out of there fast enough. It was those men, right? They somehow took Puck and got me to leave, then they set fire to the house."

"But why? Why would they do that? What have you done that would make them target you like this?" Red wanted to know.

"I think it's because of Alex. His mother hates me, or the idea of me. Her father is very well off but has a finger in lots of unsavoury pies."

"This is too far-fetched for words. Why on earth would Alex's mother and grandfather go to such extremes?"

"Jealously—hatred, even. I don't know, but she is one very strange lady. From the little Alex told me, her father will do anything she asks."

"Are you sure you didn't leave anything on that could have caused the fire?" Jem asked gently.

Ginny shook her head. "I'm sure." At the back of her mind, a small doubt crept in. She went over what she had done once she'd returned indoors. Truth was, she couldn't remember much. She had been in such a state. "I fell asleep at the workbench, and when I woke, it was dark, so I rushed outside to do the animals. Puck came out with me but then disappeared. He does that quite often, so I wasn't worried. When I went to the workroom to tidy up later, I saw the note and then jumped in the car—no, wait. I looked round outside first. Oh God, I was in such a state. It's all blurry, but I am sure I didn't leave anything on that would cause a fire."

They sat in silence for a few minutes, then Ginny burst out angrily, "I wish I never met the Unwins. I wish I never saw Alex. I wish I could forget he ever existed. I wish—" A fresh round of sobbing took over. Red got up and put her arms around her.

"Shh, it will be all right, dear, really. You're overwrought and have been through a bad time, a really bad time, but it will be all right in the end." Later, Red would regret those words.

Ginny ate a small amount of the food Red put in front of her, but hunger was hard to come by. If anything, she felt sick. She had no idea how she was going to get started again. Despite feeling ill, she had to go and face what remained of her house.

She had just finished eating as much as she could when a police car came up Jem's driveway and stopped at the front of the house. Jem's dogs and Puck began barking. Jem ordered them to stop, and a rather worried young policeman and his older colleague got out of the car.

They introduced themselves when Jem ushered them into the kitchen. The older one held out his hand to Red and Ginny. "I'm Sergeant Tony Adams, and this is Constable Ricky Jones. Which of you ladies lost their home?" he asked, looking from one to the other, though Ginny was sure he knew who he'd come to see. It was a kind of test.

"That's me. I'm Ginny Harrison."

The sergeant nodded. He'd already realised who she was. Had he been at the fire? She couldn't remember.

"I'm sorry, Mrs Harrison, but I have to ask you a few questions. Have you any idea what could have caused the fire?"

"None at all."

"You weren't there. A passing truck driver alerted the fire brigade. He was worried someone might be trapped, but the blaze was already too fierce to try to enter. Where were you at such a late hour?"

"Looking for my dog. He was missing. I searched around, then I found a note claiming he was tied up at the old quarry on Stern Road."

"Where is this note?"

"I-I don't know. I think I left it in my house, but I can't remember. I was too worried about Puck."

"Your dog."

"Yes."

"So you drove out to the old quarry. Don't you think it strange? Why would anyone do that, and who do you think was behind it?"

"Two men in a black Land Cruiser. They were here briefly when I was out, or rather, I came back because I had forgotten my purse. They drove off when I came back. This happened the other day." Ginny looked at Jem. "I'm sorry I didn't tell you. I wish I had."

"Do you know why these men would want to target you?"

Ginny shook her head. This was getting sillier and sillier, or rather her story was. She was aware of how it sounded to anyone else's ears.

Jem spoke up. "It's probably because of Alex."

"Who's Alex?" the sergeant asked.

Suddenly, Ginny was angry. It was bad enough losing her house, and now she had to handle all these questions. Who the hell did they think she was? Some sort of criminal? Why weren't they looking for the men? They must know she hadn't set the fire.

"Yes, this whole mess happened because I took a younger lover and was expecting his child. His mother didn't like it! Satisfied?" Ginny knew she was losing it, but she didn't care.

"Sounds rather extreme to me," Constable Jones said.

"You and me both," Jem interrupted, "but it's true. Ginny has been threatened."

"By these men?"

"No—yes . . . It's a long story," Ginny said.

To her surprise, the two policemen got to their feet and made for the door. When they reached it, the sergeant turned and looked at Ginny. "That is all for now, Mrs Harrison. Your house was deliberately set on fire and is now a crime scene. We will be in touch. For now, we would like you to stay away from your house. Perhaps Mr Wakefield here can see to your stock." With that, they left.

CHAPTER 32

GINNY DID AS she was asked. While Jem went to see to the animals again, Ginny lay down. She didn't think she had ever felt so tired and dispirited. *I've cried enough tears to fill a bath these last few weeks. No more tears for me.* As she made this vow, she knew it would be hard to keep. She must have dozed off, as it didn't seem long before Red shouted that she had supper ready, and after that, she was going home. Her son was at home, and she didn't want to stay away at night.

"I'm sure he would be fine, but I'd rather not," Red said. "Anyway, I have to get back to work tomorrow."

Jem moved uncomfortably in his chair. "This might be a good time to tell Ginny. You'll tell Jackson like we agreed?" he asked, looking intently at Red.

"Yes, sweetheart, I will." Red squeezed his arm. Ginny looked from one to the other.

"Is this what I think it is?"

"What do you think it is?" Jem asked.

"Red moving in with you?"

"Not only that, but she agreed to be my wife!" Jem looked like the cat that swallowed the cream.

"That is wonderful news! You both deserve happiness." But as she said it, tears threatened again despite her resolution.

However, she got to her feet and hugged first Red then Jem. Sitting down again, she said, "This was something of a whirlwind, wasn't it?"

Red laughed. "Why pussyfoot around if we know it's what we want. Life is short. We need to make the most of it."

Now Ginny couldn't hold back the tears. "I know. That is why I didn't refuse Alex. I knew he wouldn't stay with me forever, so I thought I'd make the most of the time I had with him. It was the way it finished that haunts me, and he didn't know about the baby. If our relationship had run its natural course, I like to think I would have coped—been sad but understanding. God, I don't know, but I do know I am happy for you."

CHAPTER 33

THE NEXT MORNING, Ginny realised she wanted to go and see what remained of her house. Jem wasn't keen for her to do so, but in the end, he suggested she follow him. He'd see to the animals, and she could turn round and come straight back if it was too much.

They set off in convoy. Ginny's heart was racing as they drew near. There were traffic cones across the entrance, which Jem moved when he got to them. All that was left of her house was a big heap of blackened timber and twisted metal. Nothing was recognisable. It was still early morning, and no one was about. Ginny sat still, hardly comprehending what she was looking at. Her memory of her house and this blackened heap of detritus didn't fit. It couldn't possibly be the same place. Puck, who sat in the back of the car, gave a small bark and woke her from her reverie. Jem had driven on round the remains of the house to go down and park by the animals and was walking back, a concerned frown on his face. Ginny got out of her car and let Puck loose.

"You all right, mate?"

Ginny nodded. "It doesn't seem real. There is nothing left in there?"

"Seems not."

"Actually, there should be something. Under the house, we had a fire-proof box. It was something Jeff insisted on when we lived on the farm, in case of bushfires."

"It should still be there, but we won't be able to get to it until some of this debris is cleared, and we can't do that until we have the go ahead."

Ginny gave Jem a wan smile. "You make it sound as if you'll be involved."

Jem looked uncomfortable. "Well, you'll want some help, and I have the right equipment for the job of clearing this lot up. Wanna help with the animals?"

They went to do the animals together while Puck trotted round, looking very confused. He walked all around the blackened ruin of the house, plainly wondering what had happened. Jem and Ginny had just finished their jobs when fire investigation officers turned up. They met Jem and Ginny and told them they hadn't managed to get on with much yesterday, as the debris was still too hot in places. They asked them not to cross the police tape that surrounded the ruin.

"How long before we can start to clear this all up?" Jem wanted to know.

"If all goes to plan, you can probably start tomorrow, Mr Harrison."

"I'm not Mr Harrison. I'm just a friend. Name's Jem Wakefield."

"Oh," The man looked at him closely. "I know of you."

Ginny intervened before the man said anything unpleasant. "There was a fireproof box under the house. I'd like to have it as soon as possible."

"We'll look out for it." The two men walked off.

"They didn't give us their names, did they?" Ginny asked as they watched them walk away.

"Nah." Jem looked thoughtful. "I've seen the one who said he remembered me before. Can't remember where, though."

"He said he knew of you."

"Yes, I know, but I think I have met him before. Come on, there isn't much we can do here right now. They know and we know the fire was started deliberately, so what the big deal is, I don't quite get, but here we are."

"I'm going to hang around, take Millie out for a ride. I think it will do me good."

"I thought you kept your saddle and bridle in the house."

Ginny gasped, devastated. "Yes, I forgot."

Later, when they were back at Jem's, the two police officers who had been by the day before rolled up.

"Mrs Harrison, would you accompany us to the police station? We would like to do a formal interview."

"Can I let Jem, Mr Wakefield, know? He's checking the cattle across the paddocks."

The two men looked at each other. "Yes, but make it quick."

Before Ginny could start searching, Jem came in the back door and headed to the officers. "I saw you coming from a distance. What's happening?"

"They want to formally interview me about the fire," Ginny said.

"But why? Hasn't she been through enough? She lost her house and—"

Ginny held up her hand. She felt strangely calm. What would be, would be. At this stage, she was past caring. *Why fight it? If they think I started the fire on purpose, then let them. I don't care any more. I've lost the love of my life, my baby, and now my home. Apart from Puck, there isn't much else to lose.* "It's OK, Jem. Please don't worry. It will be fine, so just look after Puck for me, and if I'm not back soon, please see to the chooks and Millie."

Jem looked hard at her. She straightened her back and nodded. After giving her a pat on the shoulder, he stood aside and let her leave in the back of the unmarked car.

The police station in town wasn't very big, but they had an interview room, and that was where Ginny found herself a short time later.

Sergeant Adams set up a recorder then asked her to formally identify herself. Afterwards, he told her that they'd known the fire had been deliberately set from the beginning. The smell of petrol had been overwhelming, and they also thought some other accelerant had been used.

"Your insurance is up to date, Mrs Harrison?"

"Yes. I renewed it a few weeks ago."

"How long ago, exactly?"

Ginny thought back, then she realised it had been before Graham came to stay.

"About nine weeks ago, I think. I don't remember, exactly."

"You run a millinery business. Is that doing well?"

"Not as well as it was. I think the Unwins may have something to do with it."

"How so?"

Ginny told them someone had been spreading negative reviews about her business.

"Have you anything definitive to back this up, or is it just suspicion?"

"Not really, but the whole thing started after Alex disappeared."

"How did he disappear? Did he leave without your knowledge?"

"I came home, and he said his father had been in an accident, and he had to go. His bag was already packed, so he jumped in his car and that was that."

Painful memories surfaced, and Ginny had the sudden urge to cry. But she'd be damned if she let these two policemen see her cry, and she somehow managed to control herself. She saw the look that passed between them. No doubt, they thought it was a case of Alex realising what a mistake he'd made and leaving in a hurry.

"You'd told him you were pregnant?"

"No. He didn't know." Again, she could see they didn't believe her. She had now got to the stage where she was beyond caring. What did it matter? What did anything matter?

"Let's get back to the fire. You say you went out to the old quarry to look for your dog. That is a long way for the dog to have gone. Even a big dog like yours would take some time to get there."

"I told you I thought those men had taken him."

"So you did, Mrs Harrison, but it sounds like a tall tale to us. How would they have taken your dog? He's big, and I imagine quite scary if he doesn't want to do something. What made you think he had gone with them?"

"It was the note. I told you about the note."

Sergeant Adams looked down at his notes. "Ah, you did. I have to say, Mrs Harrison, we are having trouble believing your story. Constable Jones went out to look at the track to the old quarry and couldn't see where a vehicle had been down it."

"We're in the middle of a drought. The track was dry, but some of the overhanging bushes are broken from where my car brushed by them. Did you get as far as the quarry? You should've seen where I had to get a run at the slope to get out of it."

Truth was, they hadn't gone that far, as they were convinced Ginny was making it up. The whole thing sounded too far-fetched. They knew Alex was an adult and was down in Sydney and that he'd had a fling with this older woman. But the whole thing seemed a step too far. They were sure Ginny wanted the insurance money.

After a few more questions, they drove her back to Jem's. Ginny felt emotionally drained and so dog-tired she went and lay on the bed. No sign of Jem. He might be back at her house doing her animals. She ought to think about getting a meal and also what she was to do. She couldn't go on relying on Jem; she'd have to find somewhere else to camp for the time being.

She must have fallen asleep because Alex was beside her, shaking her and telling her it was OK. He whispered that he loved her and then he started to undress her gently. She woke with a gasp. Red was sitting on the side of the bed, fingers loosening Ginny's belt.

"Sorry, love, I didn't mean to wake you. This looked so tight that I thought it wasn't doing you any good. You OK, Ginny? I'm sorry if I frightened you."

Ginny turned her head away from Red. She didn't want to cry any more. "I was dreaming. I thought for a moment you were Alex. Sorry, I'll get up now and help you get the meal ready."

"No need. Jackson is with me. We are staying over. It's Friday tomorrow, and we are here until Monday morning."

"Oh gosh, I forgot what day it is. You believe me about those men, don't you?"

Red, who had stood up, sat down again. "Of course I do, and the police will in the end. They just have to make sure everything is done by the book, and you have to admit it all seems so extreme—burning your house because you had an affair. But I am sure the truth will come out in the end."

"It wasn't an affair. It was deeper than that—more important."

"I didn't mean it wasn't important, and I can see calling it an affair trivialises it, but I don't know what else to call it. Alex left. Coerced or not, he made a choice. I think you are going to have to face up to that, my dear."

For a moment, Ginny thought this remark was patronising, but she knew Red meant well.

"I am facing up to it. I knew it wouldn't last. I've said that before. It's funny because Jeff didn't want children, and I was happy with that. I never felt very maternal, and when I found out I was pregnant, I wasn't sure.

Looking back, it was more that I wasn't sure what Alex would say. I came to realise I wanted that baby, so very much. If I hadn't miscarried, I'd still have a small part of him." Ginny determinedly swallowed the lump in her throat. She didn't want to cry ever again.

CHAPTER 34

THE NEXT DAY, they were told the investigation had finished, and the police would be in touch soon.

Jem swung into action. He would take his tractor with the backhoe over and start to clear the site enough so Ginny could get to her fireproof box.

When they got there, they found that the box had been exposed already; they thought the investigators had done that. It was locked, but Ginny had a key down in the sheds at the back where she kept horse food and garden equipment. She and Jeff hadn't kept it in the house because if there was a fire, the key would be lost.

The papers inside were a little curled up but not burnt. It was heat damage alone. Ginny's passports—she had a UK and Australian passport—insurance papers, birth certificate, Jeff's death certificate, and all sorts of other important papers, including her millinery training certificate, were safe.

She hauled out her insurance papers and immediately rang the company. They promised to send someone out. She also sent them photographs, and they said they would pay for temporary accommodation for her. As the assessor was coming out from Roma, they warned her it may be a few days before he got there. Also, it was a Friday, so the weekend was in between.

"I'll move into the pub," Ginny said. "I'm sure there will be room."

"You don't have to do that. You can stay as long as you like, you know that," Jem said.

"I do, but I don't want to end up being a nuisance. I'll be happier this way. Also, I need some new clothes, and there are stores near the pub. I've been wearing these for days."

Ginny had washed her knickers and bra out every night and left them in the bathroom to dry. That morning, they had felt decidedly damp. Red had offered to lend her a bra or two, but the sizes were all wrong. Red was larger than Ginny—bigger breasted and with larger shoulders and a broader back. Ginny had borrowed a top, but it rather drowned her slimmer shape.

Before Jem could persuade her to stay, Ginny drove into town and secured a room at the pub. Jo, who had been away, also offered to put Ginny up, but she refused. There was only a very small store in town with few clothing options, so Ginny asked Jo if she would like to go with her to Roma and buy some new clothes. They would go on Monday.

Ginny soon found that people who had been cold shouldering her after hearing about her and Alex were being nice to her now, and she received words of sympathy and even the odd invitation to dinner.

She moved into the pub the next day despite Red's and Jem's pleas to stay a little longer. Seeing them as a happy family made her very sad. In one respect, she was delighted for them, but it made her realise what she was missing.

Ginny found Sunday to be very difficult. Jo and her family were off to church, and she didn't want to impose on Jem and Red, so she didn't know what to do with herself. She spent as long as she could with Millie and fiddled around in her veggie patch, but with the drought and the firefighters using her water, there wasn't that much to do. The feeling of loss was all-consuming. She took Puck for a long walk, but it didn't fill in enough of the day. Martin, the publican, had allowed her to have Puck with her, though he normally didn't allow dogs. For this, she was grateful.

Sleeping was a problem, and Sunday night seemed extra bad, so she was very bleary-eyed the next morning when she arrived to pick up Jo.

"You OK? You don't look too good," Jo said.

"Thanks for that! I've no make-up on, as you can tell. I was lucky that, for some odd reason, I snatched my bag when I rushed off to look for Puck, so at least I have my credit cards and some cash with me—my driver's licence too."

"Oh, you poor thing. I can't begin to imagine what you have been through. Rumour has it that the fire has something to do with that young bloke, Alex. Is that true, do you think?"

Ginny drew a deep breath. She knew speculation was running riot. Best to be upfront with the truth.

"It seems so. Those two thugs that were asking about me a time back, well, they turned up again a day or so before the fire. I am sure they fed Puck the chocolate, though as Jem pointed out, he may have found a bar anywhere. There was a bag of rubbish on the side of the road near my place the other day. Someone threw it out of a car or truck. I think it's revenge, though it sounds silly."

"I remember you talking about Alex's mum quite a long time ago. If she is a controlling person, it may not be silly. What is that saying? Nothing worse than a woman scorned? Something like that."

"I think it is 'hell hath no fury like a woman scorned,' "Ginny replied.

Ginny had never been in a situation where she needed to buy a whole new wardrobe. Both Jo and Red had lent her things, but she seemed to be a different shape than them. She was quite a bit taller than Jo and not so buxom as Red. She hoped the insurance money would come through soon, as she was rather horrified by how large the bill was at the end of the shopping trip. She had made a claim on Jo's borrowed computer a few days before. It was the first opportunity she had, and before, she hadn't been able to face it. Puck had stayed behind at the pub while they shopped, and he hadn't been pleased when Ginny left. He seemed very clingy lately. They didn't linger and returned as soon as Ginny finished buying the necessities. Jo drove back, which gave Ginny the opportunity to catch up on sleep, though it wasn't a restful sleep, and when she woke, she had a crick in her neck.

It was mid-afternoon when they got to Jo's house, and Ginny had a cup of tea and a sandwich before she drove to the pub. When she got there, she found Constable Jones waiting for her.

"I was about to leave and come back later. You've been shopping, I see," he said, walking up to her car as she drew in to the car park at the back of the pub.

"Of course. I lost everything, which included clothes."

Puck came bounding up just then, and Ginny bent down to make a fuss of him. It took her a few seconds to take in what the policeman was saying.

"You need me to come now?"

"Yes, Mrs Harrison, if you will. My car is just here." It was an unmarked car again, and Ginny baulked. "Can I come in mine? Then Puck can come too. He's missed me all day."

Constable Jones looked uncomfortable. "Not really an option, sorry."

"Please. I promise I won't drive off the other way or anything." Ginny was half joking or attempting to, but he looked serious.

"OK, but I will be following you."

When they arrived at the station, Jones said she couldn't leave Puck in the car.

"I had no intention of doing so," Ginny replied tartly. She got him out and tied him up to the car, then she poured a bottle of water into a bowl for him. "I can see you do this often," Jones said.

"Yes, he is happy enough under the car in the shade," Ginny replied. Several things she could say ran through her mind, but she kept quiet.

She was led to the room where they had interviewed her before. She was trying not to show it, but she was very nervous. The way the constable behaved unnerved her. What could the police possibly want now?

"This is an informal interview, Mrs Harrison—Ginny. We have been looking into your finances, which is normal under the circumstances."

"What circumstances?" Ginny could feel her temper rising but tried to tamp it down. Losing her cool wouldn't serve her well.

"The fire that destroyed your house was arson. You don't have a credible alibi—" Ginny opened her mouth to protest, but Sergeant Adams held up his hand and stopped her, then he carried on speaking. "Your bank account is very low. It seems your business isn't doing too well just now."

Ginny lost it. "Just now? What do you mean, 'just now'? I don't have a business just now at all!"

Ginny gathered herself together. "I'm sorry. I know you are only doing your job. It's true that my business has dropped off lately. I think the Unwin woman may be behind it, but of course, I can't prove anything. I certainly didn't set fire to my own home for the insurance money. If I had, I would have saved some of my precious possessions. I did go looking for my dog. I now know that it was very silly to go to the old quarry, but I was so worried, and I wasn't thinking straight. They tried to poison Puck a few weeks ago, but the vet managed to save him."

The two officers looked at each other. "We know nothing of this. Why didn't you report it or tell us?"

"I can't prove anything. Puck was given chocolate, or he found some. He was very sick and near death. Bill saved him. If you looked at my accounts, you probably noticed two hefty vet bills in recent weeks."

"We saw them, yes."

"So you also know that I do have some savings, it's just that I'm currently a bit short and worse off now after everything that's happened. I even had to buy new clothes. Do you have any leads on those men?"

The two policemen looked a little uncomfortable. "Um, no . . . not as such."

Ginny sat up straighter in her chair. "I get the distinct impression that you haven't taken them very seriously and haven't even looked for them."

This was partly true, though the policemen were not about to say so. It was all so vague, and the fact that Ginny had slept with a man much younger than her seemed to be a very odd reason for someone to set fire to her home. It wasn't as if the man in the picture was under age. That would have been completely different on all fronts. The two officers looked at each other. "We will, of course, be making further inquiries. We found out that the men were not staying anywhere local, but we don't have a registration number on their vehicle. All we know is what you told us—that the vehicle is from NSW. Can you describe your interactions with them?"

"Two days before the fire, I forgot my purse when coming to town. They drove into my driveway after I left. When I turned round and came back for my purse, they drove straight off again. It was all so quick. The first time one of them approached the house, I had two male friends with me, and they didn't hang about that time either, and besides, they were afraid of Puck. Or at least one of them was."

Tony Adams raised his eyebrows when Ginny said she'd had two men with her. Was she into prostitution? Somehow, he didn't think so. As if reading his mind, Ginny said, "One of the men with me was Jem Wakefield, and the other was an old friend from the UK—a family friend who has since returned home."

"Well, we didn't really talk about this before. Perhaps you can make another statement and tell us all you know about these men. In the meantime, what more can you tell us about the old quarry."

Ricky Jones looked sharply at his partner before realising he was trying to find out if Ginny really had gone there or if she was making it up. Questioning her on the details was one way of finding that out.

"Take us through the whole story slowly, bit by bit."

Ginny sighed then told the whole story with as much detail as she could. She even told them a potted history of Black Shuck and how she'd heard a dog howling at the quarry and thought that was the end for her. After she recounted every detail she could recall, they let her leave.

After she left, the policemen looked at each other. "What do you think, Ricky?"

"I hate to say it, but it sounds genuine—her story, that is. I think she is telling the truth."

Adams nodded. "I think so too, but she could have got someone else to set the fire."

Ricky shook his head. "Can't see it myself. Can you?"

"No, so we assume she is telling us the truth. We need to ask around more, find out what we can about these guys. They were up here a couple of months ago, left, then came back. Very odd, and we only have a few things to go on: Their car was a Land Cruiser—black with tinted windows—and they're big blokes."

"We could try CCTV. If they were in town, they will show up, and we know they were in town the first time since that is where the sighting came from. Unfortunately, there's nothing recent, only Mrs Harrison's statement."

"They must have stayed somewhere, though."

"If there is a connection to these Unwins, maybe they stayed out at his property. He has that big spread out towards Charleville. We'll take a trip out there and ask around. Meanwhile, let's see what the CCTV can turn up, though this a long way back, and they may not have those tapes any more."

Ginny felt exhausted by the interview, and once safe in bed, she allowed herself a few tears. Partly because of Alex and the baby, partly because of the loss of her home, and partly because she felt cut adrift and alone. What was to become of her? *This is all because I allowed myself to love another who loved me too. There is so much hatred in the world, but it seems love can be destructive sometimes. If you love someone, it gives them the power to destroy you. I read that somewhere once, and how true it is. What am I to do? Will I ever be happy again? Why me? Why me?*

Her thoughts galloped round and round in her head, and it was nearly dawn before she slept, even though she had been so tired.

CHAPTER 35

HER RESTLESS NIGHT resulted in her being late getting up, so she was in a rush to get out to her place to see to the animals. When she got there, she got a massive surprise. Trucks and a big grab were busy clearing up the debris.

Jem appeared, grinning from ear to ear. "Hello, Ginny. How are you on this lovely morning? Got all this organised, but we are being careful in case there is anything that can be salvaged."

"Oh, Jem, what a kind friend you are. What would I do without you?" Ginny's vision blurred. When people were kind, it touched her heart and brought her to tears.

"How much will it cost?" Ginny blurted as she walked round the remains of the house. The two drivers were having a rest.

"This is on me. If it hadn't been for you, I would still be that lonely, grumpy old farmer who wouldn't help catch your horse."

Now the tears spilled. Jem hugged her. "It's OK, mate, it's OK. You're a strong woman. You'll get through this. Come on, old girl. You've cried enough tears to fill a dam." He rubbed her back as he said all this. Eventually, Ginny got herself under control.

"I'm sorry. I made a pact with myself not to cry any more, but it doesn't seem to be working."

"It's better to let it all out than store it up. Believe me, I know. Now come on, why don't you go and see what Millie has to say for herself. I haven't filled the chooks water up yet either."

Later, Ginny told Jem all about her visit to the police station and what they had to say. "I'm not holding my breath that they will come up with anything," she said.

Her phone rang. It was the third time that morning. The calls had all been from people wanting hats, and they'd all been horrified to think she wouldn't be doing any hats for the Melbourne Cup. "One woman was cross with me and asked me whether she should take her business elsewhere," Ginny explained. "Her threat fell flat; I was not in the mood."

This time, however, it was the insurance company, and the news wasn't good. "We will be writing to you, Mrs Harrison, but I thought you would want to know that, as the fire was deliberate, we won't be paying out."

"What! But—but why not? I didn't do it! I . . . You must pay. What am I to do if you don't?"

Jem, who wasn't far away, heard Ginny shout and came across. She was as white as a sheet and shaking.

Ginny pleaded, but the man on the phone said it was policy and that the decision had been made. After Ginny finished the conversation, she told Jem what they had said, though he had got the gist of it anyway.

He shook his head. "The buggers always win, no matter what."

CHAPTER 36

TIME MARCHED ON. Ginny didn't like staying at the pub—not that it wasn't clean and tidy, but she missed her own space. Now that the house was cleared and gone, she decided to buy a tent and move back onto her own land. Spring had come, and it was already quite warm at night. Jem had objected to start with, but she'd managed to convince him. The police had been very quiet, and she'd heard nothing from them in a few weeks. Then Sergeant Adams turned up alone at her campsite.

"Ginny, how are you?" He sounded friendlier than he had before.

"I am OK, thanks. Have you any news?" She indicated one of the folding chairs she had in front of her tent. "Would you like a cup of tea or coffee?" She decided to be courteous.

"Thanks." He sat down.

Ginny already had water boiling, as she had been going to have a drink, and it didn't take long to make instant coffee. She kept the campfire going much of the time. One of the things that frustrated her the most was having no internet or computer. She hadn't realised how much she'd relied on them until now.

"We found CCTV images of the black Land Cruiser you told us about and traced it down to Sydney. However, it hasn't surfaced since. It seems the plates were false, in any case. The pictures of the men are too grainy to make a reliable identification. We have drawn a blank regarding where the men were staying when they were up here. We suspect they were camping somewhere. I'm sorry, but finding these men isn't looking good. Our colleagues down in Sydney have actually spoken to a Mrs Unwin who seems to be living with her father. She denied everything. There was no sign of anyone else on the property. We also searched Mr Unwin's spread up here and found where someone may have camped, but apart from where they had a fire, there was no real evidence. Mr Unwin denied all knowledge. I rather think we are not going to get much further with all this. They were professionals. Petrol was poured everywhere, again not purchased locally. They knew exactly what they were doing."

"There was no sign of Alex, then—Margarita's son?" Ginny asked.

"The officers who went to the house asked if anyone else lived there, and they said Margarita's son also lived with them, but he was away on a sailing trip and wasn't expected back for a couple of months. Sailing round Australia or something like that."

Ginny nodded. It was almost what she had expected.

"I'm sorry I have nothing more concrete to tell you. The case will remain open, but we do have other cases that are a little more pressing than yours. Has the insurance company paid up? I can see you are just biding time." He swung his arm around, encompassing her camp.

"They won't pay since it was deliberately set—the fire I mean."

"Jesus." Adams looked shocked. "Are you sure?"

"Yes, it's in the fine print, *very* fine print, but there none the less. Stupidly, I never read that clause."

"Well, you wouldn't. No one expects such a thing to happen. What will you do? Have you sufficient funds to rebuild?"

Ginny shook her head. "Not even close. I also have no income at the moment. I am trying to work out what is best to do."

Adams got to his feet. He felt desperately sorry for this woman. Fate had dealt her blow after blow. Her husband had suffered that awful accident which left him paralysed, she'd taken a younger lover who left her, she'd had a miscarriage, and now she'd lost her home and her income. Despite these trials, she was still trying hard to be brave. A wave of admiration swept over him, and he held out his hand. "Good luck with everything. I hope there are no hard feelings. I—"

"You were only doing your job, I know," Ginny interrupted him.

He grinned and patted her shoulder. "See you around," he said, then he was gone.

Ginny sat back down, and Puck came and sat himself beside her. "What do you reckon, Puck? He isn't so bad after all, is he?"

Puck just grinned his doggy grin and wagged his tail.

CHAPTER 37

GINNY FILLED HER days with making plans but had no enthusiasm for carrying them out. It wouldn't be long before Christmas and that depressed her. It only seemed like five minutes since Alex first appeared on her doorstep. She recalled those long months when she had resisted her feelings. What would have happened if she hadn't? What if she had encouraged him and gone to bed with him earlier? Would it have made any difference to the outcome? Somehow, she didn't think it would have, except maybe she wouldn't have fallen pregnant.

Jem popped in to see her most days, and Jo also popped in quite regularly, though she never stayed long.

In the middle of December, Jem asked Ginny over for Sunday roast. She hadn't seen Red for some time. Red had given up her rental, and she and Jackson had moved in with Jem.

Ginny nearly refused but, after realising she was turning into something of a recluse, she agreed to go. Red had already put her stamp on things, and Jem was still like a cat that had swallowed a large amount of cream. As she sat with them after a huge lunch, her mind drifted. *If only I fell for someone like Jem. Why did I have to fall for someone so unsuitable? It doesn't make sense, and it's so sad. They are so happy. I wonder if they realise how lucky they are.*

Then she remembered Jem's troubles and Red's abusive husband, so she pulled herself up. They deserved happiness as much as anyone.

"Ginny? Ginny, are you all right?" Red was speaking to her, looking worried.

"Yes, sorry. I was miles away. What did you say?"

"I said we are getting married in ten days—Christmas Eve in fact—and we want you to come. Not only that, but we want you to come and stay for Christmas."

Ginny opened her mouth to protest, but Red spoke first. "Please say yes because if you say no, you will actually spoil the whole thing for us. We genuinely want you here. Neither of us has family to invite. My parents live in Thailand and won't make the trip. We aren't close. You are part of our family, at least that is how we see you, so please don't spoil it for us. Come."

Ginny felt the familiar lump in her throat but swallowed it down. With eyes full of tears, she said thickly, "Thank you. I'd love to."

"Christmas is part of the deal," Jem said, "so with that in mind, I propose we bring Millie here and your three remaining chooks, then we can stay here and not travel to yours. In any case, you have no grass left; I was going to offer to house Millie. I think we'll be in this drought for the long haul, and she will be happy enough here. That is, if you agree."

"That would be wonderful! I've been worrying about feeding Millie in the long run. I seem to have gone through an awful lot of hay as it is. It's getting very expensive too. So what are your wedding plans?"

"We found a celebrant who will come out to the farm, and we plan to have the ceremony in the garden," Red said. "We'll invite a few people from work, you, and maybe one or two others, but there won't be more than a dozen or so. I am doing the food, but will you make the wedding cake? I know you make awesome cakes—Jem told me—and I somehow feel it might be bad luck to make my own. Silly, I know, but it's how I feel."

"I'd love to, but I'll have to do it here. I don't have the equipment to do it at my camp."

"Of course you can't bake a cake at your camp! I thought you could do it while I am at work."

"It's a deal."

For the first time in many months, Ginny felt excited about something, and for the next half an hour, she and Red talked dresses and food and flowers and all things wedding. Jem raised his eyebrows at Jackson, and the two of them retired outside even though it was a very hot day.

Red frowned as she watched them go. "I only hope it's not so hot for the big day. It must be pushing forty today. Even in here with the air con going, it seems very hot."

It was, and when Ginny returned to her camp, she and Puck were very hot and bothered. When she fed Millie, she told her she was being moved. Jem would pick her up the next day. *One less thing to worry about, and tomorrow, I am baking, which is good. I need to focus on something. I've been drifting for too long.*

The next morning, Jem was there very early—before the heat really cranked up. Millie was happy to get in the float, and Ginny had already crated her remaining three chooks. So with Puck in the car beside her, they set off to Jem's place.

It was very hot again, and Ginny felt as if she were melting in Jem's kitchen, but she pushed on and made two traditional fruit cakes. Red had got all the ingredients that Ginny needed. She and Jem knew about Ginny's financial troubles, and Ginny suspected they hadn't wanted to further drain her funds. She decided not to say anything or else they would all be embarrassed. By the time Jackson and Red came home, the cakes were hidden away, waiting to be iced. Ginny had wrapped them in foil, put them in containers, and hidden them in the spare room where she slept when she stayed over. She was a little worried that the intense heat would spoil the cakes. Red asked her to stay the night, but she declined. She'd be staying over nearer the wedding day and during the holidays. She couldn't impose further.

"Are you going away on a honeymoon?" she asked Red before she left.

"Jem is worried about leaving the animals, especially now that it's so hot."

"Why don't you take a couple of days. I'll look after everything. You might have trouble finding somewhere to go on such short notice, but go if you can. You've been so good to me. I shall feel I am returning the favour."

Red hugged her. "Thank you. We didn't want to say anything to you since we know it must be hard for you—us marrying and everything."

The days flew by for them all, and for a time, Ginny was more like her old self. If she didn't think too much, she was fine. Nights were the worst.

If she went to sleep quickly, she'd wake in the middle of the night and that was that regarding sleep. If she couldn't fall asleep immediately, she'd lay awake half the night. Her restlessness stemmed from yearning for Alex and wondering where she should go in life. Her money was dwindling, however careful she was, and she had no income. Something would have to give. She decided to live in the moment until Red and Jem came back from their two days away. They had managed to sort something out but wouldn't say what.

The big day came. Ginny was wearing the dress she had worn for her parents' party. It seemed so long ago—like another life. She had lost weight but had managed to take it in enough. Red had kept her dress a secret, and when she emerged into the garden, everyone present gasped. She was wearing an emerald-green gown which looked wonderful against her dark-red hair. The dress showed her generous curves off, and the creamy skin of her bust and neck glowed with health and happiness.

Rather to Ginny's surprise, Jo and her husband were there along with Nick who owned the pub, though he didn't stay long. The other guests were from the hospital. Ginny worried about that, but she need not have. One of the nurses, Mable, had arranged the flowers for Red. It was something of a hobby for her. Ginny was acting as maid of honour. Mable was very sweet and engaged Ginny in conversation. She told Ginny to contact her if she ever needed help with anything.

A great day was had by all. The cakes were a triumph, and Ginny slept like a log that night. She hadn't had much time to think and stress about things. Christmas morning was a low-key affair after the excitement of the day before. It didn't matter. It was a perfect day in many ways. Ginny spoke to her folks in the UK. They had been horrified by Ginny's news. When she told them about the miscarriage, their response had been kind but rather muted. They didn't know anything about Alex, and Graham had not told them much. He had reflected on a lot of things during the long journey back and had concluded that it was Ginny's business. Deep down, he had been looking for someone to take care of him rather than a partner in the true sense of the word. However, when her family found out about the fire, Ginny's father was all for coming out and doing what he could to help. He then had a very slight heart attack and was advised not to travel for the time being. It was a rather emotional phone call with her family, but on the whole, Ginny felt rather good.

Early on Boxing Day morning, Red and Jem set off. They wouldn't say where they were going, and Ginny got the impression they weren't going far.

That left her with Jackson, who suddenly seemed shy and spent most of his time in his room or out with the horse Jem had given him. However, they rubbed along all right. Ginny wasn't used to teenage boys, and Jackson didn't know what to make of Ginny. He'd heard all the rumours and was half scared of her and worried she might come on to him. Although Red had insisted Ginny was harmless, there was still that little niggle at the back of his mind.

Time went very quickly, and Red and Jem returned, content and at ease. Ginny had enjoyed looking after the place and was more relaxed than she had been of late. It had also given her ample time to think. She was staying on a few days, so she left her revelation until Jem and Red had been home a day or so.

One evening, after they had eaten, Jem got up to go into his little office when Ginny said, "Can you sit again? I have something to say."

He sat beside Red again, looking worried.

"I have given this a lot of thought, so please don't try to dissuade me. I intend to sell up. All that is there now is the barn, chook run, and dam. There's not a lot else." Ginny paused. After taking a deep breath, she said, "Once I sell up, I am going to buy a motorhome and travel round Australia and work as I go. Jeff and I always said that was what we would do when he retired. I'm going to do it earlier than we anticipated, but do it I am. Maybe I'm doing it a bit for Jeff too. Sad he never got the chance."

Red and Jem gaped at her, then they both tried to speak at once. Red stopped, so Jem carried on.

"Are you sure about this? It's a huge step to take, and is it wise to travel on your own?"

"Probably not, but I'll never know unless I try. Anyway, Puck will look after me, though I have to say he's getting on, and he's much slower since he was poisoned."

"I think you are very brave, and I shall miss you being here to help me become a proper farmer's wife, but good luck. I wish you well." Red got up and gave her a hug.

CHAPTER 38

ONCE THE NEW year commenced, Ginny put her property on the market. To start with, there was no interest. The drought had taken a hold, and her dam was still very depleted after the firefighters used it. It was also very hot, and everything was getting scorched. Even the trees looked stressed. Then, one night, there was a huge thunderstorm. Luckily, Ginny was back with Jem and Red because the heat had really got to her and Puck was better off too. He had slowed down a lot recently, and Ginny was worried about him. After all, he was an old dog.

For herself, she was mending. She had come to think that though she had lost Alex, at least she'd had a time of great happiness with him, and she could look back on that and think about how lucky she had been. She was sad because of the way Alex had been torn from her and because she had lost the baby without him knowing. Deep down, she had always felt he'd grow tired of her in time. So she squared her shoulders and decided to get on with her life.

After the storm, though it did nothing to relieve the drought, green shoots appeared all over the two-and-a-half hectares Ginny was selling. Even the dam looked better, though in truth, the storm had made little difference to the water level.

Shortly after the shoots appeared, she had not one but two people interested in her place. Both were couples who wanted to relocate to the edge of the outback, having got fed up with how the city was creeping into what had been a rural escape.

One of them had sold their previous land to a developer and offered Ginny far more than she had thought she would get because they wanted to outbid the others.

Suddenly, it seemed to Ginny that she was reasonably well off. Looking for a motorhome wouldn't be as difficult as she'd expected.

Three months later, she spent her last day with Red and Jem. Jem announced at the breakfast table that he wanted Ginny to go with him that morning, as he had something to show her.

"Let's go in my car," Ginny suggested. "I'll get to drive it one last time." Red would use Ginny's car, and Ginny had also given her Millie.

Ginny had actually spent her first night in her motorhome, which was parked outside the house. It was fitted out and quite luxurious. Ginny had bought herself a bike for doing little trips if she was camped on the outskirts of a town.

They set off. Puck wanted to come with them, but Jem said, "Leave him here. He will be cooped up enough once you hit the road."

They drove through town, then Jem instructed Ginny to turn down a long, winding gravel road. The sign at the end said it was a no through road.

They came to a very scruffy looking house, and as they pulled up, they were greeted by a tidal wave of dogs. Many different breeds were all loose and mixed up together. A big man appeared. He had the longest beard Ginny had ever seen but was bald. He held out his hand to Jem, then he shook Ginny's hand, nearly crushing her fingers in the process.

By this time, Ginny knew what Jem was up to. "I picked a puppy for you, but if you would rather have another, that is OK with me. He has no pedigree, but he will be very much like Puck, and I think you will need another dog before too long."

"I know. Poor old Puck is about fourteen, and that time he was ill really aged him."

They entered a small shed that had been converted into a doggy nursery. There were puppies everywhere.

She turned to the owner, whose name was Matt. "Goodness, what will you do with all of them?"

"It wasn't my intention to have puppies. I take in rescue dogs as an overflow for the RSPCA. The bitch was heavily pregnant, and this is the result: ten puppies." Ginny looked at the mother dog. She was an even bigger version of Puck. She had a very worn look about her but was plainly a lovely dog.

Jem bent down and picked up a squirming little bundle. The puppy was the colour of chocolate with black ears and blue eyes. "This is the one I chose. He's different from all the others, and I think he'll grow into a handsome chap."

Ginny took him from Jem. "He's gorgeous. How much do you want for him?" she asked Matt.

"All done and dusted. Jem here sorted it out the other day, along with a big bag of puppy food."

Ginny opened her mouth to protest, but Jem held up his hand. "Before you say anything, Red and I wanted to do this for you, and you are not allowed to throw it back at us. We will be offended. This is a goodbye present."

Tears threatened, but Ginny was now skilled at swallowing them down. She put one arm around Jem and kissed his cheek. "In that case, thank you so much. I love him already."

Driving back, the little puppy settled himself on Ginny's lap, seemingly unfazed by travelling and being parted from his mother and siblings.

"What are you going to call him?" Jem asked.

"That is a hard one. I can't think of anything at the moment."

Red reckoned she wanted a new puppy when they got back, but Jem pointed out that they had enough dogs as it was. He said he'd get her one soon. Red winked at Ginny. She knew he'd give her anything she wanted if he could.

"I was teasing," she told him. "I know we don't need any more dogs just now." Red had given up work and was helping Jem on the farm. It was a huge change, but she seemed to be thriving. She told Ginny she had never been so happy. She had found her soul mate.

Ginny's heart lurched. *I found mine too, but it wasn't meant to be.* But she smiled at Red. "I'm so pleased for you both."

CHAPTER 39

IT WAS A tearful goodbye the next morning. Ginny had set herself to go as far as Injune that day; she had decided to go north-east. It was winter, and she had no desire to get caught up in cold weather. Not yet, anyway.

Puck was a seasoned traveller, and the pup quickly settled down. Ginny stopped every little while where she could to give them both a break. She still couldn't decide what to call the puppy, so for the time being, he was just pup. He made her laugh a few times when he tried to chase Puck, who was remarkably good with him and seemed happy to be both protector and playmate. She found she was very tired when she got to the campground at Injune, and though she spoke to her fellow travellers, she kept mostly to herself. As time went on, she would find herself becoming more and more reclusive. She was never sure why but concluded it was to preserve her privacy.

She continued to travel slowly north-east and finally came to Port Douglas. Being winter, it was a hub of activity since people from the South invaded the North to escape the cold winter months. She was lucky to get a site at the camping ground. It was due to a cancellation.

She still hadn't chosen a name for the puppy and had the sudden thought to just call him *Pup*. Ginny, Puck, and Pup had a nice ring to it. She wanted to look for a job but worried about leaving the two dogs. She knew Puck would be fine, but she wasn't so sure about Pup. There were casual jobs advertised, but the hours wouldn't work with the dogs. Then she saw a job looking after two small children and doing a little housework at the same time. It was out of town on the road to Daintree, which would have been ideal if she'd had a regular car, but she could hardly take her motorhome to work. Despair started to take hold. Then one morning, while she walked the dogs on the beach, she got talking to a man. The next morning, he asked her if she was looking for a job. As it happened, he was looking for someone to look after his little office while he was out and about. He ran a small taxi service in and around the town. She was welcome to have the dogs with her while at work. Ginny jumped at the chance.

She felt quite nervous the next morning when she got to the office, which was along the road into town and set back from the road. She had Pup on a lead. Puck ambled along beside her.

Claude, the owner, met her at the door and made a fuss of the dogs. They knew him from seeing him on the beach, though Pup wasn't so sure of him. Claude was a big man in every sense of the word. His father was a Torres Strait Islander, and his mother was of Irish descent. He was extremely tall but very broad as well—a giant. Pup hadn't minded him out on the beach, but in a confined space, his behaviour changed. Pup growled, and Ginny laughed.

"That's the first time he has done that. I was afraid he liked everyone too much and wouldn't be much of a guard dog."

Claude grinned at her. "Glad to be of service in training your dog." He really liked this woman, but he sensed a deep sadness in her. He could see pain in her eyes. He had been divorced for a couple of years and didn't see his children that often, but he was a happy-go-lucky sort of person and never let life get the better of him. It troubled him to see this deep unhappiness in Ginny. One day, maybe he'd find out what her story was.

She settled into her job well. It was very easy, as it only involved answering the phone and helping keep the books up to date. Claude wasn't really interested in bookkeeping and was happy for Ginny to take over all the office work. His business wasn't very big, as it was all very local, and they were coming to the end of the high season. As they entered spring, things quietened down. Some days, she saw quite a lot of Claude. Other days, he didn't come to the office at all. He was big hearted and had many friends.

He tried to draw Ginny into his circle of friends, but she kept her distance, as had become her habit.

The anniversary of meeting Alex and his parents came and went. Ginny tried to ignore it, but Claude noticed a dark cloud hanging over her, though he said nothing. However, the anniversary of the fire loomed, and Ginny called in sick. When it had been a year since Alex had gone and she had lost the baby, it had been just before she started to work for Claude, and she had shut herself up in her motorhome and grieved alone. She'd realised she wasn't very good at dealing with these things, and she'd made a pact with herself not to let them get to her.

That afternoon, Claude came and knocked on the door of the motorhome. "Hello, anyone home?" he called out rather unnecessarily. Puck got up and greeted him since the door was open. Pup growled. On occasion, he still wasn't sure about this huge human. Ginny had been lying on her bed. She'd had a sleepless night and was napping. She got up and greeted Claude.

"Are you OK? I thought you looked a little unwell yesterday," Claude said.

Ginny was feeling guilty. This man was so kind. "Come in. Would you like a coffee or tea?"

Claude made the space seem small. "Coffee would be good, thank you. I like this." He waved his arm, encompassing her home. "How long have you had it?"

"Not too long. I bought it earlier this year after selling my place."

"Big step, selling up."

"It was, but there was nothing left. My house burnt to the ground, so my business was finished."

"You said you had your own business but not why you gave it away. That is terrible. How did the fire start?"

"I upset some nasty people, and the fire was deliberately set."

"Jesus, woman, that is awful. Where were you when this happened?"

Rather reluctantly, Ginny started to tell him, and before she knew what she was doing, she told him the whole sorry story. She revealed Jeff's accident and subsequent death at an early age, falling in love with a much younger man, and losing his baby while he remained unaware of her pregnancy. Claude listened while Ginny explained how Alex's family had whisked him away, and for her safety, he had cut all ties, then she recounted Puck's poisoning and the fire. The flood gates had opened, and Ginny couldn't stop. When she finally stopped speaking, she looked up at Claude, as she had lowered her head throughout her tale. His big, dark-brown eyes were regarding her with something like horror, and before she knew what he was going to do, he gathered her in his arms.

"You poor little girl. That is such a sad story. I'm so sorry. It's not surprising that you look so sad all the time."

For a moment or two, Ginny let him hold her. It was comforting to be cuddled again, then she gently pushed him away.

"It's OK. I have learned to live with it. It won't change no matter how much I wish it would, and what is done is done. I try to look forward not back."

"You are one brave lady. You had a bad time, but you pulled yourself up and got on with your life. I admire that."

"Thank you. I'll be in the office tomorrow, I just needed to take a rain check today."

"You're sure? If you want more time off, say so."

"No, it's helped talking to you. It's still eating me, I suppose, even though I think it's not. Good to let it out, so thank you."

Claude got to his feet. He seemed to fill the space, and Pup let out another low growl. Ginny gave a little laugh. "Silly dog."

"See you tomorrow, then, Ginny," Claude said as he took his leave. Ginny frowned at his departing back. What on earth had got into her, spilling her story like that?

A few days later, Claude asked her to have dinner with him.

Ginny refused. Claude looked disappointed, then he said. "Look, don't think I am asking you because I know your story. I was going to ask you, in any case. I like you, and I enjoy our random conversations. No expectations—I promise."

Claude was a superb conversationalist. He was a fount of knowledge and had some strong opinions about all sorts of things. He had travelled widely in Asia and the Middle East and had all sorts of interesting tales to tell.

Suddenly, Ginny threw caution to the wind. *Why not? I haven't been out for dinner with a man since I went to the UK and Graham took me out. God, that was a different world I lived in then.*

So she said, "OK. Thank you, Claude. I will come. I just hope this little monkey here behaves."

Ginny had bought a crate for Pup, so when they were camping, he was contained because, like all puppies, he was always in some sort of trouble. Puck would lie down and wait for her. He had slowed down considerably during the winter. Now that they were in spring, Ginny hoped he would perk up.

Claude was as good as his word. They had dinner at a restaurant that overlooked the end of Four Mile Beach at the Peninsula Boutique Hotel. It was a balmy evening, and Claude was very entertaining and great company. He made her laugh as he teased her gently, and Ginny was more relaxed than she had been for a very long time. They had walked since it wasn't that far. Now, Ginny suggested they walk back along the beach, which they did. It was a very romantic setting. The moon shone on the water, the sea was calm, the waves murmured softly against the sand, and the outline of the mountains in the distance was very beautiful. Claude took Ginny's hand and tucked it under his arm. Both were quiet, as if words would spoil the moment. When they climbed off the beach and reached the camping ground, Claude stopped. "I won't come right to the door with you, as it will set Pup off. Thank you for a great evening. I really enjoyed it."

"So have I. It's been wonderful."

He bent towards her and very briefly touched her lips with his, then he walked quickly away. Ginny watched him go. *What a lovely, kind man. I had a great evening.*

CHAPTER 40

THEIR RELATIONSHIP SUBTLY changed. Not quickly or dramatically, but slowly and quietly. Once a week, they had dinner together. There were plenty of places to eat, and they always seemed to go to a different place. Sometimes Claude would drive, and sometimes it was close enough for them to walk. He was a larger-than-life character. Everywhere they went, people knew him and engaged him in conversation. He was always patient and polite but slightly distant. He was out with Ginny and didn't want the distraction if the truth was known. He had grown very fond of her. He wasn't in love, but he felt the need to protect her and look after her. He had been horrified at the curve ball life threw at her and was determined she would feel happy and safe while she was there, on his patch.

Christmas loomed once again, and Jem and Red received a parcel full of presents from Ginny. Red had given birth to a beautiful baby girl a short time before and was already pregnant once more. "We have to go for it if we are to have a family. I am forty now, and Jem is over fifty," she told Ginny over the phone.

"What does Jackson make of all this?" Ginny asked.

"He is besotted with baby Rose. He'll spend most of the day nursing her if we let him. It's good to see. Why don't you come back and spend Christmas with us? We'd love to have you."

"I know, but I have the dogs, and I'm settled for the time being. It's such a lovely place and even better now that it's quieter."

When Red put the phone down, she looked at Jem. "This bloke Ginny says she has dinner with, do you think it's serious? It would be so good if she met someone else."

Jem shook his head. "Having seen her with Alex, I don't think anyone could replace him, but she may like this man. It might be good for her."

Jem was right. Ginny was much happier than she'd been for a long time, and she could remain positive so long as she didn't think about Alex and nothing reminded her of him. She was getting very good at living for the moment and shutting her mind off to what distressed her.

A few days before Christmas, Claude announced he was going down to Cairns to see his children, so he was shutting the office. Ginny's heart sank, though she tried not to show it. She was hoping to keep busy, so she could largely ignore the festivities. She hid this from Claude, however, or thought she did. She needn't have worried because he had a surprise up his sleeve. "I will be back late Christmas Eve, so I will see you sometime over the break," he said.

"Oh, OK. Have a good time with your kids."

"I will. See you." Claude got in his car and headed off.

After their first dinner, he'd developed the habit of giving her big hugs but very brief kisses—so brief they almost didn't happen—on the lips. Ginny had never been kissed like that before. She guessed he didn't fancy her but liked her as a friend. She was happy with that. Watching him go, she let Alex invade her thoughts. *God, I miss him. I wonder what he is doing for the holidays.* She shook her head at her own foolishness. Alex must stay out of her mind—bad enough he had her heart.

Christmas dawned, and Ginny decided to ring her family. She did not want to wait until later in the day, as she knew they would be busy getting ready for visits, preparing food, and unwrapping presents—all the chaotic things that went with Christmas in a big family. So for the next hour or so, she was occupied. After that, first Jo then Red rang her. She spoke to Jem, who made her laugh since he kept yawning. It had been a bad night with the baby, and Jem sounded exhausted. Once she finished the conversations, she started to feel a bit lost. There was hardly anyone left at the camping ground. An older couple asked her to join them for a drink later, and she said she would.

Calling the dogs, she set off along the beach. That, too, was quieter than normal.

When she got back with the dogs, she made herself a coffee and wondered what to do next. She fished out a book she was reading, but it didn't really grip her, and her mind started to slide towards Alex. Pup set up barking, and she gratefully put her book down and went to see what he was barking at behind her motorhome. He had found a big blue-tongue lizard but was half scared of it. Puck was resting in the shade.

Having got Pup away from the lizard, Ginny returned to her seat outside her door. It was a beautiful day. The sky was so blue, and as yet, it wasn't too humid and hot. She sat, staring at the printed page of her book and trying hard not to think about Alex. The words blurred, and she dozed off.

She woke with a start. A warm hand on her shoulder shook her gently. "Alex." The name was out before she realised she had been dreaming. Squinting against the light, she saw a big figure. Claude!

"Sorry I'm not Alex. Was he the guy you fell in love with?"

Ginny was very embarrassed. "I was dreaming. Happy Christmas." She got to her feet as she spoke. Claude hugged her, then he put his lips to hers and kissed her—really kissed her. He took her completely unawares. For a few seconds, she froze, then she responded. Claude drew back after their kiss deepened.

"That was one hell of a kiss. Who taught you to kiss like that?"

Ginny looked confused. Claude still had her in his arms, and when he started to chuckle, his huge body seemed to vibrate. "I'm teasing, but you are a great kisser."

"Oh."

"Come on, get your glad rags on. We are going to have the most amazing Christmas lunch ever."

"What about the dogs?"

"They can come too."

"Where are we going?"

"You'll see. You can come as you are if you like."

Ginny had clean shorts on and a new blue top, which was silky and a little revealing, but it suited her colouring.

"In fact, now that I've had a proper look, come as you are. You look great."

Claude had never really paid her a compliment before, and Ginny felt her cheeks grow hot.

Claude had his personal car not his taxi. It was a big 4WD, so the dogs settled in the back happily enough.

"Where are we going?"

"You'll see."

They took the road towards Mossman then turned off and were soon climbing the steep incline up the escarpment. When it levelled out, Ginny found herself looking at an amazing house built on the side of the steep slope.

It was all glass and steel and had the most wonderful view across the cane fields to the sea. She suddenly guessed this was Claude's home, which she had never been to. In fact, he had hardly ever mentioned his home.

He led her into the big open-plan living area with the most specular view Ginny thought she had ever seen. She suddenly realised there were two people standing in the very high spec kitchen area. By the door that opened out onto a huge verandah was a table that was almost groaning from the weight of the food on it.

"Ginny, this is Annie and John. They look after me and this place," Claude said. Ginny shook hands with them both. She guessed they were in their late fifties and of island descent. They had huge smiles and were warm and friendly. She learned they had been with Claude a number of years, and although they worked for him, he treated them as family.

Claude poured champagne, and they all toasted, then he drew out a chair and told Ginny to sit. The food was sumptuous, and Ginny hadn't come across some of the dishes and fruits before. The whole meal was a mixture of island and traditional cuisine. Ginny glanced around while the others chatted. Claude was plainly very well off—something she hadn't thought about before. Now she could see his taxi business was more of a hobby than a livelihood.

She had worried about the dogs, but at the back of the house there was a big enclosed space, so the dogs could quite happily be free but safe. At the side of the house there were steps leading steeply down to a pool that had been chiselled into the hillside. After they ate, Claude took her down to the pool and asked if she wanted to swim.

"I haven't got any togs with me," she said.

Claude, who'd had quite a bit to drink, grinned at her. "Do you need any?" Her jaw dropped, and he said, "Don't worry. I was teasing."

Ginny, who was feeling very mellow after all the lovely food and wine, grinned back. *Why don't I just go with it and have some fun? Haven't let my hair down for a long time.*

She stripped her top off. Now it was Claude's turn to look a little shocked. Smiling to herself, Ginny undid her bra, shimmied out of her shorts and panties, and jumped into the pool, leaving Claude standing on the edge with his mouth hanging open. He stared for a little longer, and Ginny, who wasn't a strong swimmer, took her time swimming towards the deep end. It was a beautiful infinity pool, and being in it was magical. She heard a splash and turned. Claude swam very strongly towards her. She waited to see what he would do.

When he got to her, he lifted her up into his arms and kissed her lips, then he trailed his lips down to her breast and took her nipple into his mouth. He, too, was naked, and Ginny found it very erotic—feeling his strong body and erection in the warm water. Claude moved them to shallower water, so his feet rested on the bottom of the pool. He lifted her again, and she instinctively wrapped her legs around him. Holding her bottom in his huge hands, he gently pushed himself inside her while kissing her and caressing her mouth with his tongue. Ginny moaned with desire and responded with a longing that surprised her.

A short time later, they both swam lazily back to the shallow end and climbed out. There were several loungers set in the shade, and Ginny went straight to one and flopped down. She was feeling mellow but confused. Had that really happened? Claude sat on the lounger next to hers.

"I'm sorry. I didn't mean to take you like that. I did mean to ask you to spend the night, but having sex in the pool wasn't planned."

Usually slightly uncomfortable naked, Ginny didn't care about her appearance. She sat up and took Claude's hand in hers. "That was great. I have no regrets, except I just realised that we didn't take any precautions. I don't want history repeating itself."

Claude grinned. "I had the snip, so we should be fine. You are an amazing woman. That was some Christmas present."

They had already had the conversation in which they had agreed not to exchange gifts. Claude had said Ginny spending the day with him was enough, and Ginny had said likewise. They dressed and then Claude showed her the rest of the property, which was actually a huge part of the hillside, though mostly bush.

When they went to bed, Claude made gentle love to her again. He was conscious of his bulk and tried hard not to make her feel overwhelmed. Alex was nearly as tall as Claude but slighter in build. Later, as Claude slept beside her, Ginny thought about him. He was full of surprises, plainly wealthy, and a gentle giant, but there must be lots more she didn't know.

CHAPTER 41

GINNY STAYED FOR Boxing Day. It seemed Claude expected it, and she didn't feel like arguing. The day passed languidly, with much eating and swimming. Claude loved books and reading. He had a small library and an office. All five bedrooms had en suite bathrooms. His home was steeped in luxury. Later in the afternoon, they took the dogs for a walk on the beach, and Ginny changed. Although Claude had toiletries she could use, he didn't have any clothes, and though she had swum and showered, she still felt uncomfortable in the same clothes.

Claude made love to her again in the pool. Ginny found it was a real turn-on. Annie and John were about and prepared their meals, but they mostly kept out of the way. While Ginny floated, she asked if the housekeepers were being discrete. Claude threw back his head and laughed. "No. They know me well and know when to give me space."

This answer made Ginny wonder. "Do you do this often, then? Bring women here."

Claude looked at her with a strange expression on his face. "No, not for a long time. When my wife first ran off, I played the field because I was so hurt. I wanted to prove to myself that I was still worthy of a woman's affections. But I haven't brought anyone back here in two years—not until you. You are different. I know you don't love me, and if I'm honest, I don't love you, or at least I'm not in love with you. But I admire you, and the sex is good. I am happy you are in my life. Trouble is, I still love my wife no matter what. Silly, isn't it?"

They were still in the shallow end of the pool, and Ginny leaned against him and kissed his cheek. "Not silly. You are a lovely man. I wish I could love you as you deserve."

Her breast brushed his arm, and he stroked it gently. "You do in one way. You are making me hard again!"

That night, Ginny woke to find Claude sitting on the edge of the bed, his head in his hands. She sat up. "What's the matter?"

He turned to her, and in the dim light from the moon outside, she could see his face was wet with tears. "Claude, what is wrong?" She pulled his head gently, so it was against her breast.

"I should never have made love to you. You deserve better. You love this young guy, don't you? You mutter his name in your sleep, and I can almost feel that cold, hard lump of hurt you carry round inside you, and me having you here—I shouldn't have been so selfish."

Ginny was shocked. She didn't know she spoke of Alex in her sleep, though she often dreamt about him. "Shh," she murmured. It was the only response she could think of just then.

Claude sat up. "What a bloody muddle. We both love other people and are drowning our hurt with each other. Is that sensible? Being with you has made me realise how much I miss my wife Natalie—ex-wife. What a fool I was to let her go. I was so busy making money that I forgot about her needs."

"I don't know if it's sensible either, but since meeting you, I've been happier than I've been in a long time. Let's just go with the flow and enjoy this time together. Alex is in the past. I may dream of him, but it's over. Let's enjoy the now. Lay down and try to sleep. Everything will look better tomorrow."

Still half asleep, Jem shambled out to do the morning chores. Rose had had another bad night, and Red was still having bouts of sickness with the new pregnancy. The dogs set up barking, and a battered, old ute drove up to the front of the house. "Who the hell?" Jem muttered to himself as a tall man with a baseball cap pulled down over his face got out and looked around. Seeing Jem, he strode towards him.

"Jem. Jem, it's me."

Jem stared. "Alex! What the hell!"

"What happened to Ginny's house? It's gone, and she's gone. Is she OK? Is she here? Has she returned to the UK? Where is she?"

Jem stood stock-still. Alex was plainly very distressed and ignorant of all that had gone on since he'd left twenty months before. Jem, who had been so angry with Alex, softened. "You had better come in. So much happened after you left, and not much of it was good."

An hour later, Alex was sitting in Jem's kitchen looking completely shattered. He had hardly taken in Red, the baby, or Jackson. He was having trouble processing what had happened to Ginny and their baby.

"Why did Ginny miscarry? Do you know?" he asked. Suddenly, he was overcome with emotion. His baby! Some of the things that had happened now made sense. After a call from his father, his mother and grandfather had become even more extreme in their treatment of him. He had been a virtual prisoner until these last few months. He had been told it was for his own good, and he had taken it to mean they thought he would forget Ginny in time. He guessed they had been horrified when they'd found out she was pregnant.

He told Jem and Red a little of what his grandfather and mother had done to keep him away. They found it unbelievable that he had been treated so badly.

"How come you are here now? Have they given in?" Jem asked.

"Hell no. I escaped a month ago, but I didn't dare come here straight away. They are looking for me, which is why I'm in that clapped-out old ute. Do you know where Ginny is? I mean to go and find her. I love her, and I want to be with her."

Jem looked hard at Alex. "I'm not sure I should tell you. If you shoot through again, it will destroy her completely. Her love for you has resulted in her losing so much: her home, her business, and her self-esteem."

For the next three days, Ginny stayed with Claude. They understood each other better now, and they both knew where they stood. Ginny parked her motorhome at the back of Claude's house and moved in with him. Neither of them knew how long they would last but agreed to take each day as it came. He went about his business but only half-heartedly. He admitted it had only been something to do until she came along. His father had got lucky in the stock market, and Claude had a gift for making good investments too. His parents lived in PG and were elderly, so they hadn't visited for a long time. Claude hadn't told them about Ginny because he was waiting to see how things panned out. Ginny was too.

On New Year's Eve, they decided to go into town to see the fireworks. Annie and Ginny had planned a special dinner. They got on well, and it was plain Annie liked Ginny. In fact, while preparing the food, Annie said she hoped Ginny would stay with Claude. Ginny knew this wouldn't be the case. She felt it in her bones and knew she was on the rebound, as was Claude.

He was great company and a good lover, but there was something missing; she wasn't sure if Claude felt it or not and wasn't quite brave enough to ask.

Things came to a head in an unexpected way on New Year's Day. It had been so busy lately, and Claude was getting tired of the driving part of his business, so he had decided to hire someone. He had been interviewing a few applicants before the holidays. He and Ginny were discussing the pros and cons of the candidates as they drove up to the house. There was a strange car in the driveway.

"Bloody hell! Now what?" Claude burst out. He scrambled out of the car. A blonde woman came rushing out of the house and threw herself at Claude, who put his arms around her and held her tight. She was sobbing uncontrollably. Then two children in their early teens appeared, and Claude held out his arms to them, and it soon became a group hug.

Ginny didn't need to be told it was his ex-wife and his two children. She got out of the car quietly, let the dogs out of the back, and retreated with them to her motorhome.

It was hot and stuffy, as it had been shut up while she stayed with Claude, though she did regularly open it for an hour or so. Pup was all for going and meeting these new people, but she made him stay. He was becoming a beautiful dog. He had grown to be slightly bigger than Puck with a dark-brown coat, black ears, and a black muzzle. Puck, on the other hand, seemed to be fading away. Ginny knew he didn't have long, but since he was happy and didn't have any real issues, she hoped it would stay that way.

Shortly afterwards, Annie tapped on the door, which Ginny had left open. "Can I come in?"

"Of course," Ginny said.

"You've guessed who the visitors are? It looks as if they will be staying for a bit. Claude is trying to calm Natalie down. She is very upset. Her new husband beat her, and she left him."

"It's OK. I will stay here, out of the way, but can you either feed me or let me come and get some food? I have nothing here."

"Oh for goodness' sake, come to the kitchen and eat with us. I wasn't implying you should stay here. I was only trying to warn you about what is happening."

"I appreciate it, but I will sleep out here, anyway. I don't want to add to Claude's drama, though if you could retrieve my toiletries from Claude's bathroom, I'd be grateful."

Annie shook her head, her dark eyes glistening with tears. "I think he will have her back, which will mean it will be time for us to move on too. We never got on, and John and I were on the point of leaving when she took off. I don't understand what Claude sees in her. You have been so good for him, Ginny. I haven't seen him so happy since that woman left."

A lump formed in Ginny's throat. It was the most Annie had ever said to her, and she felt closer to her than she ever had before.

"Thank you so much. He has been good for me too. He helped keep the black dog at bay. I'll just have to make sure it doesn't come back."

CHAPTER 42

A FEW DAYS LATER, Ginny was packed and prepared to hit the road once more. She had only seen Claude once after Natalie returned. Annie had got all her belongings out of the house for her, and apart from eating with John and Annie, she hadn't entered the other parts of the house again. She had kept the dogs under strict control, as Claude had told her once that Natalie didn't like dogs. There hadn't been any sign of the children. Annie said they had retreated to their rooms and were playing on their phones and iPads. The whole atmosphere of the house had changed, and there was tension in the air.

Claude came to see her just before she left. Annie had told him. He came into her van and, without a word, wrapped his arms around her. His cheeks were wet, and Ginny found she was feeling more emotional than she had expected.

"Ginny, what can I say? I feel I have let you down badly. You shouldn't feel you have to leave like this."

"It's OK. We both know it was fun while it lasted, but we love other people, and while my love is impossible, at least your love returned."

"I don't suppose it will last forever, but I love her to bits, so while she wants me, I'll take what she offers. Silly, I know, but it's how it is."

He kissed and hugged her, then he was gone. Ginny was more upset than she had thought she would be as she drove away. Annie and John said goodbye and were sad to see her go.

Later, she received a brief text from Claude saying he had put the wages he owed her in her account. Since they had become lovers, Ginny hadn't thought about wages. After all, he was paying for everything. It wasn't until three weeks later that she looked at her account and found that Claude had been very generous. To start with, she thought about paying it back. She wasn't happy with the idea he was paying her off, then she thought about it and knew that Claude hadn't seen it like that. He was just a generous person, and it would never occur to him that the money might offend her.

A couple weeks later, Ginny found herself in a vet's waiting room with Puck. He was very distressed and seemed to be in pain. It was hot in Darwin, and the heat seemed to have got to him. "I shouldn't have brought you here, old boy," she said.

The news wasn't good. Puck's heart was giving out.

"It's up to you, but he will only last a short time. I can give him an injection now and end his suffering, or you can wait for nature to run its course," the young vet said.

Ginny stroked Puck's head. His normally bright eyes were dull, and he was panting hard. With tears streaming down her face, Ginny said, "End it now. Poor old chap. I can't bear to see him like this."

She had left Pup, who was now more mature and sensible, in her motorhome. When she returned, he looked to see where Puck was but seemed to know and cuddled up to Ginny.

"Just you and me now, Pup," Ginny said, her heart aching.

Alex made it to Port Douglas on January 10, then he had difficulty finding Ginny. When he finally drove up to Claude's house, it seemed no one was home. He was getting very frustrated. He had been followed after he left Jem's, and it had taken a while to shake the tail. He had swapped the old ute for a newer, faster car, but he had taken his time to make sure he lost them. No one answered the door, and he was just getting back in his 4WD when a blonde woman appeared followed by two teenagers.

"What do you want?" she asked suspiciously. She was distinctly hostile.

"I'm looking for Ginny, Ginny Harrison. Do you know where she is? I was told she was here."

"No, she's gone, thank goodness. I—" She stopped speaking as a big Mercedes drove in. A huge man got out.

"Hi there, can I help?" He sounded as friendly as the woman had sounded grumpy.

"I'm looking for Ginny Harrison. I—"

"You must be Alex."

This threw Alex completely. He just stared at this big man with his big voice and friendly manner. After a few moments, he pulled himself together and muttered, "Yes, but how did you know?"

Glancing at the woman, the man said, "Come into my office. We can talk privately."

When they got into the office, Claude set about getting Alex a cool drink from the small bar in the corner. It wasn't alcoholic—he didn't want to get Alex into trouble—but he had a gin and tonic himself.

"Ginny spent Christmas here," Claude said. "She is lonely and sad. She misses you. She told me her story. Why do you want to find her now? She has had more hurt in her life than is fair, and she doesn't need more. If you are going to find her then dump her again, please don't. She is a wonderful woman and deserves happiness not any more heartache."

Alex observed Claude for several minutes. They regarded each other, both busy with their own thoughts, then Alex said, "You were her lover when she was here, weren't you."

Claude nodded. "For a few days, yes. She needed the comfort of being loved. It wasn't just sex, but I don't love her, and she doesn't love me. I think I was a kind of substitute. I don't know, maybe she just needed the comfort of other arms. Who knows? Then my ex-wife, whom you just met, came back unexpectedly, and Ginny left. She was going to leave anyway, but Natalie's appearance expedited her plans. She cried out your name in her sleep most nights, so please, if you catch up with her, treat her well."

Alex sat with his head bowed. Jealousy flared but dissipated as quickly as it had come. Finally, he raised his head and, looking Claude in the eye, said, "I love her and want to be with her. I am being pursued by my grandfather's men. Should I go after her or leave her alone?"

"I think you should find her and let her decide."

Alex stood. "Thank you, and thank you for looking out for her. I never meant for all this to happen, but it has, and I can't change it. I just need to see her again—find out if she still wants to be with me."

"I'm not sure, but I rather think you should try Darwin and all the campsites along the way. She's a few days ahead of you, but you'll catch her eventually."

Claude followed Alex to his car and watched him drive away. Neither of them saw a figure hidden in the bushes, watching to see if Alex found Ginny.

Claude hadn't hurt her, but he'd made her aware of the fragility of human relationships, and Ginny decided not to let anyone too close again. She had a cold, hard lump of sadness inside her that would never leave her. She asked her parents to come out to Australia. They had said many times they would but had never made it out. Her mother said no, and Ginny was secretly relieved, as she had grown distant from her family.

She was too sad to stay on in Darwin, so she left again almost immediately. Little did she know, Alex was only twenty-four hours behind her.

Alex thought he had shaken his pursuers several times, but they always seemed to be just behind him. Unbeknownst to him, they had been told to just follow, as he would lead them to Ginny. This time, there would be no mistake. She was supposed to have died in the fire. Margarita wanted her dead above all else.

Alex wasted a couple of precious days looking around Darwin for her then moved on. He wrongly thought she would drive to Alice Springs. A few days later, he realised his mistake and rather recklessly drove across the Tanami after guessing Ginny had gone west. His pursuers weren't at all pleased. They were city men through and through and hadn't enjoyed this assignment at all. After only fifty kilometres, they had enough. Alex's dust was way ahead and disappearing. He hadn't noticed they were following him lately. He was so focused on finding Ginny now that he was so close.

Rix was with Luke not Lee. They studied the map after pulling over. "Look, the road pops back on the highway. It's a kind of short cut."

"I wouldn't call it a short cut, exactly. It's a long way round. Joins the highway near a place called Halls Creek. Still, if we share the driving, we shouldn't be that far behind."

"The GPS makes it sound like it'll take two or more days to drive there."

"Yea, well, I'm not game to try this way. We haven't got enough fuel and only the one spare."

They wasted another ten minutes or more arguing the point and finally set of back towards Tennant Creek.

Alex wasn't enjoying the drive at all. He'd bought some extra petrol in cans but only had the one spare tyre. The man at the servo where he'd filled up had told him he needed two to be sure, but he had decided to risk it. He was desperate to catch up with Ginny.

Ginny got to Kununurra and thought she would rest up then go on to Lake Argyle. She was feeling very dispirited. Puck's death had knocked her more than she had thought it would. He'd been an old dog, but he'd also been a constant through thick and thin.

Alex was nearing the end of the Tanami when he hit a rock with a *bang*, and both tyres on the passenger side blew. He was in deep trouble since he only had one spare. He didn't quite know what to do. He thought he'd change the wheel at the front and see how it went, but it was obvious the 4WD couldn't be driven far. There was no signal on his phone. He'd swapped the battered old ute for this 4WD before leaving Roma on his way north. It was only three years old and in good condition, though he hadn't expected to drive roads like these. One thing he was grateful for was that he had no money worries. He had inherited a large amount from his father's family after turning twenty-one.

All he could do was wait until someone came along. It was extremely hot. He was pleased he had plenty of water with him. He sat on the ground by his car in as much shade as it offered him. The sun was still high in the sky, so there was much shade, and though hot, he covered himself as much as he could to keep from the roasting sun.

His mind drifted to his mother. He didn't think she loved him. She was a complete control freak and, to a certain extent, controlled even her father because what she wanted, she got. He shivered. Ginny was so different, and he had never considered their age difference. To him, she was just a wonderful woman who had stolen his heart. There was no doubt in his mind that he would love her forever. She was his soul mate. He'd been horribly shocked when Jem had told him how she had suffered and that she had been carrying his baby. He was even more desperate to find her and put things right.

He was so deep in thought that he didn't hear the road train coming until it was nearly upon him. Help at last.

CHAPTER 43

IT WAS TAKING Luke and Rix longer than they had thought, but they pressed on. They didn't know Alex was now behind schedule, so they passed the end of the road and set off towards Broome where they were sure to catch up with Alex. Ten minutes later, Alex got onto the highway and turned back, convinced Ginny wouldn't have got that far. It was the main reason he'd taken the trip across the desert; he was hoping to get ahead of her. Back on the bitumen, he drove, rested, and drove again. He didn't notice the wonderful colours of the landscape—the reds, oranges, and dark browns—or the craggy slopes of the mountain ranges. The many shades of green in the vegetation and the vivid blue of the sky were lost on him. A few times, he saw brumbies near the road, but he was mostly focused on finding Ginny. A couple of times, he met camper vans, but Jem had described Ginny's motorhome well, and he was fairly confident he hadn't passed her.

When he finally got to Kununurra, he was exhausted. He'd hardly slept in days, let alone showered or eaten properly. He was a mess. He drove to the camping ground and blearily looked around. There was only one motorhome that looked like the one Jem had described. *If this isn't her, then I shall have to give up for a while. I can't think straight. I'm so tired. I will have to take a break. Don't think I've been followed, in any case. I wonder why they didn't try to stop me. Perhaps it's Ginny they want? I will protect her if they're after her.* His mind was wandering, he knew, but he was just so very tired.

He clambered out of his vehicle and staggered towards the motorhome.

Suddenly, a big dark-brown dog was standing in front of him, barking and snarling. He stopped. The dog looked as if it meant business.

"Pup!" a familiar voice called. "What is the matter?" Ginny appeared in the doorway. She saw a tall, dishevelled man with a bushy beard. He looked as if he would collapse at any moment.

"Ginny," Alex croaked. "Ginny, it's me."

Ginny's legs felt weak, and she almost fell over. She clutched the door frame.

"Alex!"

Somehow, they made it across the few metres that separated them and wrapped their arms around each other, tears pouring down their faces.

Without a word, Ginny finally untangled herself enough to lead Alex into her van. She gently pushed him into a seat then got him some water and put coffee on. He watched her, his dark eyes shining. Neither of them spoke. It was too emotional for words, and Alex felt so very tired.

Alex gratefully sipped his coffee and started to speak.

"Shh, it can wait. You need a shower and sleep. I think you look done in," Ginny said quietly.

He was. He'd eaten only a few snacks since Jem had insisted he have some food, sleep had hardly been an option, and washing had been low on his list. The more time he'd spent looking for Ginny, the more desperate he had become.

Ginny led him to the shower then left him to it. She was in turmoil. She didn't know whether to laugh or cry. She felt shaky and weak. She had come to terms with never seeing him again, but here he was. She was sure of one thing: If he only wanted to check up on her before disappearing again, she would tell him to leave as soon as he was able.

She picked up his keys and moved his vehicle closer to her van, then she picked up his bag and brought it in. Pup watched these proceedings with his head tilted to one side. He wasn't sure about this strange man his mistress had cried over.

Alex was out of the shower and wrapped in a towel when Ginny came back inside. She silently handed him his bag. He rummaged around and found his razor, then he dressed himself in clean clothes. Ginny had retreated to the living area and begun cutting fruit and making sandwiches.

As he came through, she turned towards him. He stopped in the doorway.

"You look washed out," Ginny said. "You need to sleep."

"What I need, above all else, is to talk to you. I have been following you for a while, and I began to think I would never catch up with you. I went to your house, and it was gone! Gone! I went to Jem's, and he told me everything—about the baby and the fire. I didn't know. I'm so sorry that I brought all this down on you. I love you, and I need to know if you can forgive me and if you still love me a little."

As he spoke, tears welled in his eyes again, and Ginny found she had tears running down her face too. But she held her ground.

"Have some food, then we will talk."

Alex did as she bade him, and as he ate, his eyelids started to droop.

When he finished his meal, Ginny led him through to her bed, and he collapsed onto it. He put his head on the pillow and immediately fell asleep.

CHAPTER 44

GINNY SAT STILL, wondering how she felt. She had bustled about after Alex had fallen asleep and prepared an evening meal for herself. She had fed Pup who, having picked up on his mistress's mood, was acting needy, or maybe he was trying to comfort her. Ginny didn't know, nor did she know what to think now.

Her feelings for Alex hadn't changed at all, but her sense of self-preservation had. Before, she'd been willing to take a chance at happiness when it came her way. Now she thought the possible fallout was maybe too high a price to pay. So she sat and waited. It would depend on what Alex said when he woke.

Rix pulled the car over to the side of the road and looked across at Luke, who had been dozing.

"We are stupid bastards," Rix said. "If we got in front of him, which we might have done, he could easily have turned back towards that place called Kunun—whatever it was. I think we should backtrack."

Luke pulled himself into a better position and yawned. "Let's go back to that one town, Halls Creek, I think. We both need a shower, good food, and sleep, I reckon. Then we will decide what to do. I'm getting fed up with this wild-goose chase. I'm so tired that I couldn't shoot straight even if the bloody woman was standing right in front of me."

"You have got it stowed away, haven't you? We have been lucky we haven't come across an RBT or any other police checks. NSW number plates stick out to those nosy bastards."

Luke nodded. He was confident no one would find the gun. "Alex finds her, we find Alex, we do the business, then we hightail it back."

"Well, that was the plan, but it doesn't seem that simple. I'm still unclear about what we are to do with Alex."

"Knock him out and take him back with us, so the boss said."

"Might be easier said than done. We need to make sure there is no one about, then. No witnesses."

They set off back to Halls Creek.

It was dark when Alex woke, and for a split second, he couldn't remember where he was. He sat up with a jerk. "Ginny!"

"I'm here." Ginny appeared and flicked on the light as she did so. "How do you feel?"

"Much better, thank you." Alex wanted to hold out his arms to her but knew they needed to talk before anything else.

They sat on either side of the table. Ginny had got a jug of cold water, and she poured them both a glass.

"First of all, you need to know that I knew nothing about the baby, the fire, or anything until Jem filled me in. I made him promise not to tell you that he had seen me. I asked him where you were after I managed to get away from my grandfather's men. It took me time to plan it all. I wanted to find you then take you abroad and settle down. I had to carefully plan my every move since I was watched. Grandfather even kept an eye on my bank account. So it took a long time, and I was afraid you would find someone else—someone nearer your own age or even that bloke from the UK. But I carried on planning and hoping. I won't bore you with the details now, darling Ginny, I just want to be with you and love you now and forever. You are my soul mate. My everything. I don't care about our age gap or that you might look older one day. I love the person you are, not the shell that your body is. It's the core of you, the—"

Alex stopped because, with tears of joy pouring down her cheeks, Ginny leaned over and put her lips to his.

Moments later, they were back on the bed, feverishly undressing and making love. Pup watched the proceedings with a big doggy grin. His mistress was happy, and that was all that mattered, even if she was behaving strangely.

Later, they got up and ate the cold supper Ginny had prepared earlier. Then they talked some more.

"I know I was followed to Jem's place," Alex said. "I tried to dodge them, but I had a rather clapped-out old ute. I changed cars in Roma. They were still following me, but I think I lost them before I got to Port Douglas, though I can't be sure. Then I saw them again in Alice Springs. I thought that was where you had gone. However, I took the Tanami, and if it was them, they didn't follow me."

"But why follow you? Why not try to get you to go back with them?"

Alex looked very worried. "I think they were hoping I would lead them to you. I might be wrong, but maybe they want us both together. It was a risk I had to take. I couldn't put my life and yours on hold forever."

"I am so pleased you came, and if they are after us, then so be it. We will confront that when it happens, if it does. With you by my side, I can cope with nearly anything."

During the time she had been away, she'd lived in her own world and liked it that way. She'd listened to local news wherever she was but nothing more, and she had found herself retreating more and more from society. Now, as if a window had opened, she felt completely different. She was so happy that she wanted to shout from the rooftops. Everything she looked at seemed to sparkle with gold. It was amazing the difference just a few hours had made to her perspective on life.

Then she caught sight of herself in the mirror, and her doubts returned.

"Alex, you are nearly twenty-three, and I am fifty-one. The age difference—"

"Stop right now. What I said earlier holds good. Age doesn't come into it. When will I convince you of that? Will I ever? Now, let's go to bed. I'm still tired, and a little cuddle might be in order."

CHAPTER 45

FOR THE NEXT week, they reconnected and caught up with what had been happening in their lives. Each was horrified by what the other had gone through. Alex asked Ginny about Claude. There was a worm of unease within him because Ginny had started a relationship with the man so easily. Ginny had a hard time convincing him, but in the end, he saw she was being truthful.

They left Alex's car and moved down to the village at Argyle Lake. The lake was so stunning and peaceful, though Ginny noticed Alex was on high alert whenever a new vehicle appeared. "Pup doesn't bark like Puck used to, does he?" Alex asked.

"No, he growls deep in his throat. He barks with joy but not with menace."

After they had been there for four days, Ginny said they should move on. Alex was edgy, though when she asked him about it, he brushed her concerns aside.

"Tell me what the matter is," she insisted.

"Nothing."

"If we are to sustain a good relationship, you have to be honest with me. Something's up, I know it."

Alex got to his feet and walked away. Ginny watched him go; this was something he wouldn't have done in the past. He had changed. *But so have I, and he had a rotten time with his mother and grandfather, and he doesn't see his father at all, and I always thought they were close.*

A little while later, he came back, and without saying a word, he put his arms around Ginny and held her close. She resisted the urge to push him away.

"I told you about being followed. I'm scared, scared of what it might mean if they catch up with us. Every time I hear a car, my heart rate shoots up. Let's move on. I'll feel safer if there are more people around. I want to protect you, but I'm a coward for feeling scared. I—"

"Shh, you're not a coward. I think you shook them off, and we are safe, but I already said we should move on. We'll go back to Kununurra and pick up your car, then we'll drive on convoy back to Darwin. Once there, we will review the situation. But I am sure you are worrying unnecessarily."

"Great minds think alike. I already thought exactly the same thing. I'm just so worried they mean you harm."

When Luke and Rix got to Kununurra, they rested then explored the town. It didn't take them too long to spot Alex's car.

"We know that the woman is driving a camper van, and I reckon he met her. If we wait and watch, he'll come back. Much of his gear is still in the car, so he will return for sure," Luke said.

Three days later, they were getting fed up. They had taken it in turns to watch the car but were so bored. "I reckon the boss owes us big time. We've driven halfway round the bloody country. I just want to get back to civilisation."

"Me too. He'll owe us a lot of dosh by the time we get back."

Just then, a shiny motorhome drew up by the car, and Alex and Ginny got out. They conferred for a minute, then they got into their respective vehicles and drove off.

"What does that mean? Are they splitting up?" Rix muttered.

"Doesn't matter. She is on her own. We can get her then worry about getting his lordship back."

However, it was easier said than done. Alex wasn't leaving much space between Ginny's motorhome and his vehicle. Also, there seemed to be quite a bit of traffic coming the other way.

Rix was getting worried. Neither of them had thought about filling up with fuel, and they were getting low. Alex and Ginny likely had plenty and didn't need to stop.

They were staying well back by now, as they had come to realise their previous plan to stop Ginny on the road wouldn't work very well.

"I'll have to stop at the next roadhouse and fill up," Rix muttered.

"You silly bugger. Why didn't you fill up before?"

"Because you said we had to keep watch. There wasn't time."

Timber Creek finally arrived, and they drove into town with the hope they could catch up later. When they got to the roadhouse, they saw Ginny's motorhome parked out front but no sign of Alex's car. They didn't know what to make of it. There were one or two people sitting outside eating their dinner, though it was still quite early. Again, they didn't know what to do. In the end, Luke went into the bar area and asked for two steak sandwiches to go. He was sorely tempted to order a beer, but he resisted the impulse. While he was waiting, he asked the barman about the motorhome.

"Looks like the real deal—that motorhome. Is it yours?" Luke asked.

"Nah, it belongs to some sheila. She went off with a young bloke in his car to look at the old crossing. They won't see much this time of the year, but tourists still feel the need. Pretty rough track down there too."

When Luke got back to Rix, they discussed going to find Alex and Ginny and decided they'd been given an ideal opportunity to quietly deal with them both. Off they set. Turning off the highway, they found the track, which was indeed very rough. Lurching into a big, long pothole, they heard a *bang*, and sure enough, they had a puncture. A sharp rock had shredded their tyre. They both scrambled out. It couldn't have happened at a worse place, as the track was narrow and rough, and where the car was made it difficult to jack it up to change the tyre.

However, they set to work getting the spare tyre out and attempting to jack their car up.

"We need two jacks. This won't work. Bloody hell, why did we come down here?" Rix was losing his cool.

For the next half an hour, they struggled, then they heard a vehicle coming, and around the next corner came a big all-terrain vehicle. There was just enough room for the driver to pass them, but as the vehicle drew level, it stopped, and the driver leaned out of the window.

"Hey, mate, you like you need a hand there."

Half a dozen people climbed out, and between the eight of them, they got the wheel fixed. The vehicle belonged to a tour company, and the driver was an instructor showing prospective tour guides round the various places they would be taking people to.

"The track is worse up ahead. Not sure it's a good idea for you to keep going now you have no spare. You need to be careful driving. Look out for these washouts." Gerry, the instructor, told Rix and Luke.

"We were hoping to catch up with some friends of ours—a man and a woman. Are they still down there?"

Gerry instinctively disliked these two and wondered at this remark. However, he was quite honest. "No one else down there, mate. It will be dark soon. You must have missed them." He saw the look of annoyance pass between the two men and guessed they were trouble of some sort. Ginny and Alex had been leaving when Gerry and the others had got to the riverbed where the old crossing used to be. It was a wild place, and the river was very wide there, but it was also shallower. The old crossing was still visible when it was the dry season.

Gerry and the others had engaged in a brief conversation with them before they had driven off. Little did Rix and Luke know, they had passed them going back to the roadhouse when they had been driving to the riverbed nearly an hour before.

Alex and Ginny had been behind a road train, and Rix and Luke had been so focused on their mission that they had failed to spot them. Alex, however, had seen them and had let out a curse.

"What's up?" Ginny asked.

"We are being hunted. I worried about them finding us, and now they are closing in. We need to move on."

"You really are scared, aren't you. You think they really mean to harm us? Not you, surely. Your mother—"

"My mother wants revenge, and she hates you. I think they will kill you if they get the chance. As for me—" Alex shrugged.

"Oh God, this is awful. We should go to the police."

"And say what? We can't prove anything. They would laugh at us. No, we try and outsmart them."

Ginny could see Alex had made up his mind, so she gave up arguing with him, but she, too, was scared.

CHAPTER 46

SO THEY MOVED on. They stopped briefly in Katherine overnight then decided to drive to Darwin. There, they would sell both vehicles and buy another. Pup had taken a great liking to Alex and made it plain he wanted to ride in his car instead of staying in the motorhome with Ginny. Neither of them slept much, and every little sound had them flinching. They left the camping ground at four thirty in the morning, and Rix and Luke drove in ten minutes later. They drove round but could see no sign of them. Finally, they questioned an old man sitting outside his caravan. Truth be told, he wanted to smoke, and his wife had banned him from smoking inside their van.

"We were supposed to meet up with some friends in a big motorhome last night but got delayed. A big silver-and-blue one with Queensland number plates. Have you seen it?"

John, the man they had asked, looked at the two unlikely fellows. He had seen Ginny and Alex drive out looking worried. He didn't like the look of these two at all.

"Nah, mate. They haven't stopped here. Try the camping ground out at the gorge. That is the most likely place. More people camp there than here."

John didn't know where Ginny and Alex had gone, but he thought it was more likely they had gone either towards Darwin or Alice. He guessed these two meant no good.

Rix and Luke looked at each other. They weren't sure this man was telling the truth, but they were getting sick of driving round trying to find Alex and Ginny. It was worth a try.

Three hours later, they were on the road to Darwin. They'd decided that was the most likely place for Alex and Ginny to go.

CHAPTER 47

SELLING ALEX'S CAR was easy enough, but it was going to take time to sell the motorhome. In the end, they came to an arrangement with a big car dealership; they could leave the motorhome there and pick it up later. They bought another big 4WD and a camp trailer, and four days later, they set off once more. It had been four fraught days of hiding as best they could. Ginny dyed her hair blonde, and Alex took to wearing an old beanie pulled down low. They were both aware that the two men knew what they looked like, but somehow, their disguises made them feel better.

Rix and Luke drove into the dealership ten minutes behind them. They had searched and searched and had finally spotted Alex's vehicle in a car yard. After money passed through hands, they got the information they wanted, and they set off once more in hot pursuit. It didn't take long for them to spot their quarry in front of them.

"Let's get this over with. There aren't too many cars about. Hang on, we'll do it now." Rix put his foot to the floor, intent on getting in front of Alex, who was driving. The idea was to pull up in front and force them to stop, then they would have them.

From the other direction, a police car came cruising along, and after seeing the speed Rix was doing—well over the speed limit—he turned on his siren. Although Rix dropped his speed straight away, the cruiser did a U-turn and signalled them to pull over. Ginny and Alex, who were aware they were being targeted, breathed sighs of relief and carried on. Alex wondered how far they would get before Rix and Luke caught up with them again.

They weren't that far from Katherine but decided to press on. They reckoned if they shared the driving, they could make it to Tennant Creek. If they were among people, Rix and Luke would be less likely to accost them.

"Mataranka—I've always wanted to go to the Elsey Cemetery," Ginny said as they drove on without stopping. They'd had a comfort break earlier and filled with fuel, though they were carrying extra.

Alex, who was driving, patted her knee. "One day, darling. I promise."

"I haven't actually asked you what you think they would do if they caught up with us."

Alex glanced across at Ginny. *God, I love this woman so much. My soul mate. My whole world. She is strong. She deserves the truth.*

"I told you I think they mean to kill you, but you might have a bad time beforehand. As for me, well . . . As I said, I don't know."

"But why? Surely your mother can't really be this bad, can she? She wouldn't want anything bad to happen to you."

"She hates to be crossed. She will never forgive me, of that I am certain. I am fairly sure you were meant to be in the house when it caught fire. Lee is no killer. I think they ensured you were out of the way, but I'm not positive." Alex shook his head. There was much he didn't know—he didn't want to. It was a sobering thought. His mother was so evil, as was his grandfather.

Ginny shuddered. *God, what a family. Thank goodness Alex is the real deal—I am certain of that if nothing else. I love him so much. I haven't worried about the age thing during this nightmare journey. He is just Alex, and we are in this together, come what may.* Ginny suddenly felt extraordinarily happy with this realisation, and she pressed a lingering kiss on Alex's cheek.

He gave her a quick grin. "We haven't had time for a good fuck lately, have we? I am going to give you the time of your life when this is over. That's a promise."

"I'll hold you to that," Ginny replied with a smile.

Rix had to hand over his licence. He'd got quite a few demerit points on it, but they were mostly around Sydney, and he hoped they wouldn't show up here. Then he had to do a breath test and a drug test, which came up positive. Luke made a face at him. The police officers didn't like the look of the two thugs and searched the car, but Luke had hidden his gun well, and they were looking for drugs not weapons. They were not far from Katherine, but Rix had to go with the officers and do another test at the station. However, it had been some time since he'd had the cannabis, and the second test came back negative.

As the officers drove Rix back, they thought a second, more thorough, search of the car would be a good idea. However, they were called to break up a fight near Pine Creek. After issuing Rix and Luke a warning, they drove off. The two men resumed their journey but were now unsure of the route Alex and Ginny had taken.

Ginny and Alex decided to go back to Queensland. It was an unexplainable feeling, but Ginny told Alex it might be a homing instinct. By sharing the driving, they made good progress. However, they had to make comfort stops, and Pup needed to stretch his legs too.

Finally, they were nearing Tennant Creek. They planned to cross over back to Queensland via the Barkly.

Not feeling like spending the night in town, they decided to camp at the Threeways Roadhouse. They would recharge their batteries, have a short sleep, then move on. They rented a cabin instead of unpacking the trailer. Pup was a little peeved he had to sleep in the car alone, but he accepted it. He was now a very big dog, bigger than Puck, but now that he'd grown, he wasn't quite so boisterous as Puck had been as a puppy. He was of a more serious nature.

They went to bed early, as they intended to leave before the sun rose. Alex made gentle love to Ginny. They were both very tired and emotional. The strain of keeping one step ahead of their pursuers while wondering what the future held was taking a toll. Neither of them knew what to think. They were living in the moment. Alex had seen Rix and Luke being pulled over in his rear-view mirror but had said nothing to Ginny. Now, he told her what he thought had happened.

"Do you think they will guess we are going back towards home?" Ginny asked.

"I think they may, yes, but I think going home is still our best option. We will go to Dad's place. We will be safe there."

"But you said your dad was the one who told your mother about me and the baby. He'll be hostile."

Alex shook his head. "Dad has no time for Mum, and he isn't one to hold grudges. I know he likes you, he told me so ages ago, and maybe he was jealous of me, but he will help us—of that I am sure. We will be safe there."

"Why don't we just go to the police?"

"As I said before, what will we say? We haven't been threatened—just followed. The police would tell us it's all in our heads. They would have found any weapons if they searched the car, which I am assuming they did back there. I would think they questioned them well too, as they stick out like sore thumbs. They certainly don't look like tourists."

Neither of them slept well, and they were on their way early. They knew the Barkly was over five hundred kilometres and was flat and straight. They decided to have a quick stop at the next roadhouse for a comfort break and breakfast. Stomachs rumbling, they set off in the pre-dawn darkness.

Their hunters had also slept badly. They had checked into a motel in Tennant Creek and had sat up trying to decide which way their quarry had gone.

"I think they'll make for Queensland—home territory and all that," Rix said.

"I dunno, maybe. One thing I'm sure of is I'm sick to death with this. I'll tell Marcus to shove his job up his backside when we get back. I've had enough."

Rix shook his head at Luke. Hard man though he was, he hadn't much sense. "You know too much, mate. You try to leave Marcus and you'll be helping prop up a new bridge somewhere." Rix shuddered. "A concrete coffin doesn't appeal to me."

Luke looked worried then said, "Well, getting back to Sydney is what we need to do. Get this over with."

They, too, set off before sunrise. "Take it steady today, Rix. We don't want a repeat of the flat tyre or the coppers."

As Alex drove, he constantly looked in his mirror, and Ginny sat stiffly in the passenger seat. She could feel waves of stress coming off Alex as he drove. Pup, too, was restless in the back. He had picked up on the tension.

They stopped briefly at the roadhouse and got takeaway coffees and breakfast. Ginny drove for a bit to give Alex a rest, then Alex took over again. They came up behind a drover's plant. It was a convoy of vehicles: a caravan, two trucks with horses, another small trailer, a trailer with three quad bikes, and a couple of old utes bringing up the rear.

"I'm going to need space to pass this lot. I haven't got that much power towing our trailer either. There seems to be quite a headwind," Alex said worriedly.

They trundled along for a bit while Alex debated what to do. They weren't going that slowly but too slow for his liking, then the inevitable happened. He spotted a black 4WD in the rear-view mirror, rapidly getting closer.

"Shit, they caught up again."

Ginny, heart racing, glanced behind them. "You'll have to overtake this convoy. Try to shake them off." But as she said this, the convoy in front turned off slowly into the entrance of a cattle property.

As they turned, they slowed and blocked Alex from getting by, as they had to swing across the road.

As soon as he was able, Alex floored it, but Rix was quicker. He didn't have a trailer to slow him down. He roared in front of Alex then drove on for a few hundred metres. Jerking the wheel to the side, he swung the car and blocked the road, forcing Alex to stop.

The front of Alex's car was actually against Rix's when he came to a halt. Ginny was hanging onto the doorhandle, terrified, and as soon as Alex opened his door, Pup barged out. He wasn't a happy dog.

"Stay in the car," Alex told Ginny as he faced the two thugs. Ginny complied for a moment, but then Rix took a swing at Alex and caught him on the side of his head. It was as Rix had hoped. His manoeuvre made Ginny get out of the car and go towards Alex, who had staggered but not fallen. Luke raised his gun. It was now. He had a clear view of the woman. Before he could pull the trigger, a mass of dark-brown fur leaped onto his chest, sending him over backwards. The gun went off then skittered away as Luke fell heavily onto his back. Pup held him down, his teeth bared at Luke's throat.

Alex grunted and fell slowly sideways. "Alex!" Ginny screamed.

Bill Forbes was running late. His load of electrical equipment for the power station in Alice was needed urgently, but he had experienced delay after delay with loading. The manager of the depot he'd got the machinery from had been excessively meticulous about the security of the load. It had been a hellish morning so far, and now, in the distance, he spotted vehicles by the side of the road, but as he got closer, he realised that one was partially blocking the road.

He cursed. He was going way over the speed limit trying to make up time. As he approached, he saw a bloke run and get into the car that was in his way. Good. There was room to get by now without stopping. Then, to his horror, the car spun round right in front of him. His load was heavy. He needed at least a kilometre to stop, and he didn't have that now!

Rix panicked when the gun discharged wildly, and the bullet hit Alex. Not even noticing the road train bearing down on them, he jumped in the car, intent on driving off. The two vehicles came together with a horrendous sound of screeching brakes and screaming metal. The transport truck collected the 4WD and scraped it along the road. It caught the trailer, which swung around straight onto Luke, who was still trapped on the ground with Pup on top. Pup jumped away just in time.

When everything was still again, the only sounds were metal settling, oil dripping, and Ginny sobbing.

Pup went to his mistress and licked her face then Alex's, which was deathly white. His eyes flickered. "Ginny," he murmured, then his eyes closed, and he was gone. Pup put his head back and released an unearthly howl.

A couple in a caravan stopped to help. Ginny clutched Alex's lifeless body, Pup howled, and Luke drifted in and out of consciousness. Rix was dead, his lifeless body tangled in the remains of the 4WD. Bill was trapped and couldn't move, though once free, he was uninjured apart from cuts and bruises.

The paramedics arrived shortly after and had trouble prying Alex's body from Ginny's arms, and Pup also made it difficult. In the end, as she wasn't injured, Ginny and Pup were allowed to travel in the police car back to Tennant Creek. The police transported her to Alice where she was questioned at length. They worried about her mental state, but once she was away from the scene, she seemed to pull herself together, and a strange calm overtook her.

The camp trailer was nearly a write off, and the Jeep they had been driving wasn't good either. The force of the trailer being spun had twisted the Jeep's framework.

When she'd asked about Luke, the officers had told her that all the ribs on his left side were broken. He also had a collapsed lung, a broken arm, and a bang on his head. He would survive.

Eventually, Ginny found herself driving her motorhome back to Queensland.

CHAPTER 48

RED AND JEM welcomed her. "You can stay here forever if you wish," Jem said. "We could do with help around here, what with the children and the cattle and everything." Red had recently had another baby. "We are feeling our age," Jem said.

Alex's body, when released, had gone to his father. Ginny had heard nothing from Charles. She wasn't concerned about attending a funeral. She'd said her goodbye as she'd cradled Alex in her arms. She didn't know how long she had sat with him, but he was gone, and that was that.

The police had told her, after many sessions and interviews, that Luke would be charged with murder. He already had a long criminal record. Margarita had been charged with conspiring to murder Ginny and was in jail, as was Marcus. Their reign of terror was ending, as the police had been working undercover to expose their criminal activities.

Jem and Red were constantly worried about Ginny. It was as if nothing had happened. She didn't cry or seem upset. But they both knew all the hurt and sorrow was buried deep within her, and she needed to release it, or it would eat her up. However, she flatly refused to talk about Alex. No amount of coaxing could persuade her.

Three weeks after Ginny returned, Red took a phone call from Charles. He asked to speak to Ginny. She was playing with the children, and she shook her head when Red told her who wanted to speak to her.

"I think you should," Red said. "The poor man sounds so defeated. He lost his only child, don't forget." Ginny reluctantly went to the phone.

"Hello, Charles."

"I'm sorry to bother you, but I'd like you to come out to the farm. Please, I need to—I need . . ." He trailed off. Ginny could hear the sorrow in his voice and, remembering what Red had said, her heart melted slightly.

"When do you want me to come?"

"Now would be good."

Ginny hesitated, but what did she have to lose? The poor man was suffering, after all, and he had never really been a threat.

"I'll be with you in an hour or so. I'll have my dog with me, though, if that is OK?" Pup hadn't left Ginny's side since the accident.

Ginny had never been out to his place and was taken with the beauty of her surroundings. The house, a large Queenslander, was immaculate, and the gardens were extensive and beautifully maintained. Large gums lined the driveway, and the late afternoon sun bathed everything in a magical light. Ginny cursed herself. She would be driving home in the dark. She had borrowed Jem's old ute instead of taking her motorhome, which would have been too cumbersome.

Charles must have been watching for her, as he was waiting at the top of the steps leading up to the verandah and front door. He made no attempt to kiss her cheek or shake her hand. Ginny realised he was nervous like her, though she wasn't sure why.

Then she saw he had a cloth-covered platter set on a little table, and a minute or so later, they were sitting and enjoying cheese, biscuits, and other little nibblies. They each had a glass of wine, though Ginny said she could only have the one since she was driving.

For a few minutes, they talked of everything else. Ginny had been shocked when she first saw the usually immaculate Charles. His hair was more white than dark, and he'd not shaved very well. His jeans looked grubby, and he had lost weight.

Then he said, "I thought we could do what we did that time Alex and I came to you after having upset you over Margarita's hat. You remember?"

"Of course I do. That is where it all started."

He gave a bitter laugh. "It started when I was stupid enough to get involved with that woman. Alex was the only good thing that came out of our relationship, and now he's gone." Tears started to run down his face, but he seemed unaware of them and made no attempt to check them.

Ginny was out of her depth. She fished a hankie out of her pocket and tried to wipe them from his face. She couldn't reach very well, so she got up and squatted by his chair. He continued to speak of Alex and how he was gone and how he didn't know what to do with himself. He was so grief-stricken. He turned towards Ginny and rested his head against her breast, sobbing almost uncontrollably. Then the dam holding back Ginny's grief broke, and she was crying too. They clung together, both sobbing. After a bit, Charles poured them more wine, and they both talked of Alex and what he had meant to them. Without really noticing, they drank all the wine. Charles had another bottle in the fridge, and Ginny accepted a full glass. She couldn't drive any more, so she threw caution to the wind.

Finally, it was dark, and they were both rather drunk. They talked and talked and cried on and off. Ginny got up again to dry Charles's tears, but he caught her hand and pulled her to him. Somehow, they kissed, and their kisses deepened.

Charles drew back. "Sorry."

Ginny shushed him and kissed him again. Five minutes later, they were undressing each other in Charles's bedroom. Their coupling was urgent and needy, born out of despair and grief for a man they had both loved deeply.

Later, when they were both calmer than they had been for a long time, they talked again. "I admit I liked you the first time I set eyes on you, but I knew young Alex had stolen your heart. I was jealous but thought if he came and helped you, then the attraction would dissipate. It didn't, and I was so jealous—of my own son, for God's sake! I know you loved him and will always love him, as do I, but can we please be friends?"

Ginny gave a wry smile. "After what we just did, we are already more than friends, wouldn't you say?"

For the first time since Alex's death, Charles gave a brief smile. "Later, I will take you to his grave. It's down near the creek where he loved to sit when he was here. I'm sorry I didn't invite you to the funeral."

Ginny shook her head. She wouldn't have come anyway. "Thank you. I'd like that. I also think Alex would be happy we have each other."

"I think so too, though some might consider it odd."

CHAPTER 49

"HAVE YOU GOT the passports, Charles?"

Charles patted the top pocket of his shirt. "Yep, let's go."

The helicopter lifted off in a swirl of dust, the pilot setting a course for Brisbane.

It was now eighteen months after Alex's death, and Charles and Ginny had married a few days before and were heading to the UK to see Ginny's family. Pup was staying behind, but he was happy. He'd made a new friend in a little girl who was one of the manager's children. His wife helped in the house.

Jem and Red had initially expressed concern about Ginny's relationship with Charles, but she had reassured them. She had made the best choice for her. They had both loved Alex deeply, and it was a strong bond they shared. It was the nearest either of them would ever come to complete happiness. The love they had for Alex and for each other would see them through whatever trials the future held.

www.ingramcontent.com/pod-product-compliance
Lightning Source LLC
LaVergne TN
LVHW031539060526
838200LV00056B/4568